WHISPERS *from a*
TROUBLED HEART

WHISPERS *from a* TROUBLED HEART

RIQUE JOHNSON

A

S*B*I

PUBLICATION

A STREBOR BOOKS INTERNATIONAL LLC PUBLICATION

DISTRIBUTED BY SIMON & SCHUSTER, INC.

Published by

Strebor Books International LLC
P.O. Box 1370
Bowie, MD 20718
http://www.streborbooks.com

ISBN 13: 978-1-59309-020-3   **ISBN 10**: 1-59309-020-X
LCCN 2003112282

Distributed by Simon & Schuster, Inc.
1230 Avenue of the Americas
New York, NY 10020
1-800-223-2336

Cover Design: Brian Marilla

First Printing July 2004
Manufactured and Printed in the United States

10 9 8 7 6 5 4 3 2 1

DEDICATION

THIS BOOK IS DEDICATED TO MY PARENTS.
To my Father for showing me that love and caring for people is not limited to it being biological. I thank you for your silent strength. Through this I've learned how a calm demeanor can carry one through the toughest times. Thank you for always having the right words at the right time. Thanks for your love and most of all, thanks for loving my Mom.
To my Mother for just being great. You have always been there for me, no matter what. I often look beyond you in search of the wings that I know you possess. God has blessed this Earth with a living Angel and that is you. You have been and still today are my greatest inspiration.
If I could define you in one word, the word would have t o be Triumph. Because, with all of the trials and tribulations that life has presented you, you have overcome all obstacles.
You've raised the bar on how to cope with life.
I strive to follow in your footsteps and
be a mirror image
of your spirit.

ACKNOWLEDGMENTS

I'd like to thank my wife, Sharon, for living through my writing escapades away from home and for understanding how my creativity works. Thanks for your understanding as I travel the country promoting my work. You're the best.

Myoshi, Sondra and Myra: What would I be without you three? You three along with Sharon get to read and edit my work in its rawest form. If not for your input and editing powers, my creativity might be less than desirable.

Charmaine Parker, thanks for your patience with me. I know that you coordinate events for other members of the Strebor family, yet daily, sometimes many times daily, when we talk you always make me feel as though I'm your only client.

To my fans, thank you, thank you, thank you. Your praises, comments and best wishes are heartfelt. I truly mean that I'm nothing without you. I'll never forget this. Blessings to you all.

ONE

Slam!

Jason's and Sasha's heads turn toward the door in time to see that it virtually bounces off the wall. The forceful impact leaves a perfect imprinted circle of the doorknob. Julie enters the room wearing her customary full-length mink coat. This time its arrogance is being over-shadowed by the fury in her eyes. Smeared mascara blackens her drowning enraged eyes, and streams of tears flowing down her face leave a trouble-some trail before falling from her chin. Her body trembles with rage as she studies Sasha—the competition, the foe—with all the intensity that her piercing eyes will allow.

"You can't get away with it," Julie cries uncontrollably.

"Jason, who is she?" Sasha questions concerned with the appearance of the distraught woman. "What is she talking about?"

"I'll tell you," Julie jumps in, abruptly dismissing Jason's chance to reply. "Your beloved Jason made love to me, fucked me, used me, all in one single night. I am," Julie states with a long pause, "Julie Jerrard and I'll be his wife forever. I will not be replaced by some slanted-eyed bitch that he's using to get over me!"

A bewildered Sasha directs her attention to the panic-stricken Jason, who is too shocked at Julie's words to do anything more than look at her with his mouth open. Julie reaches into her coat pocket, pulls out a small-caliber handgun that ironically, Jason taught her to use. In a quick lapse of time, she empties the six-shooter. Three rounds enter Sasha before Jason can respond or cry out. He watches terrified as Sasha's life-force seems to leak out of her, dissipating into nothingness as it fails to wrap itself around him. The tension inside of him accelerates. He feels as though his ears are escape valves for the unwanted pressure that rapidly sweeps his being, but that wouldn't suffice. It couldn't. His pain needs to be released from its main source before he explodes from within.

"Saaaa...shaaaa!"

His cry echoes vibrantly throughout the room and halls, sending shock waves reminiscent of an atomic blast raging throughout the corridors, disintegrating all in its violent path. Jason panics as his happiness is ripped from his insides, boiling over like an overcooked pot, contaminating the very happiness he has just recently rediscovered. Looking above him, Sasha's heart-monitor display screen has flatlined coinciding with the sour tone echoing between his ears.

"Please don't die; don't leave me," he begs.

Jason's eyes widen with fear. He shuts off the alarm on Sasha's monitor and performs every form of CPR his knowledge allows but the desperate attempts to save her fail to bring her rhythm back to the room. He flops down in his chair, grabs her hand and cries heavily, tormented with grief. He sits and weeps for what feels like hours but in reality is only a small moment in time. He feels his heart harden with each breath of air he exhales.

"I just wanted you to feel the pain you've caused me," Julie utters. "The humiliation of what I feel for you seems like an all-too-familiar game. You of all people, you toyed with me!" Julie yells with the gun pointed at Jason.

Jason looks at her blankly, evidence of pain showing on his face. Julie has succeeded. The gun releases two more rounds.

"No!" Jason screams.

"Mr. Jerrard...Mr. Jerrard," Dr. Bodou says while shaking Jason's leg. "Wake up."

Jason Jerrard is a six-foot, medium-build, moderately toned man in his early forties with graying hair that all but consumes the remaining blackness. He is Virginia City's finest, Sixteenth Precinct's shining example of what a detective should be. However, a matter of a shattered heart has afforded him an undesired stay in the hospital where he awakens feeling groggy, unaware of his surroundings with a nagging headache and sore shoulder. He tries focusing his eyes on the person who rescued him from the worst part of his dream. Immediately, thoughts of Sasha invade his mind and bring on a mild case of depression while making him wonder why he couldn't subconsciously recall the joyous part of the events that occurred. But now, conscious, his heartfelt words vividly splash through his mind as if they were just spoken.

"I've made all kinds of excuses, lying to myself while concealing my true feelings for you. Before I wouldn't let myself tell you that I loved you, but the greater truth is, I'd be lost without you. Now, I want all of my tomorrows to be shared with you. I do love you more than words can explain and I'm going to tell you repeatedly until my spoken words transform themselves to something tangible and wrap around you, concealing you, securing all of what we have."

Jason smiles as his sudden recollection reveals a vision of Sasha's happiness before Julie took it all away.

Dr. Bodou is a tall foreigner with silver gray hair; he has a mustache of matching color, a distinctive voice and big round eyes. Standing beside Jason in his smock, he readies his stethoscope to listen to Jason's racing heart.

"I'm happy to see your body move after so long, but, the way you were tossing and tearing at the sheets, I imagined you were having some sort of uncomfortable dream."

"I was...Dr. Bodou?"

"Yes...it's me."

"Damn, I was dreaming about my last night with Sasha. But, it was different in that it kept repeating itself over and over again in one continuous loop. I kept seeing the terror in Sasha's eyes just before she was shot...what a nightmare."

"That dream might haunt you forever."

"Somehow, that statement holds more merit than you know."

"How are you feeling?"

"Drained, sore and I've a terrible headache."

"Considering the fact that both bullets entered and exited your body without any serious harm or disfigurement, the blood you lost should be the cause of your discomfort."

"I suppose that's something to be grateful for. I've been blessed. How long have I been here?"

"Three…actually you're working on your fourth day."

"Four days!" Jason responds astoundedly. "Why is this thing sticking in my arm?" Jason questions with his eyes focusing on the IV.

"We had to feed you somehow. Your strength was very low."

"Sasha?" Jason questioned, already knowing the answer but a glimmer of hope forced the question.

"We tried everything humanly possible to save her," Dr. Bodou recites somberly. "But…" he continues with his head bowed. "Maybe if her strength were one hundred percent, she would've been able to pull through. Miss Fong was in the morgue for two days while we tried to locate a family member."

"And Julie?"

"Apparently, after she shot you, she turned the gun on herself, taking her own life."

"You can't be serious."

"Sadly, it's the truth. Her family came and made arrangements to have her cremated the next day."

"Where is Sasha's body now?"

"I believe she's being buried today."

"Today? Where…what time?" Jason questions with much anxiety.

Dr. Bodou glances at his watch and replies, "In about three hours."

"Who arranged this?"

"Your department. They figured you'd want her properly taken care of."

"They were right," Jason responds firmly. Ignoring his physical condition, he picks up the telephone and dials his precinct.

"I'll leave you now," says Dr. Bodou.

Jason nods.

"Sixteenth Precinct, Sgt. Austin."

"Kevin, where is the burial?"

"Burial? Jason, Jas you're all right. How are you?"

"Where's she being buried?" Jason demands without entertaining any form of small talk.

"So that's why…"

"Where?" Jason interrupts forcefully.

"Memorial Cemetery."

"Thanks," he says and hangs up the telephone without a return reply.

Jason sits on the side of the bed, gathers himself before snatching the IV from his arm. The tiny puncture bleeds. He attempts to stand but his weakened knees wobble, forcing him to sit back on the bed to regain his composure. Dr. Bodou reenters the room just in time to watch Jason's dilemma; he places a hand on Jason's good shoulder.

"You can't even stand; how can you possibly make it to her funeral?"

"I can. I will make it," a determined Jason recites. "I just need a moment to get my act together."

"More like a few days," Dr. Bodou counters.

"I'm beyond that decision. I can't let her be buried without me being there."

"Detective," Dr. Bodou says firmly, "my professional opinion suggests that you stay hospitalized for a few more days."

Jason's stubbornness shows. "No further discussion required. I'm attending the funeral."

"But…"

"The only but that I'm concerned with this very moment is…where are my clothes?"

"In the small closet next to the bathroom."

Jason stumbles over to the closet and the all-too-familiar hospital gown reveals his rear-end. In a weakened state, he grabs his clothes and slowly continues the stumble toward the bathroom. He then splashes some water on his vital parts and dries himself with a face cloth before using the door for support while sliding his pants underneath the gown. He is barely able to balance himself during the act of putting on his pants. He removes the gown exposing his hairy chest, slides one arm through a sleeve, and a sharp pain quickly reacquaints itself, reminding him of his injured shoulder. Jason pauses to examine the bullet holes in his shirt before carefully sliding the other arm through the sleeve to minimize the pain. He stares at himself in the mirror and realizes that by his own high standards, he looks terrible. But, the multi-day facial hair, the scrambled hair on top of his head nor the wise words for rest by his physician are not justifiable reasons to ignore the calling of his beloved Sasha. Back in the room Dr. Bodou watches his every move with care and a high degree of concern about Jason ignoring the obvious physical pain. He reaches into his smock pocket, pulls out a tiny bottle of pills and a written prescription.

"Here, I didn't think I'd convince you to stay so you may want to take these," Dr. Bodou responds while handing Jason both items. "They will help ease your pain."

"Pain pills…I can use these now."

"Please be careful; they're very strong. You should be cautious of your shoulder. Too much activity will reactivate its bleeding and hamper the healing process."

"Advice taken."

Jason opens the door; his pride takes over his demeanor. It forces him to camouflage the pain he feels by straightening his posture and pulling his shoulders back before beginning proud steps. He turns for his final words to Dr. Bodou.

"Did my department do anything with my car?"

"Sorry, can't help you there."

"Thanks, take care."

"You must sign out to be discharged and procedure dictates that you leave in a wheelchair."

"I don't have time for all of the formalities, but I will come back to sign out after the funeral. Is this acceptable?"

"That will suffice," Dr. Bodou replies, realizing that more rebuttal is fruitless.

"Once again, take care," Jason states as he opens the door.

"You too, Detective…oh, let's not meet under these circumstances again."

"Don't worry, we won't. Goodbye."

The closing door drowns out Dr. Bodou's remaining words of caution. Jason walks down the corridor greeting and thanking anyone who may have taken care of him during his brief residency. Winded from the short walk, aided by an energy level well below normal, Jason rests his weary body against a wall. He uses the water fountain next to the elevator to take the medicine. He waits in serious discomfort for the elevator to arrive.

Jason enters the cemetery groggy, but mildly pain-free from the medicine he'd taken earlier. A small crowd consisting of mostly police officers surrounds Sasha's gravesite. The minister dressed in a long black robe is concluding a passage from the Bible. He closes the Bible, and he positions his hands crossed in front of him and allows the gathering to recognize his queue. All heads bow.

Jason approaches from behind and takes a place next to the minister. His mind blackens with dark clouds at the sight of Sasha's coffin. He falls to his knees in silent prayer and diverts the attention of the small congregation to him. Captain North attempts to bring him to his feet, but Jason refuses without uttering a single word or taking his eyes away from the coffin. Instantly, as Captain North's hand touches Jason's back he knows it is a wasted effort. Jason continues praying until his emotions transform into a silent weeping. Tears fall from his chin for several minutes before he mumbles something vaguely heard by Captain North's ears.

"No more," Jason says sorrowfully.

"What was that?" Captain North questions.

"I said, no more."

"No more what?"

"Love, never again."

"You're upset, your pain and grief makes you say this. Take some…"

"Yes, I am," Jason interrupts. "That's why I mean what I say."

"You are trained to handle death."

"True, but no training in the world can prepare you for a tragic incident when it hits this close to home. I happened to love this woman. She exposed feelings that were concealed in me for a long time. I never thought I'd love this way again."

"You will, again, in time."

"No...never like this."

Jason finally stands and the coffin is lowered.

Simultaneously as the coffin descends, Jason feels his inner being changing. His heart was opened by love but now is hardened by life, closing with every breath he takes. It hires a mason; soon he feels little people inside of him building walls many feet high around all organs that allow him to care. The process places his feelings in hibernation, confined in their own solitude...afraid, afraid to mend and give love another try.

That's twice, his mind thinks. Activating signals that change his mental structure in ways he never thought possible. He stares at the dirt as it is shoveled into the grave. The sound of the loose gravel dancing across the structure of the coffin somehow triggers his memories.

Each time a shovel full of dirt hits the coffin, a shared moment with Sasha dances across his blank eyes, losing him to thoughts of her.

"Jason," Captain North says. "Jason," he says while shaking his shoulder. "When this is over, I order you to go home and get plenty of rest. Take some time to pull your emotions together."

"I don't need time. I need to keep myself occupied. Therefore, I'll see you tomorrow at the station."

"That's too soon and you know it."

"I know me so much better than you...working tomorrow will be good for me."

"How are your wounds?"

"My heart will mend."

"No, your gunshot wounds."

"Nothing I can't handle."

"Do yourself a great favor and come down off of your high horse. Accept that you're human. A body needs time to heal. Your body, believe it or not, is included in that."

"I don't need to be idle. I can't have a devil's work place. Not now, especially now," a saddened Jason continues.

"Okay, okay," Captain North says in frustration, "you don't have to take a forced absence, but I don't want to see you before Thursday."

"But…"

"Not before Thursday and that's an order," Captain North states firmly.

"What's special about Thursday?"

"Thursday is when you'll be recognized for your outstanding efforts."

"I don't need an award ceremony for doing my job."

"It's settled already. The Mayor is making a big commotion over you ridding the city of the serial rapist."

"It's a good thing I'm out of the hospital," Jason replies in a tone that is nearly disrespectful to his superior.

"I know, knowing him, it would happen anyway. It's political, good for his image since he's thrown his hat in the upcoming gubernatorial race."

"I don't want a ceremony or to be used like a pawn."

"Enough talk, just be at the fairgrounds Thursday afternoon at three-thirty p.m. sharp."

"Maybe," Jason replies while shaking his head.

"Be there and be on time," Captain North directs.

"Jason," an officer replies, "I'm very sorry for your loss. I truly know that this is a bad time to mention this but…here are Sasha's things from the hospital. If you don't want them, I will have them put in the evidence room."

"No," Jason replies as he takes the small box, "I'll take them."

The minister delivers his closing remarks over Sasha's grave. Afterwards, they all join in a silent prayer. Jason receives several condolences from the attendees and is soon left standing alone over Sasha's grave. He sits in the grass and talks to her for hours, reminiscing on the wonderful times they shared. Smiling, laughing loudly occasionally, and knowing that she's sharing the same special moment with him. He recalls the knock-knock jokes she favored, how her wit and charm warmed him.

The setting sunrays bathe the clouds, tainting them the customary shades of orange before darkness approaches. Without an additional thought, Jason stands quickly, brushes himself off and sets his sights for home. However, that feeling really doesn't reach his feet. They become stationary, stuck and embedded in the ground. Jason's only recourse is to shower himself in the oncoming darkness and let his mind take him where it deems necessary.

Thinking back to the many adventures they shared, he clearly remembers a gorgeous day some time ago when he picked Sasha up from her home late one afternoon. Their encounter destined for the seclusion of a place called Three Pond Park.

It is a huge park containing acres of trees and wildlife of all sorts. It derives its name from the three manmade ponds developed within its boundaries. Jason parks his car a few yards from the water's edge of one of the massive ponds. They step out onto thick, plush, freshly cut grass. Its aroma cleanses the air. Sasha lays down a queen-sized quilt for their use. On one end she empties the picnic basket containing two crystal glasses, a bottle of moderately priced red wine, cold cuts with all the trimmings, and dessert. On the other end, Jason places cheese, grapes, and a portable CD player with soft romantic music leaving its speaker. He sits, Sasha joins him and they both watch nature in its usual state. A pleasant breeze warms their bodies while sounds of jumping fish invade their ears.

Ducks, geese, and other birds float in the pond. Some venture closer with hopes of finding food. All is perfect.

Jason glances toward the other end of the blanket and snickers at the birds waddling.

"What's that thing down there with the long neck?" Jason asks.

"Which one? They're all ducks of some sort."

"With a cork?"

"Oh that." She smiles. "I remembered your story about the champagne, so I brought something alcoholic."

"It is fine of you to remember that alcohol makes me horny."

"Will you join me in a glass?"

"Okay, you get in first," Jason jokes.

"Would you like a glass of wine? Fool."

"You're asking for trouble."

"I'll take any trouble you dish out," she says before leaning him back and giving him a passionate kiss.

Jason submits to her dominance, enjoying her actions.

"We'd better stop," Jason urges, "before the birds eat our food."

They quickly prepare and devour their mini-meal while the multicolored sunset adds more ambiance to their romantic picnic. Sasha lies with her head in his lap, gazing into his dark brown eyes while Jason gently strokes her face. His fingertips are awed by her softness.

"I think you're feeling the effects of the wine now," Sasha says, smiling.

"No, I'm fine."

"Are you sure?"

"Yes." Jason pauses. "Why?"

"Your friend is poking me in the back of my head."

"Really, I hadn't noticed."

"I guess I'm lucky we're not at home."

"Wrong."

Jason excuses himself, opens the car's trunk and pulls out something reminiscent of a huge umbrella with Sasha watching his every move. He stands in the middle of the quilt and opens the oversized contraption into a huge dome with dimensions of approximately six feet long in diameter and four feet in height. Parachute material covers the aluminum supports and a zipper runs from the center of the dome down to an edge. Sasha watches Jason conceal himself inside of the dome followed by the sight of the zipper going up and Jason crawls out.

"Ta ta!" Jason boasts. "Instant shelter."

"This is not your home."

"It's my tent, right?"

"Yep."

"Then it's my home."

"What if someone comes?"

"You mean...before you do?" Jason jokes.

"No, Jason!" Sasha glances in awe. "You know what I mean."

"The thrill of getting caught doesn't excite you?"

"Yes, most definitely."

"Ah, the freak in you is coming out, isn't it?"

Sasha splashes a devilish smile.

"That's good enough...let's party," Jason suggests.

Jason grabs her hand, falls to his knees and crawls into the instant sanctuary. Sasha crawls inside leery of making a spectacle of herself, but the eagerness for a little romance quickly devours those feelings. The zipper comes down; moments later heavy breathing escapes from inside. The heavy breathing transforms into more passionate moans causing their temperature to rise to the point where tiny sweat lines roll off them wetting the quilt. She moans louder while Jason's eyes roll back into his head as they both near their climax.

Many birds leave the water to investigate the sensuous sounds from within the tent. Some devour food scraps; others circle the tent like an Indian tribe about to attack a wagon train. Sasha's moans become uncontrollable; her body trembles, recklessly responding to Jason's movements. Her passionate cry is exerted loudly, seemingly triggering a more subdued moan from Jason. His tense muscles indicate to Sasha that he followed immediately behind her. The birds, frightened by the loud scream of passion, fly away and unknowingly provide their own form of approval as their flapping wings create an unusual method of applause. Soon the only sound they hear is the clap of human hands given by a park policeman.

Jason and Sasha scramble to get their clothes back on. In a short time, Jason's head peeks from inside; his hair is massaged all over his head.

"Hi, officer," Jason says, smiling.

"Jason," he says. "I should've known it was you when I saw the BMER. Get your butt out of here before someone comes along that doesn't know you."

"I knew that this was your day for this area."

"Just leave before you cause me trouble," the officer responds while shaking his head in disbelief.

"You got it, Cliff."

Jason leaves the tent proud of their experience while Sasha looks around embarrassed that they are caught. They pack their belongings and depart with silly grins plastered across their faces.

Jason returns from the dream state wearing the same silly grin. He searches for the proper words to end his stay but only finds the ones that were important to her when she was living. His heart flutters with every passing beat, filling his eyes with tears as he turns to walk away seemingly ashamed to let her see him in his emotional state.

"I love you," his heart pours. "I really do. My actions from this point may not prove that to you or anyone else but, hopefully, you will understand that they are being done because…I love you."

As Jason returns to his car, thoughts of Sasha seem to blanket him, diverting his mind to the thing that helped him solve the murderer-rapist case: Sasha's journals. He wants all of them, not just the one that contains information that helped him because he knows they were Sasha's prized possessions. He is fully aware that she wrote intimately, passionately, and that she poured her soul into each letter, each syllable, every written word that the pages contained. Somehow, having them in his possession will keep her near and have her remain forever close to him. After all, something is telling him that Sasha wanted him to have them. It pains him to think that they would be discarded like common trash by whoever cleaned her condo.

Without consciously being aware of his driving activities, Jason finds himself sitting in Sasha's condo's parking lot, hoping he's not too late. He uses Sasha's key from her belongings to enter the condo and a welcoming feeling warms him. Jason takes a moment to bathe in the sensation before retrieving the journals from the bedroom, then exits her place with an eerie feeling that this will not be the last time he feels her presence.

TWO

A couple of days pass. Jason has hibernated in his home since the funeral. As a result, dishes are piled in the sink and clothes are laying all over the house. This neat, organized person has temporarily abandoned his daily principles and become what many would consider a slob. The only thing he's done constructively, despite medical advice is work on his body with a weight set in his basement. He has concentrated mostly on his legs and stomach and used lighter weights to tone his damaged chest.

Jason's psyche seems to tell him that his mourning period has ended. Therefore, in an effort to get back to the norm, Jason shaves, showers, and sports one of his finest suits before venturing into the city for a change of scenery. Riding down the main thoroughfare, the growl of his stomach taints the soothing jazz playing on the radio.

Not willing to relive the last week or so with his friends at his usual restaurant, he makes an unexpected turn away from breakfast food. He finds himself at the valet parking of La Magnifique, a French restaurant known for its crepes, wines, and other fine authentic foods.

You enter the restaurant through etched-glass doors. The walls are painted baby blue with navy-blue, hand-carved chair railings. The woodwork and window frames are of matching color. A flowery mixture of baby and navy blue along with beige separate the walls from the cathedral ceiling. The table settings are romantic. A long stick candle with a dim flame burns on each table, not to be overshadowed by the huge crystal chandelier that hangs from the ceiling. Carmen, a charming young woman with dark brown eyes, seats Jason. She has thick black eyebrows and a head of matching hair color pulled back into a long braid hanging down her back.

"What do you suggest?" asks Jason.

"Depends, what you are in the mood for...seafood?"

"Tempt me."

"The chef's specialty is a seafood crepe topped with a creamy cheese sauce hiding a hint of burgundy wine."

"That sounds delicious."

"Would you like a cocktail before dinner?"

"Yes, make it leaded."

"Huh?" she says while raising an eyebrow. "Make what leaded?"

"Coffee, caffeinated."

"And the decaffeinated is unleaded?" she asks, trying to follow the strange dialogue.

"Correct."

"I'll admit that it is an unusual way to refer to coffee," Carmen confesses. "I'll return in a moment."

"Which way is the restroom?"

"Follow me and you will walk right past it."

Jason follows a couple of strides behind her. When he returns to his table, a hot steaming cup of coffee awaits him; its aroma can be enjoyed from a distance. Oddly enough, across from his coffee sits a woman of more than average height on a small frame. Her hair is pinned on top of her head with the front pulled down and teased covering most of her forehead. Her features are strong: a squared chin, high cheekbones, pointy nose and a long neck of tanned color. As Jason gets closer, he notices her most outstanding feature: her seemingly black eyes.

"Excuse me," Jason says, "I've not dined here before so I may have lost my bearing, but, isn't this my coffee?"

"Yes."

After sitting, he asks, "Do you come with the meal?"

"Not exactly…I'll leave if you'd prefer."

"No, you're here now. However, I'm curious as to why?"

"I came in after you; you look gentlemanly and quite frankly, I can use some company."

"Deja vu, this type of thing seems to follow me wherever I go."

"So, this has happened to you before?"

"Sometime ago."

"Forgive me, I'll leave. Sorry to intrude."

"Your intrusion is welcomed. Even your boldness."

"You like bold women?"

"At times, and you?"

"Bold women do nothing for me," she jokes.

"A sense of humor, good."

"However, bold men ruffle my feathers."

"That can be taken as a positive or negative."

"Positive…definitely positive."

"What's your name?"

"Is that important?"

"It can be; I don't want to be addressing a lunatic."

"You can tell this from a name?"

"Okay, what do you do?"

"Occupation, hmm…next is what do I drive?"

"Are you normally this evasive?"

"Normally, I don't greet men I don't know; besides, those questions aren't necessary. We can enjoy each other's company without the privilege of a history lesson. So," she ponders, "what do we talk about next?"

"Let's talk about that wedding ring you're wearing."

"If it meant anything, I wouldn't be sitting here so pay it no attention."

"It means enough for you to wear it."

"It's all about imagery. On paper, I'm married. My emotions are not. My husband has no time for me."

"I've heard that a time or two."

"You married?"

"Divorced," Jason pauses, "Widowed…something like that."

"Which one is it?"

"With the recentness of it, it's too emotional to get into right now."

"Sorry, I'm not trying to pry."

"Don't be; I've recently regained my mental and I would like to keep it that way for a while."

"I've a feeling I'll be divorced soon. I'm not going to put up with his…why are you staring at me?"

Jason says nothing while staring deeply into her dark mysterious eyes, silenced by the ache for passion they reveal.

"Talk to me," she states, intrigued by Jason's glaring.

"You're beautiful."

"You're staring at me because you think I'm beautiful?"

"Precisely."

"That's the first compliment I've had in years; too bad it didn't come from my husband."

"Is that any relation to, behind every successful man is a woman; far too often, it isn't his wife?"

"There's a lot of truth to that." She nods. "You're quite handsome yourself."

"Thanks."

"Stop it," she demands, "you're making me nervous."

"I'm just trying to discover the true reason you're sitting here."

"Must there be an ulterior motive?"

"There must be. Simply by the way you're dressed, I can tell that you are no ordinary person."

"How can you be so sure or," she ponders, "are you sure of yourself?"

"Both."

"Is this where you become bold?"

"You call it boldness; I call it being a realist. Before I'd sit here and wonder how it would be to take you to bed, but a few days ago I changed."

"Something to do with being divorced and widowed at the same time?"

"Yes."

"And now?"

"I'm sure you are aware that I've already compromised my position."

"Meaning?"

"By the simple nature of entertaining thoughts of having you physically."

"Surely, you can be more direct," she states, willing to see how far Jason will go.

"Cut to the chase."

"Please."

"Now, I simply ask, would you like to be fucked crazy?"

Her eyes widen as she stumbles for a response. "Is this a question or part of your sentence?"

"You answer that."

The waitress places Jason's food on the table and asks, "Miss, would you like anything?"

"Yes, I'll have what he's having."

"Leaded also?"

"What?" she asks, not understanding the question.

"Coffee, too? I assumed that since you're sitting here, that you were versed in his dialect."

She flashes Jason a puzzled look before replying, "No, bring me a rye and ginger, please."

"Right away, Ma'am," she replies before leaving.

"What was that all about?"

Jason shrugs his shoulders. "It's not important at all. Shall I wait for your food?"

"No, by all means, eat before it gets cold."

"Excuse me while I dance," he states before bowing his head to recite a silent prayer.

As Jason consumes his food, she thinks back to his question and a horny feeling overwhelms her. Her nipples become erect and broadcast through her blouse, sending tingles wildly down her spine as she begins to gaze at him.

"Now, who's staring?"

"Uncomfortable?" she says while biting her finger, very much turned on by her new acquaintance.

"Is that seductive gesture a yes to my question?"

Her food is placed on the table; very few words are spoken while they watch one another with anticipation—intrigued with what the evening might bring.

"Where and when?" she states unexpectedly.

"Now," Jason replies. "There are a number of places within walking distance from here."

"You choose, but before we go, may I ask you a question?"

"Shoot."

"Is there anything I should know?"

"Be prepared for the ride of your life."

"No, the word nowadays is safe sex. That's what we'd be having, correct?"

"Correct."

"You feel that the question is unwarranted?"

"Kinda, how do you know I'm not lying?"

"The windows of your soul..." As an afterthought, she replies, "I think it's best if we leave the city. The outskirts will be more relaxing for me."

"There's a Kings Inn at the city limits."

"I've seen it."

"Meet me there."

"I'll be right behind you."

After a small debate that Jason wins, he pays for their meals. They hurriedly retrieve their cars from the valet and depart in separate directions. She rides to the destination eager, longing to be touched again but unsure of the consequences that may follow.

Jason rides to their destination in awe. He is surprised that the recent change within himself allows him to pick up a perfect stranger. He's unsure of the outcome of their encounter. Nevertheless, he quickly gets a room and stands inside leaning against the door waiting for sounds of the mysterious woman. Seconds later, he opens the door to the cry of the woman's knock.

"Well, here we are," she responds after entering the room.

"We're here."

"Look at this room…"

"Suite," Jason corrects.

"Suite, it's large, plush and expensive-looking."

"Don't worry about the cost."

"What now?"

"A little conversation."

"Talking? Will that set us in the proper mood?"

"It will relax me."

"Your actions don't fit your boldness at the restaurant."

"I've never done this before."

"It's beginning to show."

They engage in meaningless talk for several minutes before she smoothly attempts to unbutton Jason's shirt.

"Wait a minute," he says.

"What's wrong?"

"Nothing. I just want to see you do what you're trying to do to me."

"Undress myself?"

"Yes."

"Let's do it together."

"Agreed."

They stand on opposite sides of the bed and have a silent count-off. The woman unfastens a button. Jason duplicates her action. They follow this routine until their tops hang open, revealing part of her bra and Jason's hairy chest.

"Muscles," she replies. "Impressive."

"Thanks, but my upper body has been ruined."

"How so?"

"You'll see when I completely remove my shirt. I've a permanent wound, a result of being a victim of revenge."

"What?"

"Let's save that conversation for a time when we are not about to get our freak on," Jason suggests, smiling.

"That's fine by me."

She removes her blouse, and Jason stares at her nicely shaped breasts covered by a lace bra. She reaches behind her back and unfastens the hooks. Slowly she removes the bra, teasing and tantalizing him with every action. As the bra hits the floor, the light from her high beams is blinding to Jason, indicating that she is already aroused or very cold. The sound of her skirt's zipper overtakes the room's silence. In one motion, she lowers her skirt and pantyhose to her ankles. She sits on the bed long enough to remove her pumps and free her ankles of the hindering clothing. Quickly, she crawls between the sheets and rests her back against the headboard.

"Now," she says. "I get to watch you."

"You slick devil."

"I can be at times."

Jason crawls across the bed in search of the miniature radio located on the nightstand and flips to a station whose musical format is slow romantic songs.

"That will do it," he says.

"Do what?"

Without saying a word, he crawls back across the bed, deliberately brushing her breast as he stands.

"Clever," she says.

"At times," he returns with a devilish grin.

She only smiles.

"Come here, closer…about this close," she directs while placing her index finger on her lips.

Jason sits on the bed and leans toward her, gazing into her eyes, anticipating the closeness he's craving. Their lips meet; the softness each of them feels sends warm rays through their bodies. He kisses her lips gently, teasing and caressing them with his tongue but not parting them.

"You shouldn't do that," she suggests.

"I know…I should do it like this."

He brings his lips to hers and slowly part their lips. The kiss is hard, passionate… hungry.

"Uh," Jason grunts, breaking their embrace.

"What's wrong?"

"This is a good song."

"Good song, what?" she replies baffled.

Jason stands and his feet begin to work. Smoothly, he glides in the limited space, dancing to the song. Imitating a male stripper, he makes an effortless transition of removing his shirt. His muscular chest conveys balance as he flexes, boasting his chiseled physique. Even with his injured shoulder, his build awes her. Jason begins by making slow seductive circles with his hips, gyrating in the open air while pretending to have an imaginary partner. He steps out of his shoes, dancing, alluring her more with every move. He runs his hands firmly down his chest with her eyes following the trail to his belt. The sexy facial expression Jason delivers is captivating, inviting, and warming to her sensual parts. He tackles his belt with an effortless movement making her mouth open, watering in anticipation. His pants are lowered simultaneously with a waving motion from his hips to his knees. Suavely he sits on the bed, winks and kisses her while he removes his pants from his ankles without her really noticing the action.

With each passing moment her body temperature rises, dictated by an ever-increasing desire for Jason. He stands; his nude frame has her caught in the moment of her private show. It doesn't take long for her to realize her womanhood is soaked. Jason climbs between the sheets and softly caresses her breast. He wraps his strong arms around her and gently walks his fingers down her spine playing each vertebra like a piano key.

"I can't wait any longer," she cries desperately. "I want to feel you inside of me."

Jason continues his foreplay as she submits freely to what seems like a thousand hands.

"I need you," she pleads. "Please don't make me wait."

Listening to the woman's woes, her cries for passion, it is all too obvious that her words lack an ingredient, which is important to Jason: conviction.

"I'll give you what you need," Jason replies before lying beside her.

He positions her head on his chest and gives her a tight securing hug.

Seconds later, he feels his skin being moistened by her falling tears. He strokes her head gently. Soon the tears dry and her breathing thickens. They sleep.

Later in the wee hours of the morning, she wakes Jason by her soft lips kissing one of his nipples. Jason kisses the top of her head while giving her another strong hug.

"I adore your firm embraces," she moans with approval.

"It's the only way to do it."

"Why?"

"Why do I hug this way or why didn't I finish with you?"

"The second question."

"Did I not give you what you needed?"

"Yes, but how could you have possibly known?"

"Just something I sensed."

"You're right, having sex wasn't important as the affection I needed. Thank you."

"No thanks necessary."

"Really, it is. You showed me respect and at the same time made me feel whole...special...attractive, all of that. I feel like a woman again; that's why I cried."

"Truly, there is no need to explain."

"And now?"

"Now, you should go home. It's very late; your husband will be waiting."

"What about the ride of my life?"

"It will happen when fate says so."

"I feel awful. You saw right through me; that's why you didn't continue."

"Don't feel bad; I believe I helped you more this way."

"What about this expensive room?"

"No biggie."

"You're a generous man."

"Don't get me wrong. If fate presents us a next time, you will most likely not be so lucky."

"How can there be a next time? We don't know each other's name."

"You'd be surprised how uncanny fate is. However, just in case, how often do you eat at La Magnifique?"

"Once a week."

"That's a possibility."

"I'm feeling better now. You're sure you don't want to do what we came here for?"

"Tempting, but I'll take my chances. You have nice curves; everything is proportional."

"What is it then?"

"Timing, let's wait. We both need clearer thoughts."

"What's bothering you?"

"My fiancée recently passed."

"Fiancée, widowed and divorced. It must've been a mess."

"Emotionally, I need more time to recover."

"Sorry."

"You didn't know."

"Enough said. I understand now."

"Come here."

Jason hugs her tightly.

"This is nice," she says, moaning with approval.

"The moment feels good."

"The moment?"

"Yes, we live many years but only one moment at a time."

"Are you always analytical?"

"It is a habit."

After putting her clothes back on, she reaches into her purse, grabs a comb and dashes into the bathroom. A short while later she reappears as luscious as she did when they met.

"I must get going now. I don't want to be much later than it already is."

"I know what you're about to say," Jason suggests, "nice meeting you."

"Next time."

"Wait," Jason responds as she reaches for the doorknob.

It is expected, anticipated without a doubt. Jason's last words, his eleventh-hour plea for her body is lingering in the air. She is ready, wanting, and hungering for him even as time is her enemy. She leans against the door expecting a few words from Jason. Instead he climbs out of bed toward her. His private part is swinging, inviting her, stimulating her already enhanced mood. She tries not to stare, but her eyes widen as she's drawn into a trance of his nakedness.

"I forgot something," he says before embracing her and gives her a deep passionate kiss that seems to entice them to lose all touch with reality.

She pushes him away. "I'm so wet."

"I'm sure you are."

"You're cocky, too."

"He is, isn't he?" Jason replies while pressing his hardened member against her.

"I'd better leave before I lose all control and attack you."

"That would take some time."

"What are you going to do?"

"Stay until morning. I have nothing better to do."

"I see…well, enjoy yourself," she states as she strokes his hardened member.

She leaves abruptly—seemingly unfitting for what they almost shared. Moments later, in the room's solitude, all is quiet. He lies, content that he did the best thing for the mysterious woman, yet in the back of his mind, pictures of her naked body dance vividly in his thoughts. He ponders how a woman so gorgeous and seemingly educated, can be trapped in a relationship with no ending? Soon, he starts to fade as slumber relaxes him, drifting down a peaceful river until he hears the mating rituals of a couple in the next room.

"Oh boy," he sighs before covering his head with a pillow.

THREE

"How much money do you think we'll make tonight?" asks Reggie.

"Make, you sound as if we're going to a job, but there's no telling how much. If this works, we'll round up our most trusted partners and venture citywide. We could be overnight sensations," he boasts.

William "Sly" Butler, a street-educated scholar with a survival degree derived from the school of hard knocks, speaks these words. He is of average height and build with a smooth face. A fast-talker gifted with gab. When he talks, people follow. Persuasion comes easy for him. Public education failed him, however, judging from the amount of money concealed in his pocket, something big is working well for him.

Unlike Sly, Reggie is a spoiled upper-middle class tyrant. Twelve years of schooling and a taste of college hasn't swayed his desire to obtain things without effort. Fast and easy—that's the way he likes to get his money. His well-to-do parents hindered his quest for success by trying to make him happy and failing to instill the meaning of a hard-earned dollar.

"Are you ready for this?" asks Sly.

"I was born ready."

"Packing?"

"Guns, you didn't say anything about guns."

"Be real, man. How do you expect to get our fucking point across?"

"But…"

"Oh I see, we're supposed to politely ask for their money," rages Sly.

'Excuse me, may I pretty please have your money,' Sly sarcastically remarks. "Remember, people are afraid of death; guns represent death."

"Give it to me but I'm not doing any shooting."

"Whatever. Take this one," he says, tossing the revolver at Reggie.

"Is it loaded?"

"Yep, the safety's on."

"Let's do this."

"That's the spirit."

Moments later, they conceal themselves in the darkest shadows of a bank parking lot, waiting for their first victim of the night. The wait is tedious and Reggie grows impatient.

"Sly?" Reggie whispers. "Sly?"

"Why the fuck are you whispering? No one is here."

"I gotta go."

"Go where?"

"Piss… real bad."

"Why didn't you go before we left?"

"I didn't have to go then."

"Just make it fast."

"Where?"

"For Christ's sake, man," Sly yells. "Must I tell you everything? You want me to hold the fucking thing for you, too?"

"The hell with you, I'll be right back."

Soon after Reggie relieves himself, a white Camaro pulls into the parking lot. The headlights darken and the driver's side door swiftly opens. A pair of two-inch-heeled shoes, supporting luscious legs, sound on the pavement. Nice curves and other bodily dimensions complete a woman's frame. With bankcard in hand, she dashes to the ATM, punches a secret code, followed by other numbers and like magic, crisp dollar bills appear. She removes the money, card, and receipt. Seconds later, she has the car door opened two inches when Sly's body suddenly plunges into it. The handle is snatched out of her hand, slamming the door shut. She jumps back startled, very afraid as her heart starts its own marathon, pounding heavily inside of her chest.

"Boo!" Sly laughs.

The frightened woman is astounded, expressionless, with her heart winning the race.

"I'll take this," Reggie demands, as he grabs her things from behind.

"Please don't hurt me," she cries with a tremor in her voice.

"Don't worry, Miss...Miss Clemens," Reggie replies after reading her bankcard. "I don't think causing you undue harm will be necessary."

"We can do this calmly," Sly says while flashing his gun, "or...simply put, your ass can die here and now. Your cooperation is all we need."

"What more do you want?" she pleads.

"Money."

"But...he has my money," the woman states confused.

Sly cups her chin in one of his hands, turns her head toward him and conjures his next thought.

"Here's an educated guess; you didn't withdraw your maximum daily limit. Did you?" he questions while moving her head left to right, answering his own inquiry. "Give me her receipt...hum, you certainly have enough to cover that and more."

Tears fall from the terrorized woman's eyes.

"Don't cry, Babe; I assure you all we want is money," he says before snapping his fingers. "Card, please."

Reggie hands him the bankcard and after a quick glance, he gets excited.

"What's going on?" Reggie asks. "Why the sudden grin?"

"How much money did she get out of the machine?"

"Six fresh smelling twenties," Reggie replies while literally sniffing the bills.

"Well then, luck has blessed us with a few hundred more dollars."

"How so?"

"This is one of those Checkcards. A gold one..."

"I can withdraw a maximum of six hundred dollars a day," the woman intrudes, trying to help her cause.

"Exactly," Sly responds. "Now, let's get the remaining five hundred, well, four hundred and eighty dollars to be exact so that everyone can leave on their own accord. Catch my drift?" He frowns his brows for more effect.

The woman nods. Sly and Reggie stand on each side of the woman, out of the camera's view while she retrieves more green peacemakers. The cash appears in the slot, Sly grabs it and they vanish in opposite directions. The woman sits on the cold cement with her back against the building trying to regain her composure while attempting to put some life into her rubbery legs.

Sly and Reggie continue their escapade at several other locations throughout the city. With a reasonable amount of success, they head back to their origin to discuss plans for a more widespread operation. As they drive down the street, Reggie continually counts the profits.

"How do you feel?" questions Sly.

"Terrific. Money seems to have a soothing effect on me."

"You did good tonight. I'm proud of you."

"Yeah, I was pretty smooth," boasts Reggie.

"Carrying a gun is not so bad, is it?"

"Piece of cake."

Sly builds Reggie's ego with more flattering remarks. He easily convinces him that he is born for this lifestyle, knowing that with a little praise, Reggie would do almost anything.

"Now, when we get back," Sly says, "I'll show you something that could be very profitable."

"What could be more profitable than what we accomplished tonight?"

"Tie what we did tonight in with a detailed robbery plan and we're in there."

"Who are we going to rob?"

"Some of the same people from tonight."

"Okay, I'm confused. I'll admit."

"Let me see how well you paid attention tonight."

"Shoot."

"What was the first name of our first victim tonight?"

"Monica," Reggie replies positively.

"Close, it was Monique Clemens."

"Okay, but how does that help us?"

"We'll look into the phone book or search for her over the Internet and once we have her address, we pay her dwelling a visit."

"Burglarize her home…why not simply pick out a place as we drive down the street?"

"Too simple, besides, from the amount of cash she had remaining in her account, she's bound to have nice expensive things just yearning for a new home."

"Smart idea and all the low balances that we come across, we'll forget about them."

"You catch on fast. Let's come up with some partners so we can hit several ATM locations simultaneously."

"Why share our wealth with others?"

"We need a few others to make my plan work effectively."

FOUR

Thursday afternoon Jason sits in La Magnifique on a hunch that the mysterious woman might reappear. He waits anxiously, periodically checking his watch in an impatient manner. Time grows short, forcing Jason to leave to attend his unwanted event.

Jason wears his police dress uniform. All buttons are highly glossed and his uniform creases are sharp. His many accomplisments and honors decorate his chest proudly. Jason greets his superior with an uneasiness unfamiliar to Captain North. He takes a seat next to him on the platform visually demonstrating his contempt with the whole idea. A high school band is playing various marches while many citizens of Virginia City sit and wait for the festivities to begin.

"Are you nervous?" Captain North asks.

"Irritated is more precise."

"Well, contain that emotion a little longer and be that proud servant of the people you are. The festivities will begin as soon as the Mayor arrives."

"I see that," Jason sighs, waiting for the Mayor's fashionably late arrival. "I just want this unnecessary event over with."

"I told you the reason behind this."

"Right, I'm being used to enhance his political career."

"All a part of politics, my friend; you should know this."

A black stretch limousine arrives and parks on the side of the platform where the steps are located. The chauffeur quickly opens the rear door and the Mayor steps out. He's a short balding middle-aged man wearing a black tuxedo with the cummerbund failing its attempt to hold in his bulging stomach. The gleaming sun draws automatic attention to his bald spot. A pair of white pumps hit the ground; an overpowering woman standing a few inches taller than the Mayor retrieves his waiting arm. The Mayor's wife is many years younger and wears a white sequined dress which hugs her nicely. They ascend the four steps of the platform while the band plays a rendition of "Hail to the Mayor." Once at the microphone the Mayor waves a hand and the music stops. He makes a small speech about the city's reduction in burglaries, homicides and other crimes in all areas of Virginia City during his tenure in office. He draws a light applause with talk of becoming the Governor.

Next, he mentions the outstanding efforts of all the precincts under his jurisdiction. Special attention is made of the Sixteenth Precinct. Notably, he recognizes the efforts of Detective Jason Jerrard and his key role in releasing the city from the wrath of its most vicious murderer-rapist.

His congratulatory remarks about Jason for his dedication to duty and superior performance all through his years on the force make him sound inhuman. Soon, Jason is asked to come to the podium. After a quick hand-shake, he's presented a plaque, which the Mayor reads to the audience.

"This plaque is presented to Detective Jason Jerrard for devotion to duty, above and beyond all expectations. Virginia City is proud to have an officer as fine as you. Sincerely, Mayor Blake and all of the citizens of Virginia City."

The second award presented to Jason is the symbolic key to the city. Mayor Blake takes a few steps back allowing Jason to enjoy his fifteen minutes of fame. Jason nods to the applause, delivers a brief speech, pauses, and then addresses the audience with one question.

"Which door does this key fit?"

Several chuckles roar through the crowd. Afterwards, a small receiving line consisting of the Mayor and his wife, the Commissioner, Captain North and other city officials form to greet Jason. As the band plays their final number, Jason reluctantly walks down the line for his final congratulations.

While shaking the Mayor's wife's hand, her eyes widen and embarrass-ment immediately shows. An uneasy feeling consumes him as he instantly realizes that she's the same woman from the restaurant and motel. Trying not to look surprised, he smiles to himself as she stumbles for words.

"Congratulations, Detective Jerrard," she says.

"Thank you, Mrs. Mayor?" Jason says puzzled.

"Crystin."

"Thank you...Crystin."

Jason walks off the platform and is followed by the receiving party. The crowd begins to disperse and the receiving party gathers for their last goodbyes. The Mayor calls Jason over for a formal introduction to his wife.

"Detective Jerrard," the Mayor addresses, "thank you again for your extreme dedication to our fine city."

"No thanks necessary, Sir. If I may use a cliché, I'm just doing my job."

"Jason, I'd like you to meet the backbone behind my sanity. This is my lovely wife, Crystin."

As if the Mayor needs to impress all within his hearing range, he continues his bellow.

"Look at those dark mysterious-looking eyes. Aren't they gorgeous? Because of them, I call her Shadow. Shadow, this is Detective Jason Jerrard."

"Call me Jason," he interjects.

"Pleased to meet you again," she responds.

"Likewise."

Their handshake is quite different from the one on the platform. She reaches out her hand and squeezes his more caressingly, reminiscent of a few days past. However, her hand is clammy, as more nervousness shows, driven by an unexpected lustful feeling. Jason tenderly holds her hand and fights the urge to gaze into her eyes.

Jason is pulled to the side by Captain North to discuss his return to work. With some masterful maneuvering, he is back in Shadow's company as the Mayor is standing nearby being occupied by the Commissioner.

"What time is it?" Crystin questions.

"Three-oh-six," Jason says while intently gazing into her eyes.

"Excuse me, Jason," the Mayor interrupts. "It seems that your watch is malfunctioning. The correct time is 4:56 p.m."

"Really," Jason announces anxiously. "I have approximately two hours to prepare for another engagement. I must get going. Thanks for the recognition. It is nice when a public servant is seen in a positive manner for a change."

"I agree with you wholeheartedly."

Jason leaves abruptly. Later, he finds himself preparing for an evening that may never occur. He showers, changes clothes and heads for his predicated destination. After settling into the temporary domicile, he immediately orders the necessary ingredients to make the evening magnetic. As luck would have it, these ingredients arrive before his unconfirmed guest. He's careful in placing everything in its proper place. Sitting in a chair he runs over in his mind the plan for the evening.

Precisely at 7:00 the door blossoms with a knock. Jason dims the lights and slowly answers the door with a warm smile. No words are spoken as his guest adorned in a long elegant dress with a zipper down the back enters the room. Without a sound he grabs her sweaty palms and pulls her near.

"I hoped you'd come, Mrs. Mayor Blake," he whispers.

"Please don't call me that. I hate that."

"I'm sorry…Shadow is your pet name, isn't it?"

"That's worse. Crystin will do fine."

"I knew you'd come, Crystin," Jason says before kissing her neck.

"I didn't want to, knowing that you know who I am, but, I am driven. There is something irresistible about you. Besides, there is some unfinished business between us."

"I'm glad you caught my clue."

"Simple logic. This is room 306. It was something to five when I asked for the time and approximately two hours from then is now: 7:00."

"Maybe, you should be the detective. Anyway, I'm pleased that we are on the same frequency. However, I was a little leery about you remembering the room number."

"Are you kidding? It's the only thing I've thought of since I was last here. Hell, I even played the number in the three-digit lottery."

"How did you get away?"

"Like I always do, I just leave. He doesn't care about my whereabouts as long as I'm there to look pretty for him in public. Of course, you know I can't stay too long."

Jason believes that her last two sentences contradicted each other, but, he does not express his concern.

"Understood, but what did you say to him when you returned home last time?"

"Nothing. When I got home he was asleep. I removed my clothes and climbed in bed. The next morning when he asked me what time I got home, I told him a time hours before I arrived."

"It was that simple? I imagined you'd have a difficult time explaining your whereabouts."

"I have two things in my favor. One, he usually goes to bed early. Two, he sleeps very sound."

"I say you're lucky because that isn't the impression he instilled in me."

"We put on a good show, don't you think? That comment he made about his backbone is bullshit; excuse my French."

"Seriously though, I think you should've told me that you were the Mayor's wife."

"Would you have talked to me?"

With the lift of a brow, Jason replies, "Only at the restaurant."

"Well then, my disclosure was the proper thing to do. After all, you invited me back. Why did you, considering how I acted the last time I was here?"

"Your emotions aren't anything to be ashamed of; besides, now I can find answers to so many unanswered questions."

"And all of this?" she states while glancing at his preparations.

"It is all part of the unanswered questions."

"It appears that you've thought of everything."

Jason has a small candlelit table setting placed in the center of the room. Silver candlestick holders and matching food warmers decorate the table. Covered on the table are several delectable seafood dishes and a vegetable, each being warmed by a flame underneath. There is Burgundy wine to be consumed in long-stemmed crystal glasses and one red rose placed perfectly across her plate.

"I can't remember the last time I had one of these," she responds after smelling the rose.

"Just enjoy it with no remorse."

"What's on the menu?"

"Besides you?" he jokes. "Close your eyes."

She gives a bashful smile obeying the command. He lifts each cover one at a time, fans their aroma in her direction.

She inhales deeply, holding the aroma within her for a few seconds before replying, "It smells scrumptious. Seafood!"

"I figured I couldn't go wrong with seafood. It's a standard with women according to the woman's handbook, page twenty-seven."

"And who wrote this handbook?"

"Me, of course...am I correct?"

"In most cases you are, this one included," she confesses.

Jason seats her and takes his place across the tiny table. He seizes one of her hands, and inappropriately caresses it considering his head is lowered for a brief prayer. Crystin's head awkwardly bows. Afterwards, Jason gives simple but different dinner rules.

"No talking while we eat," Jason replies.

"What? How are we going to figure this all out?"

"Talk with your eyes," he instructs before motioning her to begin eating.

Crystin looks puzzled, wondering what to make of the odd dinner rules but complies with his wishes. Jason feels excited and intrigued. It falls short of how he felt when he met Sasha. However, it ranks high on his scale of lustfulness. This time though, the entire scenario is more baffling than ever.

Several times Crystin attempts to talk, but Jason quiets her by placing his index finger over her lips. The advantage she gains by forcing Jason's finger to her lips allows her to delicately suck on it, which she did on a couple of occasions. Crystin sees that he is affected by the playful move. She imagines that jolts of electricity are stimulating his sexual appetite. It compares little to the demanding hunger that sweeps over her each time she sucks one of his fingers. She imagines herself doubled over with cramps, hungry for his kind of food, his manly sensuous touch. The silent dinner allows her mind to wander into different fantasies, wondering what's in store for her. Jason sips on his wine contemplating how to move into the next phase of the evening.

"We can talk now," Jason instructs.

"Dinner is finished?"

"I'm stuffed...you?"

"I couldn't swallow another morsel. Besides, this silent business is not an easy thing to do."

"I noticed your eagerness to talk. What would you have said in lieu of sucking on my finger?"

"I would've questioned why the silence."

"That's all you thought of? What were you really thinking?"

"Some of the things that crossed my mind would make your blood boil."

"Like the unfinished business from last time?"

"That and other things. So, Mr. Twenty-One Questions, what crossed your mind?"

"Did you bring makeup?"

"Makeup, that's an odd thing to ask."

"Hopefully you did. Let's move into the bedroom."

"Is this where you seduce me and we have never-ending sex until I beg for mercy?"

"Wouldn't you like to know," Jason answers with a devilish grin.

Jason disappears into the bathroom and returns with a big bowl filled with hot steamy water. Crystin's eyes widen as a slight nervousness takes over her.

"What's that?" she asks.

"Nothing that will hurt you. Lie back, relax and enjoy. This is your night."

She takes a deep breath, releases a sigh of approval as Jason reaches into the bowl and produces a medium-sized towel billowing with steam.

"Relax," he says while wrapping the towel around her face. "Too hot?"

She shakes her head no. He presses the towel to her face and massages with his fingers. The warmth of the towel coupled with his gentle caressing make Crystin moan with acceptance.

"Hurts?"

Muffled words express, "Feels good."

After the towel cools, Jason removes it and holds it in the air by two of the corners. He looks at her while holding the towel and then repeats the procedure again.

"What's wrong?" she questions.

"Oh nothing...I'm looking at the makeup that the hot towel removed and can imagine your makeup-made face intact on the towel. Watch me as I peel it away from the towel and place it across the palm of my hand."

"You're silly, you know that?"

"You don't need this one."

"This one what?"

"This face, the one with makeup."

"Why do you say that?"

"Because in comparison, both faces are gorgeous but, hidden under your makeup is a warm natural beauty."

"That's a kind thing to say."

"Kind but true."

"I only wear it because Mr. Mayor expects me to. I have to look the part he says."

"Be your own woman."

"Come again?"

"Nothing," Jason lies.

"Be my own woman...I am...that's why I'm here with you."

"I can't argue with that."

"What comes after the face massage?"

"The rest of your bod."

"Am I the only receiving party tonight?"

"Most likely."

Smiles highlight her face being overwhelmed by her pampered treatment.

"What am I to do?" she says.

"Stand, please."

Jason gives her a firm hug, bites her lower lip and holds it between his teeth with minimal pressure as he unzips her dress. He walks his fingers down both sides of her neck toward her shoulders. The dress easily slides off of her shoulders and falls to the floor. Crystin stands with only a pair of pumps, sheer stockings and no bra. Her firm breasts reveal excitement being given away by her erect nipples. Jason stares drooling over his favorite look on a woman.

"Bra-less, huh?"

"Why not, they are firm and all natural," she boasts. "Besides, I didn't think I'd need the extra clothing."

Jason negotiates her pantyhose down to her ankles; eagerly she steps out of her shoes allowing him to remove the hose from her feet. She is left standing nude, bashful of his wandering eyes.

"What about your clothes?" she questions.

"Mine will follow soon, but for now, close your eyes."

"Why?"

"This is not for you to see first; you must feel it first."

"Feel what?"

"Shhh."

Jason slowly pulls the bed covers back and a fresh aroma overtakes their senses.

"What's that? Smells like springtime."

"You'll know soon enough; for the moment, keep your eyes closed."

He scoops her up into his arms and lays her down on the king-sized bed covered with red rose petals. Immediately, her nakedness absorbs the rose petals' softness. She wiggles on them in disbelief before grabbing a handful of petals and brings the clutched fist to her nose.

"Roses?" she responds enthusiastically while opening her eyes.

"Surprised?"

"Very, this is quite unusual. You have unique ways."

"Pleased then?"

"Extremely."

"Go ahead, roll around a bit, enjoy yourself while I get hotter water."

Crystin tosses and turns in the petals like an adult stuck in adolescence. Jason returns naked with the hotter water and joins her in bed. Crystin's eyes devour Jason's powerful frame as she wonders if he can feel her eyes drawn to his manhood. She willingly accepts his instruction to lie on her back. He covers her body with a steamy hot towel that extends from her shoulders to below her waist. His massive hands begin working on her tense shoulders. Soon, her entire upper body is placed into a relaxed state by the soothing massage. The tender caressing of each breast feels more erotic because of his gentle touch. Jason moves to her upper inner thighs, deliberately brushing her womanhood as he switches from one leg to the other sending strong cravings throughout her body.

"Jason…Jason?" Crystin cries.

"Yes."

"Forget the massage."

"Doesn't it please you?"

"Yes, yes, yes!" she urges. "I can't wait any longer."

"It isn't time."

"Don't make me wait. I want to feel you inside of me."

"All right, join me in the bathroom."

"What's next?"

"Wait, you'll see."

She steps off of the bed, hair flowing behind her, aided by the brisk walk toward the bathroom. Jason watches her toned body float effortlessly as if it were not moving at all. They enter the huge bathroom that has over-sized mirrors, an oversized separate shower and a gigantic Jacuzzi tub that comfortably seats four. The Jacuzzi jets send the aroma of more flowers into the air.

"More roses, Jason?"

"Let's say they are a substitute for bath oil."

They engage in hot and steamy necking for minutes before Jason swoops her into his arms and steps out of the tub. Quickly he turns on the heat lamp, grabs a towel and begins to dry her wet body.

"Jason, why all of this?"

"All of what?"

"Dinner, roses, basically pampered treatment. I came here willingly. I'm a sure thing."

"As someone from the hood might say, that's just the way I roll," he replies with exaggerated movements. "Seriously, though I barely know you, I didn't want it to seem like a physical thing only."

"What else could you possibly call it?"

"Yin and Yang."

"What?"

"I give you what you want and you give me what I need. We both gain."

"I never looked at it that way."

"Look at it this way," Jason says as he begins to nibble on her neck.

"I like it this way."

His hands squeeze her back firmly. Initially, Crystin's body cringes to his roughness, but soon responds favorably sensing her womanhood moistening. Her nipples harden as she becomes sensitive to his touch. Jason drops to his knees and his nails claw down her back during their descent. The slight pain is overshadowed by the pleasure of the act, sending surrender thoughts throughout her being. He nibbles on her inner thigh which makes her jump uncontrollably. Jason attacks her wet-box hungrily, eager to please. Her head falls back, and her back arches as she begins to move to the rhythm of Jason's mouth.

Along with his actions, the soothing heat from the sunlamp beaming on her face and breast places her into another dimension. She finds herself wandering around in a land called ecstasy, searching for the only known route back to reality. Her mind and body pass through many forms of pleasure until she reaches a neon-lit tunnel called climax. Slowly, she enters the passageway following imaginary signs that read, "This way to pleasure." Her body begins to tremble as she glides through various sensations while becoming more and more excited.

She begins to moan upon reaching the end of the tunnel. Having followed her only guide—a blinding burnt orange warm light that enhances sensuous feelings throughout her body—out of the tunnel, her moans become deep and broken, letting loose a vibrant cry as Jason continues his actions bringing her to a tremendous orgasm.

"Oh, Jason," she moans while falling to the floor.

"Are you all right?" Jason says concerned. "You fell pretty hard."

"No, yes!" she pants. "What an incredible journey."

"Journey?"

"Never mind, wow! Are you always this kind?"

"Always, care to join me in bed?"

"I don't have the energy to get up."

"Sure you do," he says while running his hand through her wetness then places the fingers into his mouth.

Jason leaves for the bed while Crystin attempts to regain her composure. Finally, she stumbles into the bedroom finding Jason lying on his back with his member erect. She climbs onto the bed and strokes it softly.

"Seeing you like this makes me hungry," Jason says.

"For food?"

"Me want human," Jason jokes. "Are you going to feed me?"

"With pleasure." Crystin mounts Jason and takes a deep breath as their midsections meet. "You're a hard man to handle."

Jason only smiles. Slowly, she begins hip movements that fill her body with sensual pleasure. Initially, her pleasure movements are short up and down on his penis moves. Later, they are replaced by such long, hard body-waving motions that Jason swears he sees her body ripple from her breasts to where their bodies connect. Jason grinds his hips into hers, literally doubling the effect for both of them. In a short while, their bodies moisten with sweat from a sudden accelerated tempo. Their wild bucking begins their race to an orgasm. Reminiscent of stage actors, they bellow as explosive screams leave their mouths. Crystin falls forward exhausted.

Jason pulls her wild wet hair from her eyes before replying, "I like this on you."

"This what?"

"The just-fucked look; it's radiant on you."

"I've never heard that one."

Silence consumes the room as her hard, heavy breathing quickly softens to normal, below normal, then in a deep sleep, slower breathing takes over. Jason hugs her firmly, securing her in his embrace. Hours later, they awake.

Crystin frantically grabs his watch.

"Oh shit," she says excitedly. "I told Mr. Mayor I'd be home hours ago."
She runs into the bathroom, quickly bathes, dresses hurriedly and applies more makeup while apologizing for being abrupt. Jason steps out of the bed.

"You look so appealing like that," Crystin pleads, "but I must go."

"I understand."

"I'll call you...Sixteenth Precinct, right?"

"Yes."

"You've been fantastic. Got to run, bye," she says after kissing his cheek.

"Quick question, how are you going to explain your tardiness this time?"

"I'll think of something creative."

"Do that. It might be best."

They kiss passionately under the open doorway, mostly concealed from the outside view of a naked eye but, unsuspecting to them, a camera's shutter clicks repeatedly.

Crystin enters Astoria Estates, the most prominent area in all of Virginia City. The who's who of the city claim their homes here. She turns into the circular driveway, approaches a huge multistory house with large columns. She's uneasy with her explanation of her whereabouts. However, after a quick glance into the mirror to summon her courage and face the dilemma at hand, she dashes for the door. Upon entering the house she finds Mayor Blake pacing the entrance foyer anticipating her return.

"My darling Shadow, where have you been?"

"Oh, honey it was awful," she pretends. "I've been a nervous wreck."

"Why, what happened?" he questions with concern.

"First of all, I was run off the road by a car which came up behind me speeding. It didn't look like it was going to stop. I had to actually drive on the median to avoid being hit. I sat there shaking trying to get my rattled nerves back together. When I pulled back on the road, I'd swear that same car began following me."

"You should've gone to the police."

"That thought didn't even cross my mind. All I wanted to do was to lose that car. I made several turns in my escape attempt and found myself on the outskirts of the city. Being that far out, I became even more frightened so I checked into a motel called the Kings Inn under a false name. I should have called you once I got into the room but I wasn't thinking clearly, emotionally disturbed and all. I fell asleep. When I woke up, I rushed home."

"Why didn't you just drive home first?"

"Surely, I didn't want that person to know where I live."

"You should've called for my help."

"I know, I know, but then you would insist on me taking bodyguards with me everywhere I go."

"They're escorts."

"Bodyguards. As I've said many times before, I don't want any."

"After tonight's episode, you really shouldn't be so stubborn."

"I'll take my chances. There is a slight chance that I'm being a bit paranoid."

"Okay, it's late. We can talk more about this in the morning."

"My answer will be the same."

"Let's go to bed. I'm feeling lucky." He smiles. "That's if you're emotionally okay."

"You mean sex?" she replies with false excitement.

"Yes, let's play house."

"We can do what grownups do?"

"Possibly invent something new of our own."

"Maybe I should disappear more often if it brings on this type of mood."

"That is not funny."

Crystin's lie is taken as the truth. But now having to engage in sex with a man who she hates to be touched by makes her cringe. As her head hits the pillow, immediately her thoughts turn toward Jason.

FIVE

Friday morning on Jason's first day back to work, he is greeted with a small welcoming committee of fellow officers. Throughout the station he is congratulated on his speedy recovery. After all the hoopla dies, Jason settles at his desk and plays with paperclips while wondering what his next assignment might be. Sgt. Kevin Austin approaches his desk with a slight smile.

"What's new around here?" Jason asks.

"SSDD."

"Okay, my slang is rusty these days."

"Same shit, different day."

"Surely you have something more positive than that to say?"

"I'm dieting," Sgt. Austin boasts. "I'm positive that I'll stick to it."

"Really, that's great. What is your motivation?"

"Our conversation in that coffee shop sometime ago."

"I didn't say anything about your weight."

"I know, but after it, I felt I should take charge of my life, starting with my weight. I've lost eight pounds already."

"Really, I'm pleased to hear that."

"Well, I see you're still the same."

"Meaning?"

"Look at you, wounds to the chest and shoulder and no type of harness."

"A sling, it goes well with my attire," Jason says sarcastically.

"Sorry, I forgot that you were Mister GQ."

"In my defense, it didn't fit comfortably over or under my clothes."

"You left the hospital so quickly, me and the boys bought you something special. Top drawer on the left." He points anxiously.

Jason reaches in the drawer and pulls out what appears to be a blue cloth wrapped in plastic. He removes its covering and is disturbed—not slightly amused with the cape with a Superman emblem on the back.

"Cute, real fucking cute. You all are still trying to make me out to be some sort of superhero. I tell you, if assholes could fly, this place could be an airport."

"It's just a gag, Jason; don't get upset. We thought it would ease the tension."

"With all the rumors floating around, this seems to be a bit unpractical."

"All right, I'll return it for a real gift."

"No, no, that would spoil all of your fun. I can play along. I'm damn happy to be out of the house."

Jason ties the cape's string around his neck and imitates Superman's best stance while standing on his desk.

"How's this?" Jason asks.

"Great, really great. The guys would die," Sgt. Austin replies. "Oh, before I forget, the Captain wants to see you."

"The last time you said that, I was assigned that madman."

"This time, he only wants your report on the murderer-rapist's downfall."

"That's easy...I'll take it to him now."

Jason reaches into his briefcase, pulls out a folder and flies down the hall creating wind-gust sound effects with his mouth. He lands and rap's lightly on the door.

"Enter," Captain North instructs.

Jason slings the door open while imitating his best Superhero stance.

"Boy Wonder, come in. I trust you're feeling better."

"Yes, remember, I'm Super Somebody."

"Take a seat, fool. It is time for business. We found all kinds of incriminating evidence in the rapist's home. Many loose ends came together. This, incidentally, is why your unprofessional conduct was dismissed. I expect a complete report on what happened the night he died."

"Right here, Sir," Jason replies while holding up the folder.

"Covering everything including the severed ankle?"

"It's all in here."

"Excellent. Now, I don't want you involved in any stressful cases until your health is one hundred percent."

"Come on, Frank, you know that isn't my style. I'd go crazy."

"It's either that or forced leave. Take it easy for a while; after all, you're the city's hero. You deserve a break from all the stress and strain of detective work. Hell, you don't have to drive all the way here from the country. A call a day would be sufficient for the time being."

"That sounds like forced leave."

"Not really, it's your call. You can stay home; otherwise, come here and do nothing. Just give yourself some time to get healthy."

"Okay," Jason reluctantly responds, "but I don't see myself pushing papers."

"When your health is back at its full capacity, then you can wear that cape again as it's meant to be worn."

"Fine, well then, I'll just fly out of your hair."

"Going where?"

"To visit an old friend. I'll return shortly."

Jason returns to his desk. Heading toward him is Chris McAllister, Jason's rival dating back to the academy and another officer named Mike. They are laughing and joking about how Jason's near-death experience hasn't changed him.

"Nice cape." Chris laughs. "Why don't you fly around the office and show us your true ability?"

"My," Jason jokes. "If it isn't the Off Brothers."

"The Off Brothers. I don't know of them."

"Yes, you do. Jerk and Jack," Jason replies while pointing at each respectively.

Mike begins laughing hysterically while Chris turns different shades of red, embarrassed that the unsuspecting ear has heard the comment.

"Anyway," Chris says, "I'm glad you're okay and back to work. One day," he replies with envy, "I'd like to know how you do it."

"How I do what?"

"He's referring to me," a woman's voice answers.

Chris and Mike part, and stepping through the middle of them is Monique Clemens, Jason's first, true love.

"Let's leave Romeo alone," says Chris. "Remember, if you need any help, I mean anything," he says, scanning her body, "call on me."

"You see something you like?" she asks.

"Yes indeed," Chris answers lustfully. "You are tempting, tantalizing, and sexy, all in one package."

Monique takes a couple of steps toward him, presses her breasts against his chest and leans toward his ear.

"Do you think that you can actually handle this package?" she asks while highlighting her figure in the fashion of a game-show hostess.

"Oh Chris," Mike replies, "she burned you."

"If I can," Chris says somewhat ruffled, "I win. If I can't, I still win."

"Just like I figured," Monique says before directing her attention to Jason. "All talk and no stamina."

"Mike," Jason says, "take this crash and burn victim and get him some first aid."

"Funny, Jason," Chris responds.

"Goodbye, Chris," Jason says abruptly.

Chris and Mike leave Jason's desk with Mike ragging and laughing about how Chris had gotten pie thrown in his face.

"Monique," Jason conveys pleasingly surprised. "When did you get so testy? I don't remember you being this way."

"I'm not testy, but that Chris person could have behaved like a gentleman and kept his sexist remarks to himself. He's lucky that I'm not overly sensitive with the sexual harassment thing."

"I can be a third party witness to it."

"Don't bother. What is his problem anyway?"

"He envies me. Right now, I envy me, especially with you standing here. Have a seat and tell me when did you get back in town?"

"I came back a few days ago," she replies with a puzzled look.

"Oh, excuse the cape," Jason explains while untying the string at the neck. "It's a gift the guys gave me."

"Signifying?"

"A rumor…oh, never mind, how in the hell are you?"

"I'm terrific, but tell me why they think you're Superman. That should be quite intriguing."

"If you say so, but on another note, I'm overwhelmed to see you. I apologize for not stopping by your motel when you were last here."

"That's okay; you had a lot of drama going on then."

"I will make a point to see you this time. Are you in the same motel?"

"No, try apartment."

"Apartment, this sounds permanent."

"Yes. Well, until I can find a townhouse or single-family home to purchase."

"This is fantastic news. You must tell me all about it. I was just about to leave for a quick bite. Care to join me?"

"I'd be delighted."

"I'm heading to…"

"Rosalina's," Monique interrupts.

"It's still my favorite place. I even tried a fancy French restaurant. The food was good but it just didn't have the same atmosphere as Rosalina's."

"Will you ever forget that place?"

"No, someplace deep inside tells me if I forget Rosalina's, I lose cherished memories of you."

Monique smiles.

Arriving at Rosalina's shortly before lunch hour, Jason is greeted with a warm smile from the establishment's maitre d' and Jason's close personal friend, Alfredo. Alfredo is an older gentleman, many years Jason's senior.

"Good day," Alfredo states surprisedly. "I'm very pleased to see you're well."

"Thanks."

"I was so worried about you. I dropped by the hospital on several occasions and each time you were sleeping. The doctors didn't understand why you slept so, but Dr. Bodou assured me that you weren't in a coma."

"Maybe that's why I had a speedy recovery. I rested well."

"Yes, how are your wounds?"

"I'm fine. I get the most pain when I do something I shouldn't do like lifting weights."

"You're lifting already," intrudes Monique. "When did you do this?"

"A few days ago…very light weights though."

"You're crazy, are you trying to cause permanent damage to yourself? This explains the cape…good thing, I'm here," Monique says, purposely letting her leading remark linger, "to help look after you."

"Let's talk about why you're here…Monique, meet Alfredo, Alfredo…"

"I remember this charming woman from the last time," Alfredo ensures. "It is very nice to see you again."

"Likewise," Monique responds.

"I'll seat you now, follow me."

"Thank you, old friend," Jason says, "that will not be necessary. I could find the booth blindfolded."

"I'm sure of that," Alfredo concurs by stopping in his tracks, letting Jason escort his guest to his table.

Jason stops to express his gratitude for Alfredo's concern over his well-being.

"Dear friend, thank you…" Jason pauses extremely intrigued and tickled that Alfredo's attention is drawn in a hypnotic glare deliberately fixed on Monique's butt. Jason stands in place, chuckling internally and wearing a dumbfounded expression. "…for…coming…to…see me," he slowly continues.

Alfredo's eyes meet Jason's. Instantly a rose color overtakes his face.

"My friend, what's gotten into you?" Jason questions barely able to contain his laughter.

"Was it that bad?" he replies with an embarrassed tone, one that's new to Jason's ears.

"Bad, real bad. When did you get like this?"

"In which way are you referring?" Alfredo asks, attempting to regain himself.

"You know very well what I'm talking about. The way you are admiring the ladies."

"My apologies, it has been a long…well you know what I'm referring to. You are actually going to let me suffer through this?"

Jason smiles. "There is nothing wrong with that; you just have to be more discreet while you're checking out the goods."

Again, Alfredo blushes in a way unfamiliar to him.

"Yes, I must," Alfredo agrees as he places his arm around Jason's shoulders. "Pardon me, Madam," he delivers while walking Jason away from her, stopping behind the podium to conceal himself. "I don't want to be heard."

Jason remains silent, awed by his peculiar behavior.

"This stuff I'm taking finally worked. Viagra." Alfredo pauses, waiting for some response from Jason.

Again, there is silence but this time accompanied with a huge smile.

"Don't be too amused," Alfredo defends. "We old dogs often think about how it was to be young. Viagra may provide that for me."

"That's wonderful news. Just don't hurt anyone," Jason jokes.

"Today is the first time I've seen results. Just now, it stood like a natural man."

"What, now?" Jason asks after noticing Alfredo's rouge-colored face for a third time.

"Why do you think I'm concealing myself."

"Aw, you go, boy. For your sake, I hope no other female customers arrive. You could be standing there for hours."

"Indeed, Sir. I believe I've taken you away from your lady friend long enough."

"We will talk later," Jason assures and approaches Monique with the most inquisitive expression freely showing.

"Well, spit it out," Monique demands.

Jason's smile is a sure indication that she may not want to know the answer.

"Boy talk," Jason replies while using all control to contain the laughter raging within him.

"Boy talk, that's all you have to say. I sense something more than that. Alfredo's mannerisms are extremely different from the last time," Monique states defying Jason's defensive overtures.

"Let's sit. I know the way."

Monique's feet are planted, hands on her hips. An expression occupies her face coinciding with the "duh?" that blurts out of her mouth.

"To respect his and my confidence, I can't tell you. But, boy," Jason delivers devilishly, "I'd love to."

"Okay, out of respect for your friendship, I will not pressure you."

"Thanks, it's appreciated."

After they're seated, Monique's order is placed. Immediately Jason drills her about her sudden return to Virginia City.

"Nothing has changed with you, has it? We sit at the same booth as before," Monique says.

"I told you once that this is considered my booth. Tell me dear, what brings you back to this city?"

"I'm here because of concern."

"For me, I suppose."

"Yes, I caught the news and realized that you must be going through living hell."

"You mean Sasha?"

"Yes, her death must've been devastating to you. Did you actually witness her being shot?"

"Yes."

"That is something I don't think that I could bear."

"It has been difficult."

"I can tell by the way you talked about her that you cared for her deeply."

"Unfortunately, I realized that I loved her a little too late. However, I did get to tell her before she died. It was a most glorious moment."

"And she died shortly after that?"

"Yes, you see, she regained consciousness and we talked long enough for me to get an acceptance to my marriage proposal. Moments later, Julie took her away from me."

"So the murder-suicide that flavored the airways is correct?"

"Yes, only the part about her not regaining consciousness seems to be misreported. My police report has the true story."

"Jason…" Monique pauses. "Is this too difficult to talk about?"

"No, I have a good handle on it. Well, let's say I had a good talk with her at her grave. When I left that day, I could somehow feel that she wouldn't want me to be sad. She'd want me to live my life…a full life. I'm thankful that she's in a place where I hope to someday be."

"What placed her in the hospital?"

"I can't remember if I told you about the case I was assigned to the last time we talked…the murderer-rapist. Does that ring a bell?"

"No, but I remember reading about him in the papers."

"Well, it turns out that Sasha knew him. One night while I was sleeping, she went through my files and discovered some small clue that connected him to several rapes in the area. It was a long shot, but instead of telling me, she set out to help me. They were to meet here, the same night we were here together."

"So, that's how she came to be here on the very same night that we were here," Monique interrupts.

"Correct."

"How did you discover all of this?"

"She kept a journal on every aspect of her life. A very personal, detailed one depicting her childhood memories, things she cooked, romances, successful dates and failed dates. This is where it detailed her suspicions. So," Jason continues, realizing he had not thought of the painful memories since he had written his police report, "the night she was attacked, somehow she managed to escape. She came to me in the exact place where you left me."

"At the telephone outside of Rosalina's," Monique adds.

"Correct. She was so hysterical, I can't recall exactly what she said to me, but I knew that she was in danger. I pursued him; he eluded me and stole her car. I don't understand why she came back toward the scene, but when she did, he turned the car toward her. She hid behind a dumpster and he rammed it with her car, knocking her unconscious."

"The impact caused her coma?"

"Yes, but most damaging to me," Jason continues with a more disturbed tone, "is the baby we lost."

"She was pregnant?" Monique says surprised. "Did you know?"

"No, she started hemorrhaging while in the coma. After a thorough examination, a D&C was administered."

"Damn, that's awful," Monique responds in shock and with concern.

"The bad part is…that was the second time. The poor woman should not have had to go through that procedure twice in a lifetime."

"You're absolutely right. So," Monique asked, needing an answer to a burning question, "how did it affect you?"

"When I found out that my baby was lost, I lost me, too. I became more determined to find this madman. Out of sheer desperation, I searched her place based on something she said to me."

"What could have stuck in your head that much to make you want to search her place?"

"You remember, we were sitting as we are now, and Sasha screamed with frustration that she was trying to help me. It plagued my mind, driving me to believe that she was hiding or not telling me something, so I went on a wild-goose chase. I stumbled across her journals; one of them detailed her suspicions about possibly knowing the man I was searching for. I really lost my senses and revenge dominated me from that point until I took the bastard down," Jason states more emotionally.

"You don't have to continue. I can understand your rage."

"Okay," he agrees relieved with not having to rehash the ordeal. "Now you, why so much concern over me?"

"We have a past, a history together. I just want to be here if there is ever a time that you need me."

"That's sweet, but I think I'm ruined."

"How so?"

"Sasha's death delivered a powerful blow to me emotionally. I made myself change; I hardened my heart. Already, I've done things that I'm not exactly proud of."

"You're afraid of relationships now?" she replies in a dismal tone.

"Self-preservation, that's all. I couldn't stand another hurt."

"All relationships, Jason?"

"I'm afraid so."

Monique's eyes close for a few seconds as if to banish the words that just intercepted her ears.

"I hadn't planned on bringing this up," Monique states with summoned courage. "But, now is a better time than any. I came back to town so I could be available for you when you got your emotions back together. It's selfish of me but I live with the dream of you and me together. That precious day will be many years late, nevertheless, a happy day."

"Wow," Jason responds. "After all this time, you still want us?"

"Based on your comment as we left the precinct, *you* may still want us. I've never stopped wanting us. Fate was unfair to us early on in our lives…so, fate has me back in town for another chance at what should have been."

"I've a special place in my heart for you. I believe it can grow, but at this very moment, I'm afraid to let it go."

"I know, Jason; believe me, I understand more than you think I do and I'm not trying to force you into anything. No pressures—I just want to know what your feelings are toward me."

"I know that we have feelings that are embedded deep in our hearts. Just give me some time because there's one thing I learned. I can love again. It's a matter of deciding to let my hardened heart roam freely."

"Understood. I've waited for this opportunity for over two decades; a little more time won't kill me."

"How's Jason?" Jason asks, referring to Monique's son.

"He's fine. When I told him that I was relocating back to Virginia City, he became excited."

"Excited about coming back to Virginia City?"

"Actually, he is excited about meeting you."

"Me?" Jason replies surprisedly.

"Yes, remember, I raised him to be like you."

"My unseen son. It's still hard to believe that you named him after me."

"You said our feelings are deeply embedded. I also happen to know that the thought of us getting together excites him as well."

"He told you this?"

"In his own bashful way, yes."

"Where is he now?"

"He is out of college and working as a software engineer. He will visit when I get settled."

"Speaking of which, where are you staying?"

"The Arbors."

"The ones outside of the city?"

"Yes, and I know that they are a stone's throw away from your house."

"How convenient?"

"I moved there because they were the only apartments in the area that allow me to rent on a month-to-month basis. I plan to buy a house as soon as I can," Monique explains.

The food is served. Quickly they devour their meals almost without stopping to breathe. They stare at each other with uncertainty, but not enough uncertainty to keep their minds from entertaining erotic thoughts. However, neither will voice their private notions.

"Okay," Monique asks, "why the half-smile?"

"Oh...nothing."

"I want to hear those things you just expressed with your eyes."

"I'm just thinking about my sixteenth birthday."

"What about...oh," she replies. "We've done that a thousand times or more in my mind."

"You know, I'm having an anniversary of my sixteenth birthday soon."

"I know it's coming soon."

"That's strange," Jason jokes. "I don't feel a thing."

"Comedian, are we?"

"Humor never hurt anyone."

"Good humor doesn't. Is it a date; do we indulge in frustrated sex on your birthday?"

"Why frustrated sex?"

"Well, I figure after all these years, some frustration must be present."

"Yes, but why sex?"

"I thought it would sound better than frustrated fucking."

"My dearest, Monique, the only thing that our separation hasn't revealed to you is, I don't fuck or have sex with someone I have feelings for."

Monique hopes that Jason can't see that his comment makes her blush; it warms her and verifies things she's known for years.

"Should I have said, making love?" asks Monique.

"That would have been better but, being intimate would be more precise."

"If my choice of words has provoked you in a negative way, then accept my deepest apologies."

"I did not say all of that because I'm upset. I simply stated it for clarity."

"Things are clear now," Monique states. She pauses and smiles before continuing her words. "But, frustrated intimacy seems to lose something."

Jason shakes his head and smiles.

"Mind you, I'm not saying that it won't be good," she boasts.

Alfredo places the check on the table. Jason pulls out a credit card and places in on the check. Nervousness coupled with fright immediately consume Monique's facial expression. She tries hard to contain her sudden mood swing while reflecting on her robbery last night.

"Yes," Jason says.

"Yes what?"

"You look like you want to say something…hmm, more like you've just seen a ghost."

"Nothing is wrong, seriously," she replies defensively.

"Whoa there, horsey…is something really wrong?"

"No, I just had a chill," she lies.

"Are you sure?" Jason double-checks, almost positive that he'd been told an untruth.

"Yes, I'm fine."

"All right, if you ever need me," Jason assures, "I'll be there for you."

"I know you will," she says while glancing at her watch. "Must you leave at this moment?"

"Actually, the Captain has given me strict orders not to get involved with anything strenuous until my health is one hundred percent. So, I don't really have a reason to hurry back."

"Unfortunately, I've an appointment with a client shortly, but I can call you later this evening."

"Great, maybe I can come over and help you unpack boxes."

"I can use all the help I can get. But, I will not be the person responsible for you straining yourself."

They leave with unclear thoughts. Monique is anxious but cautious not to push too hard for Jason's feelings. Yet, her heart motivates her to run full steam ahead. Jason's thoughts wander to the deep dark cells of his heart. They examine the structure of his encased emotions, knock and slide a note under the door advising that it may be too soon to release.

SIX

Sly and Reggie walk into the camera shop to retrieve the pictures taken Thursday night. Anxiously, they tear open the package with hopes that the photographs will prove to be rewarding.

"I don't see how they can come out," Reggie says. "It was dark outside."

"With the right film and lens you can shoot under almost any condition."

"What made you follow this guy anyway?"

"I have a personal vendetta against him. Well, I guess more like a pet-peeve."

"You know him?"

"Just like you, I know of him. The city recognizing one man when hundreds of officers risk their lives daily is absurd. That's what I'm upset about!"

"Yeah, but he did rid the city of an evil person."

"Yeah, yeah." Sly sighs in disgust. "Like thousands of other officers don't risk their lives every day doing the same thing."

"You want revenge?"

"I want something better than revenge. I want to get even. I'm going to destroy him just to show the public that their golden boy is not all that he portrays. His rise to fame will be short. This I promise."

"I sense lots of ill feelings in you."

"That's only half of it. I do feel strongly that others should have been awarded with him."

"Man, you got issues. Anyway," Reggie says, sensing Sly's anxiety. Changing the subject, he states, "It's too bad we didn't see which room he rented."

"That's okay; we know where he lives. He's not going anywhere. These pictures of Mrs. Mayor Blake are something to concentrate on."

They view the pictures; most are incriminating to Crystin. Wondering what the Mayor's reaction will be, Sly plans his course of action.

"It's too bad we can't make out her lover," Reggie says. "It would be the icing on the cake."

"We'll make do with these."

"What's our plan now?"

"Somehow we have to get a private meeting with the Mayor. He'll have a strong interest in these."

"How can you be so sure?"

"You heard him at the ceremony; he's running for the Governor's office. He will want to pay us hush money for these pictures. If not, I'm sure one of the local or even national tabloids will have a field day with them."

"Now, I see the grand scheme of things."

Bright and early the next day, Sly and Reggie are at the post office. They express mail a brief note and a photograph of Crystin standing outside the motel. The envelope is addressed to Mayor Blake, Virginia City, City Hall with no return address. The following day the Mayor is greeted with the envelope. Immediately, he questions its origin. After opening the envelope he reads the note:

Hopefully you have an interest in seeing the other pictures that accompany this one. I prefer a private meeting. 397-1324.

The Mayor views the picture of Crystin. His first reaction is extreme anger which later turns into sympathy for his wife who seemingly likes playing with fire. He summons his most trusted friend, James Freeman. He is an enormous, burly man standing well over six feet four inches with a deep baritone voice. Junior in age by a few years, he is considered point guard to the Mayor by taking on and tying up the Mayor's loose ends of a business and personal nature which would require the Mayor to remain anonymous.

"Yes, Sir," James replies after answering the intercom.

"I need to see you urgently."

Seconds later, James is standing in the Mayor's office.

"What do you think?" Mayor Blake asks after handing him the note and the picture.

"I don't get paid to think, but, I'll have it taken care of. Just say the word."

"No, we'll wait on that. I'd like to see the other pictures and discover their intention."

"It could be dangerous to your political future if the pictures ever became public."

"Play along with me. If this person wanted a quick buck, he could easily sell his evidence to the *National Enquirer* or any other tabloid for that matter. I think he wants me to buy them. Oh, the honor of it all," the Mayor adds, attempting to mix humor into the situation.

"Are you going to meet with him?"

"Yes, that's the plan."

"Of course," James defiantly states, "I will not let you attend this meeting alone."

James dials the number on the note. To his surprise the contact number given turns out to be a pager. He enters his return number and waits anxiously for a reply.

"What was that all about?" the Mayor questions.

"I left this number on a pager. Whoever this is should soon reply."

"We'll just wait and see."

"Do you recognize anything on the pictures?"

"Just my bitch of a wife. Do you see what I see?"

"You mean her seemingly waving goodbye to someone?"

"You see it also; otherwise I wouldn't care. She had already told me her whereabouts."

"I'm not trying to pry, but I warned you that she was a gold digger. Just looking at her, all I see is greed and a love for money."

"I should've been more selective but I was more or less blinded by her beauty. And, the physical stimulation caused by gazing at her was amazing. Honestly, it stood to full attention just being around her. That had never happened before...I figured she couldn't be but so bad. Besides, she seemed genuine with her love."

"We all make mistakes. It's time for you to rectify that situation, however, a divorce is definitely not appropriate with your political plans. Nothing wins an election like an untimely accidental death of a spouse."

"I don't want her dead. Cheating on your spouse is not punishable by death. If it was, I would've been hung a long time ago."

James nodded as if the Mayor has just spoken some form of revelation.

"I've a better..." The telephone rings interrupting his thoughts. Immediately, he picks up the phone. "Mayor Blake."

"Ah, Mayor," Sly replies. "I'm glad you found that picture intriguing enough to call me. After all, we wouldn't want these pictures to fall into the wrong hands."

"All right, who are you and what do you want?"

"We are both businessmen. I like conducting my business affairs in person and privately. I assume you feel the same."

"Where and when?"

"At the docks, there's an abandoned building called the Far East Import Company. Can you make it there tonight, around eight-thirty?"

"Consider it done. You'll have the remaining pictures and the negatives?"

"Will you have compensation for my time?"

"How much money do you want?"

"Somewhere in the neighborhood of ten-thousand dollars."

"That's a respectable neighborhood."

"Based on your comments Thursday afternoon having your personal life wrung through the mud would be disastrous."

"What comment?"

"The ones when you referred to yourself as Governor."

"I see. Blackmail."

"No blackmail.. let's call it securing your future and padding my pockets."

"Okay then, I'll see you there."

"Come alone."

"I'll have my closest colleague with me. He's already seen the picture."

"Him only, goodbye."

Sly hangs up abruptly. The Mayor holds the receiver in his hand wondering how the encounter might unfold. Briefly the authorities come to mind, but his best decision is one which entails handling the matter personally.

"Well, what did he say?" James questions.

"We are meeting him tonight at an abandoned building at the docks with ten-thousand dollars in exchange for the remaining pictures."

"That's a lot of money."

"The money doesn't bother me. I wonder, should I trust this man to have just one set of pictures."

"I tell you what," James insists, "if after tonight he tries for more money or the pictures miraculously appear in the tabloids, well...it's easy enough to trace the pager number and the rest of the story you don't have a need to know."

"Agreed."

"Do you think this is some kind of setup?"

"No, he only wants some quick money; otherwise, the amount he's demanding wouldn't be so small. Amateurs."

"Why don't we have the police arrest him after the exchange?"

"It would be hard to keep the pictures from surfacing, and the negative publicity moments before I begin my campaign will not fair well."

"Okay, we'll proceed as planned."

That evening the Mayor and his colleague arrive minutes before their scheduled appointment. A sign proclaiming the building as the Far East Import Company dangles down on one hinge while blowing in the mild night breeze. It has black painted windows with a huge metal sliding door. They open the door slightly and slip through the narrow space discovering a loft and several rows of hanging lights. Only one burn, casting a lighted circle on the huge warehouse floor.

"Are you sure this is the place?" James asks.

"This is the place that he mentioned. He'll be here."

"I'm already here," Sly says as he steps out of the shadows carrying a legal-sized manila envelope. "Gentlemen, let's make this short and sweet. You have the money?"

The Mayor steps forward with a briefcase. "A better question is, do you have the other pictures, as well as the negatives?"

"Right here," Sly says, patting the envelope.

"You're the person who spooked my wife a few nights ago?"

Sly gives a puzzling expression. "What do you mean?"

"Running her off the road. It was you, wasn't it?"

"Nope, wrong guess," Sly expresses seemingly confused. "I have no idea what you are talking about."

"Then, how did you come to follow her?"

"I wasn't following your wife. I was waiting for signs of someone else when I noticed her in the motel's doorway."

"Who were you tailing?"

"That's other business of mine; it's not important to you."

"It's just that I knew she checked into the motel. When she got home, she explained everything that happened."

"Why did you come here if you know everything?"

"I have to be sure that the picture isn't what I believe it to be."

"What's that?"

"Only you can tell me if she's really waving goodbye to someone. Was she?"

"Let me put it this way," Sly replies while reaching into the envelope for a more incriminating picture, one of Crystin kissing her unknown lover.

"This I didn't know about," the Mayor responds while attempting to control his rising temper.

"I didn't think you knew of her extra activities."

"Did you get a clear shot of her mate?"

"Nope, he stayed in the shadows. After recognizing your wife, I left knowing that my night would be profitable," Sly replies directing his attention to the briefcase.

"There are no more pictures or negatives, right?"

"You'll have to trust me on this. I don't operate like that."

"And this is the last I'll hear from you?"

"Right again."

They exchange items. Sly counts the money while the Mayor and James view the remaining pictures. After being satisfied that all the money is present, Sly silently begins to back away into the shadows.

"Gentlemen," Sly replies, "nice doing business with you."

"What is your name?" the Mayor asks.

"Just call me Sly."

"Sly, I have one remaining question for you…are you always this resourceful?"

"I'm good at what I do."

"What exactly do you do?"

"Anything, I'm motivated by the almighty dollar."

"Hum, we may do business again. That's if you're for hire?"

"Anytime."

"Good, I'll have to keep your contact number handy."

"Until then, goodbye," Sly says as he vanishes completely into the darkness.

"Why did you do that?" James asks.

"Do what?"

"He's already beat you for ten thousand and you'll be willing to give him more?"

"I just wanted to make sure he's available for possible future use. We can use someone like him on our team."

"I'm pleased to hear your confidence in me," Sly's voice interrupts. "Take this."

As Sly appears into the light, he's handing the Mayor half of the money he just received. James quickly grabs the money as if he is getting back stolen property.

"Why are you returning money?" James questions suspiciously. "None of it is marked."

"Let's say it's a matter of good faith," Sly replies.

"Now, there's a man who looks into the future. I like that," Mayor Blake responds.

"Well, you know how to contact me," Sly says as he quickly disappears.

The Mayor and James leave. James has many questions floating through his mind while the Mayor ponders his next move. After Sly is sure they are gone, a light comes on in the loft. Sly joins Reggie who has been hiding in the darkness.

"Did you get it all?" Sly questions.

"Yes, I got clear shots of the Mayor and his friend during the exchange."

"As I said, with the right film you can shoot under any condition."

"What will you use these pictures for?"

"Nothing now, originally as a precaution but since things turned out better than expected, I don't think they will be needed. However, we will keep them as our security policy."

"Do you think he'll call you back?"

"Certainly, I could hear it in his voice. Returning some of the money hooked him."

"Hopefully, you're right."

SEVEN

Late that evening the Mayor sits in the study dressed in a bathrobe watching television. He's awed by the pictures of his beloved Shadow. They lead him to find fault within himself for her actions because of his sexual appetite, but not enough to keep the anger and hurt controlled within him.

"Honey," Shadow says entering the room. "It's not like you to be up this late. Is something bothering you?"

"Just my upcoming campaign," he lies.

"Don't you worry about that; you're the favorite. I'm positive you'll get elected. Don't trouble yourself with such a meaningless thought."

"I don't know; it just seems like something always pops up to spoil my plans."

"What else is troubling you?"

"Nothing other than me worrying about you, and I still don't feel comfortable with what happened to you the other night."

"That's over with; probably some nut trying to initiate himself into a gang."

"Maybe you're right...I think though, you should let me give you some protection against people like that."

"No escorts, bodyguards, or anything of that sort. I can take care of myself. I did the other night and will continue to do so."

"That was smart of you to check into the motel and wait that person out."

"I saw fit to do that."

"What name did you check in under?"

"Reese, Gloria," Crystin says thinking fast.

"You're lucky they didn't ask for identification."

"They don't ask questions when you pay in cash."

"Regardless, I think you should accept my offer. Let me assign someone to you for a while. Long enough to make sure that nut isn't still on your trail."

"If it will make you feel any better, I'll consider it but for now, let's go to bed."

"Okay, that's a start."

They enter the bedroom; as the Mayor's head hits the pillow he's more than determined to have someone follow his reluctant wife. Crystin is relieved that the conversation has ended. Having to relive that lie makes her uneasy.

The next morning Crystin is up early. She's dressed and wakes the Mayor with a kiss on the cheek.

"Honey," she says, "see you later. I've a hair appointment."

"Okay," the Mayor mumbles.

As the Mayor hears Crystin's car drive off, he sits up in bed. Clearing his throat he picks up the telephone and dials information. After receiving the telephone number for the Kings Inn, he dials the front desk.

"Kings Inn, all of our rooms are suites," a woman's voice answers.

"Hello, may I have Gloria Reese's room?"

"One moment, please...I'm sorry, Sir. There's no one on today's register under that name."

"She would have checked in on Thursday."

"Thursday's register shows..." She pauses while scanning the book. "Ah, Gloria Reese, room 212. I'll connect you to her room."

"No need; I'll be by to see her later," the Mayor says before hanging up.

He pulls the envelope with the pictures from under his side of the mattress. He flips through the pictures and stops to view the closed motel door of Crystin's lover. He picks up the telephone again.

"Captain North."

"Frank," the Mayor says, "Mayor Blake. How's it going?"

"Fine, fine, what can I do for you this morning?"

"I'll get right to the point. I have reason to believe that someone is stalking my wife. Do you have anyone you can assign on a special project to watch her to see if my suspicions are true?"

"I'm sure I can come up with someone. When would you need him?"

"As soon as possible."

"Fine, I'll have someone contact you."

"I'll be in my office later on this afternoon. Have him meet me there."

"Yes, Sir."

Without a second thought, Captain North decides that Jason will be the one assigned to the Mayor. He believes that he has the perfect solution to give his subordinate a sense of accomplishment and provide the best man possible for surveillance of the Mayor's wife.

Jason arrives at the station shortly after Captain North and the Mayor's conversation. His mind is plagued with thoughts of Monique's actions. He can't help but wonder what was said to trigger her nervous reaction. The situation feels all too familiar. In conjunction, he ponders what kind of tedious things he'll be forced to do until he's placed back on regular duty. He finds himself doodling on a scratch pad when the telephone rings.

"Sixteenth Precinct, Jerrard."

"Jason, report to me right away," Captain North instructs.

"Right away, Frank." After entering Captain North's office, Jason is greeted with a half-smile. "Yes, Sir?"

"Damn," Captain North replies, "I thought you finally got it right."

"Got what right?"

"You called me Frank and spoiled it ten seconds later with the 'sir' business."

"I hadn't noticed...what is it this time? You're going to tell me that you want me to go home," Jason states with distraught.

"No, as a matter a fact, it's the exact opposite of last time."

"Oh?"

"Yes, I have an assignment for you. Something non-strenuous but it will at least keep you from playing with paper clips at your desk."

"I get to help little old ladies across the street," Jason states sarcastically.

"You'll be on special assignment for your favorite person."

"My favorite person? Hmm, so I'm on special assignment for myself?"

"Yeah right, the Mayor asked…"

"The Mayor," Jason interrupts. "What could he possibly want with me this time?"

"He didn't ask for you directly. He asked for help and under the circumstances you're the perfect person for the assignment."

"Which is?"

"You're to keep an eye on his wife."

"What!" Jason responds astoundedly. "Isn't this a bit unusual?"

"Yes, but the Mayor is convinced that someone is harassing his wife and asked for help. You're more qualified to detect if someone is actually stalking her."

"I'm to follow her to determine if someone is following her? Sounds like a contradiction in itself."

"I believe that's his plan."

"I don't want to be a desk jockey, but this assignment doesn't utilize my best abilities."

"I know, but you're the most likely candidate at this time. Take it; it's probably short-term anyway."

"When does he want me to start?"

"He'll tell you. Visit him at City Hall sometime later this afternoon."

"All right," Jason says reluctantly. "Awards up the ass and I'm playing babysitter."

"Just do your best and by the way, this assignment is confidential. Only you, me, and the Mayor know about this."

"Fine," Jason replies as he leaves the office.

Jason sits at his desk and the troublesome thought of the Mayor knowing about his secret affair with Crystin plagues him. The few hours before he leaves for City Hall seem like eternity as an uneasiness attempts to consume him.

Walking down the corridors of City Hall, he takes deep controlled breaths in his quest to conceal any signs of guilt. He approaches the receptionist who happens to be buffing her nails.

"Detective Jerrard, here to see Mayor Blake," Jason announces.

The woman never acknowledges Jason's presence.

"Excuse me," Jason says a bit louder, "I see that you're busy, but I'm here to see the Mayor."

"Why else would you be in his office?" she states sarcastically. "I'm sorry, Sir, I don't see you on his appointment calendar," the woman says rudely.

"Is he in?"

"Yes, but..."

"Well, tell him the officer from the Sixteenth Precinct is here," Jason interrupts. "He will know who I am."

"Susan," Mayor Blake's voice relays over the intercom. "I'm expecting an officer from the Sixteenth Precinct sometime today. When he arrives, interrupt anything I'm doing and send him in."

"He has just arrived, Sir."

Jason gives her a nod of "I told you so" as he walks toward the Mayor's door. The woman rolls her eyes and resumes her buffing. Jason opens the door; the Mayor is sitting in a highback leather chair overlooking the window. He turns around slowly while beginning his conversation.

"I'm pleased you're here...oh, Detective Jerrard," he says after recognizing Jason. "The city's finest, how did I get so lucky?"

"Good afternoon, Sir. The Captain feels that I'm not one-hundred percent healthy, so I got volunteered. How may I help you?"

"I assume you know why you're here."

"Vaguely."

"Can we talk unofficially, man to man."

"Surely," Jason replies, feeling he is about to be exposed.

"Confidentially, I wasn't completely honest with Frank. I do want you to keep an eye on my wife, but not because she's being followed. Instead, I believe that she is having an affair. I want to know when and where she meets him."

"This is a domestic matter, not police work. It's more suited for a private investigator."

"True, but I figured a cop would be more sensitive to my concerns. Me being an ex-cop myself."

"What exactly is this cop supposed to do?"

"Initially, I wanted you to escort her everywhere. I was sure someone was following her."

"She convinced you of that?"

"Yes, she told me that she was spooked the other night by someone following her, so she checked into a motel. She was very convincing...now, I'd like you to follow her and report to me her every move."

"What changed your mind?"

"These fucking things," the Mayor replies as he empties the envelope of pictures on his desk. "She has a lover. I want to know who he is. Look here. The number of the door where she's apparently enjoying herself is room 306." The Mayor pauses.

"Go on, the relation to the room number is?"

"The desk clerk at the motel gave me a different room number for the false name that she told me she checked in under."

Jason fumbles through the pictures. His eyes widen accompanying his racing heart as he views pictures of the Kings Inn to include Crystin and him kissing in the doorway. Extreme anxiety wraps itself around his neck, waiting to tighten upon hearing a slip of the tongue.

"Well," Jason says, "the pictures substantiate your suspicions. Why not confront her with these? She certainly can't deny anything."

"I want to find out who he is and confront him first. This way I'm sure this affair will end. It comes at a bad time," he says while shaking his head.

"How so?"

"It could potentially ruin my political career."

"I see. Well, how did you get these pictures?"

"Let's say I paid to keep them out of the press. My chances are favorable in the upcoming election so you can see the seriousness of my situation."

"From whom did you buy them?"

"Where I got them isn't important to you," the Mayor responds aggressively.

"That defensive posture in your response," Jason says before literally sniffing the air, "smells like blackmail."

"Blackmail or not, let's keep this entire matter confidential."

"You have my word on it."

"Then, you do accept the assignment?"

"Yes, believe me, I have first-hand experience with the wives-fooling-around situation," Jason replies, humoring the Mayor. "When should I start?"

"Tomorrow morning," the Mayor suggests while handing him a folded piece of paper with his address on it. "Most days she leaves the house after I head for the office. Keep me abreast of her wrongdoings."

"Consider it done."

Jason leaves the Mayor's office confident that his identity is unknown, yet he's uncertain how to please the Mayor and feed his uncontrollable craving for secret moments with Crystin. The Mayor places the pictures back in the envelope and stands at his window which boasts a view of the front of the building. Seconds later, there is a passing glance of Jason entering his car.

Jason settles back at his desk awed by the turn of events. Half of his thoughts are in erotica while the other half travel down an eerie path of uncertainty.

"Detective Jerrard, Sixteenth Precinct," Jason delivers, answering the telephone.

"Jason, it's me."

"Me who?"

"Crystin."

"Crystin!" Jason says astoundedly.

"Don't sound so surprised. I told you I'd call."

"I know...your timing is remarkable."

"What makes you say that?"

"Never mind that now. Can you..."

"Yes, I can meet with you," she interrupts. "This is why I'm calling."

"When are you available?"

"I'm ready for you now."

"What time...where?"

"Now, room 306."

"You're at the motel?" Jason whispers.

"Exactly, when can you leave there?"

"In a few, we need to talk."

"Dirty I hope," Crystin responds blinded by desire, not detecting the concern in Jason's voice. "See you soon."

"All right, goodbye."

"Goodbye."

Jason informs Captain North that he has accepted the Mayor's assignment and is requested to start immediately. He excuses himself from the station and makes his way to the motel awed by the tormenting sensations within him. After a knock on the door, a faint voice commands, "Enter." Jason opens the door and is presented with two hand-drawn arrows taped on the mirror in the tiny foyer. One points to the bathroom labeled, "Fuck" and the other points to the sitting area labeled, "No Fuck." He smiles and turns to follow Crystin's warm beckoning voice.

"Come on," she says, "the decision can't possibly be that difficult to make."

Jason appears in the bathroom sitting on the side of the Jacuzzi. Crystin is submerged in the water with only her head visible.

"What if," Jason replies, "I'd decided on the negative?"

"Somehow, I didn't think you would."

"Sure of yourself, huh?"

"Definitely," she replies while standing.

Jason's eyes follow the water descending from her breast, down her stomach and watches the water fall from her private hairs between her legs which she has shaped to resemble an exclamation mark.

"That's different," Jason responds, allowing Crystin to follow his eyes to her private punctuation.

"You feel like that when you are inside of me, don't you?"

"Well," Jason responds with no further comment.

"Besides," she says after giving a hard kiss. "You'll have to do something while your clothes dry."

"Wha...?"

Before Jason can pronounce the last letter, Crystin grabs his tie tight at the neck and pulls with all of her strength. She uses her weight to unbalance the load, causing Jason to plunge headfirst into the water. Engulfed instantly by the hot bubbling water, he manages to include her in the underwater dip. In a brief moment, they rise from the depths in a tight embrace kissing passionately. Crystin tears at his clothes only to be stopped by Jason's firm grip.

"What's the problem?" she asks.

"We need to talk."

"What could you possibly say that could override this moment?"

"Your husband..."

"No, no, he's not going to ruin this. I've planned this evening for days. I want you. It's all I've thought about since the last time. You definitely know how to please a woman."

"A reversal of fortune."

An inquisitive expression consumes her face. "Explain."

"I'm being used as a sex object."

"I beg to differ," she pleads. "Please don't think that. I've never had a man that's totally in sync with me sexually. You being that, I must have lost my head. I really care for you and believe that it could grow into something fruitful. As sudden as it may seem, I feel this way."

"Let's hold off on the sex for a moment. There's something more we should discuss."

"Well, at least get out of these wet clothes. You see this motel has a valet. They told me that your clothes could be dry-cleaned in a matter of hours."

"You've thought of everything, I see."

"You know there is nothing better than a prepared woman."

Crystin steps out of the Jacuzzi, leaves a wet trail to where she uses a telephone to dial the valet. She instructs someone to pick up the clothing for an immediate cleaning. She returns to Jason and they engage in a series of heavy necking before being interrupted by a knock on the door.

"That must be the valet," Crystin states, breathing heavily. "The door is open!" she yells.

"Excuse me," a teenaged boy says. "Where can I find the clothes?"

"Follow the sound of my voice and you'll find them."

To his surprise, he finds them together in the Jacuzzi. Jason sits with only his head above water while Crystin floats on her back revealing her firm breasts. Her hardened nipples place the boy in a trance. He sees Jason's clothes laying on the floor next to the Jacuzzi, but finds it difficult to not stare at her nakedness. He bends for the clothes, his head meets the side of the tub and simultaneously, he grabs the clothes and his head, turns and darts out of the bathroom. After hearing the suite's entrance door close, Crystin laughs uncontrollably.

"Why did you have to tease the poor boy like that?" Jason asks.

"Did you see the way he tried not to stare at me? Youngsters are so funny."

"You're quite an exhibitionist."

"If you were a woman, and you had these curves, would you be ashamed of them?"

"No, but..."

"My question is answered," she interrupts. "Now, what is so important?"

"Our last meeting was perfect." He pauses. "I thought."

"What do you mean?"

"First, how did you explain your tardiness the other night?"

"Simple," she boasts. "For extra security, when I left this room, I went to the office and asked if some woman had arrived. While the desk clerk was checking the register, I scanned it for any woman's name. If I recall there was a woman by the name of Gloria Reese in room...room 212."

"So, you were skeptical all along?"

"No, not until we overslept. As I said, I promised him I'd be home hours before we woke up. I decided to get an alibi just in case he wasn't sleeping."

"Was he?"

"No, so I fabricated a story about someone running me off the road, then following me until I checked into this motel."

"Ingenious, however, some of your lie may be true."

"What part?"

"The part about being followed."

"What are you saying?" Crystin asks with her full attention.

"I'm saying that you were actually followed."

"What!" she replies with worry tainting her words. "Why would someone follow me? Mr. Mayor has no cause for suspicion."

"This I don't know, but, it gets better. Your husband showed me pictures of you outside of the motel as well as a few with us kissing in the doorway."

"Who followed me?!" she asks surprised.

"I don't know. He wouldn't reveal his source."

"Probably one of his goons. Wait a minute. You're kidding, right?"

"Unfortunately, I'm not."

"He knows about you?"

"No, luckily, the shadows kept my identity concealed."

"I don't believe this," she rages. "This can't be happening."

"Are you ready for the clincher?"

"There's more?"

"I'm on special assignment. I'm to follow you and report to him with word of your lover."

Crystin sighs in relief. A more pleasant expression magically consumes her face, apparent to Jason.

"What are you thinking now?" Jason asks.

"It can't be too bad, you following me. It's unlikely that you'd report on yourself. When are you to start this adventure?"

"Tomorrow morning."

"In the morning." She nods before standing.

Jason watches her girlish figure as she steps out of the Jacuzzi.

"I've been in the water so long, I'm pruning," Crystin states.

"I am rather wrinkled myself. Jacuzzis tend to wrinkle faster than a regular bath."

"Shall we continue in the bedroom or has this news spoiled your mood?"

"Aren't you at least concerned about all of this?"

"At first I was disturbed. Now I realize that we can spend more time together. You can do close...personal surveillance."

"I know, but I'm not sure if I want to start a habit of lying to your husband."

"Don't worry, it will be all real. I'll let you know what my daily routines are. They won't be different from any other day. We'll spend lots of quality time together."

"You do realize the consequences if we get caught?"

"Yes," Crystin expresses. "Isn't it exciting?"

Jason gives her a puzzled look as his mind wonders how she can take the matter lightly.

"You sound as if you have everything planned," Jason replies.

"I'm just confident that we can get away with our escapades."

"Don't you think that it's too easy?"

"I'm not; you're the breath of fresh air I need and I'll not let this golden opportunity pass."

"Just remember, I have a say in this also."

"Now look at you," Crystin says while changing the subject. "All this talk has ruined things," she says while glancing at his member. "You've lost something."

"Don't fret that," Jason replies with assurance, "say something dirty."

"Fuck me like I'm a nasty whore," she says without hesitation.

Almost simultaneously, Jason's member becomes erect and Crystin shakes her head in disbelief.

"What are you, a machine?"

"No, I just know me."

"Okay, if those two words do that to you, you'd probably explode if I talked about licking up and down his shaft. Then, continually circle my tongue around the rim of his head. Would that do more for you?"

"Sounds intriguing, but I'll play from Missouri."

"Show you. I'm about to, but first things first."

Crystin lays Jason on his back while spreading his legs. She crawls up from the foot of the bed between his legs with his private in mind. Along the way she scrapes her nails firmly against his skin causing Jason's leg muscles to contract. Stopping less than an inch from his erect penis, she breathes heavily over it, pausing for effect. Jason waits in anticipation for the warmth of her mouth. The wet tip of her tongue descending from the top, down the shaft to his testicles, awakens erotic sensations within him. Her circular tongue motions, and gentle kissing sends twinges throughout his body.

She ever so carefully captures one into her mouth, caressing it pleasingly with her tongue. Jason's body trembles with pleasure while simultaneously fighting a slight tickling sensation. Soon she releases it, grabs his shaft and attacks his penis. She administers great pleasure with long strokes coupled with short fast ones on the head. Her nails dig deeply into his tightened leg muscles causing several places to bleed.

Jason's hips begin to move in a circular motion while Crystin works his throbbing penis. Jason is on the verge of exploding; his trembling body is tender to her touch. Crystin stops abruptly and runs her tongue up Jason's stomach to his chest hungrily attacking his hardened nipple. Lustfully, she mounts him with her already soaked womanhood, moving slowly to a rhythm controlled by heavy desire. Her head falls back while her body gyrates as she loses all grips on reality. Jason caresses her hungry breasts which are crying for affection. Pulling her near, he tantalizes them with soft strokes with the tip of his tongue. Crystin's eyes close as her movements turn into short jerky ones. Heavy moans accompany her warm release. Jason feels a rush of excitement as tiny little men dance around his sensitive member, marching to the beat of their own drum. Double-time. Jason continues with fast, hard, dominating thrusts which transform Crystin's moans into sporadic screams. She bucks wildly on her pleasure while accompanying Jason to his orgasm and her second. She rolls off of Jason and settles in his arms. His comforting hug aides her body's attempt to return her pounding chest to a normal pace. Their slumber is interrupted by the knock of the valet returning with Jason's clothes.

"I'll take care of it this time," Jason instructs Crystin. "Just leave them on the doorknob!" Jason yells at the door. "We will leave a tip on the bill for you," the valet faintly hears.

Jason steps out of the bed, stands behind the door, and cracks the door enough to allow his hand to reach around and retrieve his clothes.

"You have to admit," Crystin comments, "your approach is less thrilling than mine."

"The poor boy would probably have a heart attack if I'd greeted him naked."

"Anyway, nice buns."

After some petty necking and a brief conversation, they shower and leave determined to meet again.

EIGHT

Six weeks have passed since Jason accepted the assignment. Twice a week Crystin and Jason rendezvous in the same room indulging in lustful sex. Each day Crystin uses running errands as her major excuse for vacating her domicile. Jason's reports have the Mayor puzzled. He lies on the bed staring at the ceiling while his mind travels down dark winding roads searching for answers to his wife's infidelity. He ponders whether or not her knowledge of his alleged women is premise of her naughtiness. However, like a lion, he feels threatened by the intruder pouncing in his domain. But, the reports of her inactivity assure him that her actions were just a one-time fling. Therefore, he decides to bottle his rage in order to concentrate fully on his upcoming campaign. After long deliberation, he decides to end the surveillance of his wife, helped by the old saying, "What's good for the goose..." Like other transactions, he prefers to conduct business in person.

The next morning, Mayor Blake watches Jason exit his car after inviting him to his office to discuss his most recent thoughts. He watches Jason's proud steps as he disappears into the building. Moments later, the Mayor answers his secretary's call over the intercom.

"Send him in," the Mayor states. "Ah, Detective Jerrard, it's nice to see you again," he says just as the door opens.

Greeting the Mayor with a smile, Jason responds, "Good morning, Sir, I hope everything is okay. You sounded anxious on the telephone."

"No, don't get me wrong; things couldn't be better. I'll get right to the point. Look at these," he says while handing the pictures to Jason. "This is the last you'll see or hear of them," the Mayor states confidently.

"Oh?"

"It's time to look toward the future and bury harsh feelings. Therefore, I want you to end your surveillance of my wife."

"Oh? Splendid," Jason recites relieved.

"Yes, use your talents for more important work. Thanks to your superb coverage, I'm convinced by your reports that she had a one-time fling and I can live with that. Just between you and me, I get my share of strange," he nods. "If you know what I mean. I guess it got the best of her."

"Well, I'm pleased to hear this. You two make such a lovely couple. Now, you can concentrate on your upcoming election."

"Exactly. My mind is now free and I thank you for that."

"No thanks necessary, just doing my job."

"I'll phone Captain North and advise him that you have been released. I'm sure he's eager to get you back to regular police work."

"Okay, Sir, if that's all, I'll take my leave. I'd like to run an errand before reporting to the office."

"Fine, take care of yourself and thanks."

"You're welcome. Goodbye."

Jason leaves. The Mayor turns, leans against the window frame and flips through the pictures one last time as means of closure to his bothersome emotions. Again, he watches Jason's brisk steps to his car, shakes his head and thinks, *When I was a growing detective I couldn't afford a car that expensive.*

The Mayor's closure to the tail of his wife directs his attention to the top picture. He studies what the poor lighting allows, a black BMW, faint but unmistakable. His head remains tilted but his eyes glance out the window and see what is perceived to be a replica BMW, black and identical to the picture.

Naw, he thinks, *it's just a coincidence.*

He reads Jason's license plate as he drives off and scans the remaining pictures for a verifiable one—one that will disprove and eliminate his accelerated heart.

"Son of a bitch!" he yells. "Wait, calm down, let me think this out. I hire a man to watch my cheating wife only to discover that the man she's cheating with is the fucking man I hired. I should have known something when their eyes locked at the ceremony. The ceremony, that's it!" he rages, pounding his fist on the desk. "What time is it?" he remembers. "Fucking 306! Why didn't I make the connection the first time?"

He flips through the pictures again, this time determined to tie them together by the room number.

"They fucking match; I don't believe this! He conned me...*Me!*"

Mayor Blake dumps the remaining contents of the envelope on his desk and frantically searches for Sly's pager number. Moments after completing his call, he abruptly snatches the telephone.

"Mayor Blake."

"Mayor Blake," Sly says. "I recognized your number. What do I owe the pleasure?"

"There is no pleasure in this call so I won't waste your time pretending there is. I'd like to know more about the night you took those pictures of my wife."

"I've told you everything there is to know."

"Yes, but you also told me that you were following someone other than my wife."

"Why is this so important to you?"

"Just tell me," Mayor Blake pleads too desperate for his own liking. "I'll pay to know who you were following."

"You don't have to pay; this one is free. I was tailing that detective you had the ceremony for...Detective Jerrard."

"That motherfucker!" The Mayor sighs. "You saw him go into which room of the motel?"

"I didn't see which one. I got caught by a couple of traffic lights but noticed his car in the motel's parking lot. I sat in a far corner of the parking lot and waited. Just when I was about to leave I took pictures of his car because I didn't want to forget what he was driving. It was about then when I saw this sparkling dress hugging a woman so nicely. I peeked through my camera for a closer look and recognized her as your wife. She was waving goodbye to someone, then suddenly went back for a final kiss. I shot it all. You have the pictures of the whole scene."

Mayor Blake shakes his head in disbelief. "The fucking bastard."

"Who? Detective Jerrard? He's the one in the shadows," Sly asks. "So, you have a vendetta against him, too?"

"Too?" Mayor Blake questions quickly. "Do you mind enlightening me on what he has done to you?"

"Personally, he hasn't done anything to me but I just want to see the city's wonder boy take a fall. As if he was solely responsible for stopping that rapist," Sly says with enough contempt to fuel the Mayor's rage.

The Mayor picks up on Sly's hidden implication, but systematically decides that Jason holds a higher priority. He decides to see just how far Sly will go.

"He's fucking with the wrong person," the Mayor states, pausing to see just where Sly is.

"My sentiments exactly," Sly blurts. "He is going to fall and I'm just the one to push him."

"I like that in you. You see an opportunity and seize the moment."

"Meaning?"

"Let me hire you to watch my wife for a while. You're good with a camera; that's an added plus. I'm sure my bitch of a wife will meet with him again."

"I'll start tomorrow. What is your address?"

The Mayor conveys his address as well as directions to his domicile and the importance of keeping his actions discreet. Sly promises to report to him at least three times a week unless something earth-shattering occurs, which he'd report immediately.

"Your fee is?"

"It's not important. I'm sure you'll take good care of me."

"I will...that you can bank on. Just keep me updated on what she's doing."

"Good enough, I will be in touch in a couple of days."

"Sly," the Mayor says at the last minute. "I'm counting on you."

"Don't worry, everything will be fine. Talk to you later."

NINE

Jason sits patiently at his desk waiting for a call from Crystin to spill the news. A mild case of anxiety sets in with no call from her, so he leaves the office early and heads home to digest the evening. His emotions ride a continuous bumpy roller coaster while playing tug-of-war with the right thing to do. Jason is relieved that his assignment is over. Having to lie constantly to the Mayor really makes him feel inadequate, less than the man he really is. However, looming in his subconscious, he knows it is easier to feed his unexplained hunger for her while on assignment.

Relaxing on the sofa, Jason contemplates his predicament, all the while knowing that his involvement with Crystin is a dead-end journey. He fights the notion that she is just something to do, a temporary phase present until his emotions are once again intact. Deep inside he's confident that she's too comfortable with her lifestyle to ever give it up, yet he's compelled to explore more of her sexuality. He is tormented with thoughts of the similarities between Crystin and Julie. Are these similarities the main attraction for the ill-fated affair? Lastly, and most importantly his concern with not losing another opportunity to explore his feelings for Monique claw at the artificial walls used to protect his feelings, while his hardened heart struggles to suppress the pain felt over the loss of Sasha.

He reaches and dials Monique.

"Hello," she answers.

"Monique?"

"Yes, Jason?" Monique replies with excitement. "Where have you...why haven't I heard from you these past few weeks?"

"I've been sort of busy," Jason shamefully confesses.

"I was beginning to think that my confession to you scared you off."

"No, that didn't frighten me. My lack of communication has been a result of a simple but tedious case. Anyway, am I disturbing you?"

"Jason? You can never disturb me. I need a break anyway."

"A break from what?"

"What I've put off long enough: the task of unpacking these gazillion boxes. I never knew I had so much junk."

"May I volunteer my services?"

"Gladly, but I warn you, there are boxes galore. Should I prepare food?"

"That won't be necessary. We can always go out later."

"Fine, see you soon. I'm in building 14332, apartment 473."

"All right, I'll be there soon. Goodbye."

"Goodbye."

Jason drives the short distance to Monique's apartment complex. The Arbors consist of three high-rise buildings with mirrored outside glass reflecting the beautifully landscaped grounds and the splendid moments at the beginning and end of each day. After finding her building he ignores the elevator and dashes up four flights of stairs to her floor. Jason knocks. Monique answers the door dressed in a huge men's shirt and sweat pants. She gives Jason a one-armed hug, less affectionate than expected.

"Sorry," she states. "I'm a bit funky. Besides, it is hard to give good hugs with one arm. Take this," she replies while giving him a tall glass of hot apple cider with a cinnamon stick which was concealed behind her back.

"Thank you. You never cease to amaze me," Jason says.

"I remember a time when this was all you'd drink."

"It's more or less been replaced by coffee."

"Is that what you want?"

"Don't trouble yourself. This is fine. Besides, I came here to work. But first, if you don't mind, I'd like to revisit that hug."

Without a word, Monique's arms embrace Jason, strong and firm, releasing some of her pinned-up passion in the embrace itself. She nearly loses herself inside his arms, but breaks to recite her discovery.

"See," she states, "it's kinda hard to give a good hug with one arm."

"I see your point. We'll try this again when we have full use of both arms."

"Agreed, well, at least finish your cider. It's getting cold. These boxes aren't going anywhere."

"I like your table and chairs," he jokes. "Early American Cardboard has always been my favorite."

"Are you making fun of me? I have a long way to go to get this place in order. I promise you, it will feel like home when it's completed."

"You'd like that, wouldn't you?"

"Like what?"

"Your place feeling like home to me."

Jason's statement warms Monique's being, bringing a smile to her face and no words from her mouth. Jason quietly sits on a box enjoying his cider as Monique glances at the ceiling light fixture attempting to hide her blushing.

"This is definitely not going to work. You have to go."

"So soon," Jason queries. "I just got here."

"Not you, that blown light bulb. It's entirely too dull with only one illuminated."

She digs through a few boxes until she finds a replacement bulb, slides a steadier box directly under the ceiling light and carefully stands on it. Struggling on her toes for balance, barely reaching the screw to remove the light's base, the wobble begins just as a loud scream simultaneously exits her mouth as she falls off of the box. She lands backwards into Jason's grasp. They softly hit the floor with his arms crossed around her from behind, each hand coupling a breast.

"I thought this might happen," Jason responds while trying to gather himself. "You should've asked me. After all, I came to help."

"It doesn't take a brain surgeon to change a light bulb."

"True, however, it takes someone a tad taller than you."

"Thanks for coming to my rescue.. uhm," she says pretending to clear her throat while glancing down at Jason's hands. "Quite a unique grip you have."

Jason ponders for a short moment, then quickly moves his hands to her thigh. "Sorry, I hadn't noticed. Simple reflexes," Jason tries to explain.

"Don't apologize. You broke my fall and I can't think of anyone better for that."

Monique caresses one of Jason's masculine but soft hands. She slowly guides his fingertips up her thigh and under the oversized shirt. Her soft, silky skin sends wild thoughts of erotica throughout his mind. Many suppressed fantasies surface as years of anticipation come to a close. Monique's direction ends at her breasts where Jason takes a moment to savor their firm softness. She turns seemingly in slow motion to face Jason with his arms hugged around her until their eyes meet displaying a passion fueled by years of uncertainty. An eagerness to attack overwhelms Monique.

"Finally," she says with a tone indicating this very instant. "Nothing can disturb us. I'm sure you know what to do from here," Monique suggests.

Jason gently rubs her nipple with the tip of his finger while kissing her behind the ears. Instantly, Monique's body melts to Jason's touch like a hot knife cutting through butter. A wet steamy trail brought on by a burning desire is left as his tongue descends down her neck causing shivers and tiny chill bumps to plague her body.

"You're cold?" Jason asks.

"No, Jason," Monique cries short of breath. "This is not the time to play dumb. You know what you're doing to me."

"And what exactly is that?"

"You're driving me fucking crazy but somehow I know that you know that."

"What can I do for you?"

"Why are you asking such silly questions?" she says, showing a bit of frustration in her tone. "Unless," she pauses, "how are you handling Sasha's death?"

"I'm handling it well. Why do you ask?"

"Just your actions. Are you feeling guilty about this intimate moment?"

Jason sighs. "Why should I feel guilty about this particular moment?"

Monique's eyes widen as she breaks from Jason's grasp.

"You mean there have been others?" she questions with intrigue.

"Okay, okay, I'll come clean," he replies before standing and pacing the floor. "Am I feeling guilty about this moment? You ask. Truthfully, I don't know."

"Jason, you've never been uncertain about anything in your life, so stop pacing the floor and talk to me. Please."

"Actually, I shouldn't feel guilt over this other woman."

"Other woman?" Monique questions, interrupting Jason.

"Yes," he admits shamefully. "I've kinda been messing around with this woman, but, for the life of me, I don't truly understand why."

Monique summons her inner control to not let Jason know that this new information tears through her insides like a shark's teeth on its prey.

"Do you love her?" she asks uncertain if she really wants the truth to be revealed.

"No," Jason says firmly. "This I know."

"You like her a lot, then?" she says, feeling a weight lifted inside.

"Let's just say that I'm driven, no, intrigued by this woman."

"Please forgive me, Jason, but I don't know what you're trying to tell me."

"I'm saying that there isn't a correct answer. We met and instantly we had this strong physical attraction. The sad part of it is...I do realize that I'm traveling down a dead-end street with her, but I've continued to see her despite of it."

"You've just told yourself why."

"Why what?"

"Why you're dealing with this person. The dead-end street, it's your security. Deep down you don't want to open yourself and be hurt again. Right?"

"No one ever wants to be hurt."

"Thinking back, you indirectly told me about this."

"I did? When?"

"When we were in Rosalina's...the day after I came back to town. I quote, 'Already, I've done things that I wouldn't have normally done.'"

"I do remember saying that, and that is exactly what I meant, my relationship with this woman."

"Why do you keep her identity a secret?"

"Because you know her."

"Is it someone from school?"

"No, let's say it's someone you know of."

"Are you going to tell me or are we going to play this beating around the bush game?" Monique questions firmly.

"It's the Mayor's wife."

"What!" Monique responds astoundedly. "How could you possibly be having an affair with the Mayor's wife, Crystal?"

"Crystin is her name," Jason replies as his head is lowered. "It just happened. I was sitting alone, she appeared and minutes later we were on our way to a motel."

"This is not you, Jason," Monique says while shaking her head in disbelief. "More importantly, you can't escape."

"I'm not trying to escape from you."

"Not from me," Monique blurts, "but from the pain of Sasha's death."

"I've had my mourning period."

"I don't believe in such a thing. You can't dictate to your being how long you should sorrow over a loved one. Your inner-self naturally does that. Sometimes it takes weeks, even years to cleanse oneself. For a select few, the pain never leaves."

"You're a philosopher now?"

"I'm not trying to be one. All I'm trying to say is that you can't keep your hurt bottled inside, captive, never to be released. Sooner or later, the pressure will make you explode or slowly kill you."

"You're saying my involvement with Crystin is a direct result of Sasha's death?"

"Not Sasha's death, but of your inability to let the pain caused by her death go. You're so busy trying not to show your emotions, you do stupid things like fooling around with the Mayor's wife."

Jason pauses. His eyes are directed at Monique with a blank stare while his soul searches his heart. Deep down in the darkest corner of his heart he finds a steel cage bolted and locked. Encased within are years of forgotten pain and anguish, all being magnified by the grief of Sasha's death. Monique's words seem to add life to its dormant state. It breathes; its strength expands the steel walls weakening the seams. The escaping emotion contaminates his being, showing externally by his heavy breathing.

After a few moments, Jason responds, "You're right, I've been suppressing my pain, but, I've been doing this most of my life. I now realize that some-place, sometime it will hit me like a raging rhino."

"Why don't you just let yourself go? You can cry. Where is it written that a man isn't supposed to cry?"

"I've cried many times in my life. I cried when she got hit and at the funeral."

"No, Jason," Monique says firmly. "You shed tears. There is a difference between shedding tears and actually letting pain come from your heart causing a true in-depth crying session."

"That could get ugly."

"When did you start caring what people think about you?"

"I don't."

"Jason, I'm not telling you what to do. This is my last comment on the subject."

"What's that?"

"Let it go. You will feel a lot better."

"I will someday. Somehow, your words have made me realize that I'm causing myself more harm than good."

"Remember what you just said. It holds a lot of truth. Now," Monique says deliberately changing the subject, "what about me?"

"What about you?"

"How could you go to a married woman knowing how I feel about us being together? Knowing I've been waiting here, not wanting to pressure you into anything."

"It started before you arrived back in town."

"What about afterwards? After our talk in Rosalina's."

"I was assigned to watch her. It made things easy."

"The simple but tedious case."

"Right."

"Is the assignment over?"

"Yes, as a matter of fact it ended today."

"Does the Mayor know about this?"

"It was his idea to assign someone to his wife."

"What?"

"It's a long story and if you don't mind I'd rather not discuss it."

"Grant me one more question then I'm through with this matter."

"Agreed."

"Do you plan to see her again?"

"Yes," Jason answers too quickly for his own good and attempts to recover after noticing Monique's expression sadden. "Only to tell her that our affair is over. It wouldn't be proper any other way," Jason continues. "But first I'll start with you."

"Me?" Her heart pounds. "It's over between us before we have a true start?"

"No, I'd like to ask for your forgiveness. I feel very ashamed of what I've done."

"All I can say is that we learn from our mistakes."

"Yes, but do you forgive me? Can you dream of us again?"

"That depends on you."

"Me?"

"Yes, you. Come here," she replies while directing Jason into her spreading arms.

"You aren't using my method on me, are you?"

"Yes, we're about to hug. As you've always said, you can tell a lot from a hug."

Jason enters Monique's waiting arms. Her embrace is firm and tight, overflowing with emotion. Jason's embrace is strong, trapping her in his clutches. Monique develops anguish. Initially, her reasoning is a need to comfort a friend, however, seconds into Jason's embrace, her mind entertains thoughts of them entangled sexually.

"How's this?" Jason asks.

"Good, very good," she moans. "Just don't let go, this feels...I mean you haven't revealed yourself."

"I see you're enjoying yourself."

"I'm not a machine and it's been a while since I had a real affectionate hug."

Jason grows silent while staring deep into her eyes. His head slowly lowers to her shoulder. Simultaneously as his grip weakens, tears begin to wet her shoulder. Jason's silent cry is overpowered by his raging heart. The walls of his steel cage sound loudly, echoing through his body sending chills as the encased beast makes its escape. The door hinges tear; with a better grip the beast folds the steel door like paper. The ferocious roar inside of him leaves his bellowing mouth as a loud "Aww!" The vibrating cry weakens his body.

Slowly, he descends to his knees engaged in some form of an embrace. Hurt, pain and sorrow ascend from his mouth bursting into nothingness but carrying the fury of years of emotional restraint causing tears to pour from his eyes like an overflowing cup.

"Let it go, Jason," Monique suggests. "Let it all go. You'll feel much better."

Jason's heavy weeping absent the loud cries continues for minutes as he lies on the floor with his body curled. Monique digs through many boxes in search of a blanket and pillow. Gently, she lifts his head, places the pillow under it and covers his body with the blanket. Jason is seemingly unaware of her actions. She lies cradled behind him with her arm around his waist. They indulge in a brief slumber. Jason disturbs their peace by jumping up and quickly dashing into the bathroom. He splashes water on his face while viewing his bloodshot eyes in the mirror and dries his face with toilet paper. He walks toward Monique ashamed.

"I think I owe you a better one of these," Jason states before giving her a strong embrace.

"You don't owe me a thing...are you okay?"

"I'm much better. Actually I feel stupid; embarrassed is a better word."

"Don't be, showing emotions is nothing to be ashamed of."

"I know, but the way it happened, I was fine. Then all of a sudden Mt. Saint Helen erupted."

"You don't have to explain," Monique interrupts while covering his mouth. "I understand."

"You should be a fortuneteller," Jason jokes, trying to add some humor to the ordeal. "You called it just like it happened."

"I knew it would happen soon. Honestly, knowing you, I'm surprised that you actually let me witness it because I remember that you don't like to let people see you upset."

"I guess that I'm changing as I grow older. Would you understand if I asked for a raincheck to help unpack these boxes?"

"Of course I would."

"Then with your grace, I'll go home and finish getting myself together so the next time you see me, I will be my usual self."

"Yeah, crazy."

"Probably, crazier now. One question for you though. Can your crystal ball tell me whether or not these types of outbreaks are over?"

"Your body only knows," Monique replies with deep sincerity.

"That's what I thought you'd say. Unfortunately, I dislike you seeing me like this so I'll take my leave. I'll give you a call soon."

"Fine, and remember, when all else fails, look up."

"Thanks for everything. We'll talk later. Goodbye."

"Goodbye."

Monique closes the door behind Jason and wonders if he will be able to pull his emotions together enough to ever share his heart with her. Jason walks to his car heeding Monique's advice, praying silently for more strength to prevent the outbreaks from occurring again.

As Jason arrives home, sitting in his driveway awaits Crystin's empty car. With the sound of Jason's car door closing, Crystin sits up from her semi-prone position. Jason sighs deeply in preparation for what's sure to be an unwanted emotional evening.

Crystin exits her car hurriedly, spreading her arms as she approaches Jason.

"I've been trying to get in touch with you all day. I miss you," she says while accepting Jason in her arms.

Jason's embrace is less than cordial, lacking the excitement and emotion of previous ones.

"Is something wrong?" questions Crystin.

"No, I've had a tiring day."

"That's all...well when inside I'll give you one of my world famous massages."

"We need to talk," Jason states firmly.

Inside his home, Crystin's hands attack Jason indicating the direction she wants to venture. Jason ignores her sexual plea.

"Okay, Jason, what's wrong?" Crystin says at the beginning of frustration. "This is extremely different from the last time I saw you...so, what do you need to talk about?"

"Us, this, it's..."

"It's okay," she abruptly interrupts Jason, "the Mayor has confidence in your reports."

"He won't anymore, that is...he has no need to."

"You told him about us?" Crystin asks surprisingly.

"No, my assignment is over. I'm not watching you as of today. Your husband seems to be relieved with the fact that you had a one-time fling and has forgiven you. We should leave it at that."

"Isn't that sweet of him; it only means we will have to be extra careful in our endeavors."

"No," Jason says in a tone demanding all of her attention. "It means that our escapade, relationship, affair, whatever, has to come to an end."

"You can't be serious," Crystin responds with a flatter tone coupled with an expressionless face.

"I'm very serious. What I tried to say earlier is that this is all wrong. I suddenly realized that you exist in my life because I am, was, if you will..." Jason pauses knowing that the news he's about to deliver will be painful to Crystin. "I have been running from the pain of Sasha's death."

"Who in the hell is Sasha?" Crystin questions resentfully.

"She's part of the mental stability I thought I'd regained before we met."

"I remember you saying something like that, but I never dreamed after all this time it would come to haunt me."

"Crystin," Jason pleads, "I've done you a grave injustice. Had I known that my actions were the result of me hiding behind pain, I would have never let any of this happen. For this I apologize with the deepest sincerity. The moments we've shared have been most enjoyable, but under the wrong pretense. You deserve better."

"I deserve you, the passion, and the rage of excitement that embellishes me when I lay eyes on you. The exuberance when we touch is..."

"Something that can't continue," Jason interrupts. "To go on I'd be lying to you, but most importantly I'd be lying to myself. I've done enough of that."

"That's it, just like that, it's over."

"It truly has to be. I've lost my edge."

"What fucking edge?" Crystin asks at the beginning of anger.

"Meaning," Jason pauses to gather his thoughts, "when I refused to differentiate between the truth and lies, or accept that I'd become something that I shouldn't. I could be content with some form of relationship with you…as long as I believed the lies were true, but questioning the lies as lies has made me realize that this is all wrong. My actions with you have been all wrong."

"Damn you! Jason, how could you do this to me?"

"Believe me, at the time I didn't understand that I was doing anything to either of us."

Crystin's aggression fueled by her heated spirit directs her to pound Jason's chest repeatedly venting anger with physical and verbal abuse. Jason accepts the punishment for his crime without rebuttal.

"How could you. Jason…how could you give me everything I want, make me feel everything I need, then take it all away as if it never happened? You used me, my good-for-nothing husband uses me. To him I'm just a pretty armpiece. To you, I'm just some bitch to fuck. I'm sick and tired of being used as a piece of ass!" Crystin screams.

"Truly, it is not as it seems."

Rage flows through Crystin's body, stimulating each nerve and causing her body to tremble. Her words transpose into vulgar obscenities, which seep through Jason's skin like acid, leaving him with an uneasy feeling. Jason's astonishment occurs when Crystin's hand sounds as it meets his face, proudly leaving a full handprint.

"I'm not going to be the only one who gets fucked here!" Crystin yells from the top of her lungs. "The city's 'Boy Wonder,' some fucking man you are."

In a blink of an eye, Crystin reaches into her purse and produces a small-caliber handgun, holding it firmly against Jason's penis. Jason stares at her intensely while contemplating his next move. Crystin pushes the gun's barrel forcefully against Jason's member. Presto! Like magic, it triggers a physical response in Jason.

"You think that's funny, don't you?" Crystin argues while cocking the hammer on her weapon. Jason's penis hardens fully, bulging to her trigger finger. "You're sick, you're a fucking lunatic. I should blow the damn thing off."

"You should do whatever you're going to do and leave," Jason responds evenly. "I may be sick but I'm not the one with a loaded gun, well ... not one with bullets," humors Jason.

"You can't joke your way out of this. We will see who has the last laugh in this matter. I promise you this," she states as her hand again sounds on Jason's face. "I'll get even with you."

"Do what you must, but for now, either pull the trigger or put it away. I've had one hell of a day."

Crystin stares angrily at Jason. Another slap sounds and stings Jason's face. He has time to react and counter her aggression but somewhere inside him, he feels that he deserved her punishment. She retreats the gun and pushes Jason to the side, storming out of his home calling him every four-letter word imaginable.

Jason settles on his sofa, content that the ordeal with Crystin is over yet bewildered with her disturbing behavior. He'd wished for a peaceful ending to their affair but some part of him understood her actions. Needing a pleasant voice, Jason dials Monique. When he hears her voice, clouded thoughts delay a response prompting Monique for a second more inquisitive.

"Who is this?"

"Jason," he responds followed by more silence.

"Are you okay?"

A hesitant Jason replies, "Yes."

"Not by the way you sound. What's wrong? Tell me."

"It's over," Jason says saddened by the events prior to the call.

"Please clarify yourself," she states with her heart skipping a beat.

"I mean, it's over with Crystin."

"You let me know that this was your intention before you left here. You don't have to reconfirm it to me. I believe you."

"You don't understand.. she was here waiting for me when I got home. When I explained to her how I felt she became very emotional and enraged. It wasn't a pretty scene."

"This explains your current tone; the ordeal upset you."

"I'm shaken a little. The control I exercised when she pulled a gun on me, wel ...it's somewhat unnerving now that I've had a moment to reflect on it."

"What?" Monique shouts. "Surely, you're exaggerating."

"I wish that I were. I guess the pain she felt caused it. I handled it calmly though my actions were unorthodox. I dislike hurting people ... using people."

"This is what she led you to believe? Look at it this way. During the weeks you guys were enjoying one another or if I use more realistic terms...fucking each other, did she once mention anything leading toward the two of you being together with no third parties involved? Was anything ever stated about you two eventually being a couple?"

Jason quickly reminisces on their encounters before replying, "No, not one time."

"I didn't think so," Monique sounds confidently. "I submit to you that she was using you. Somewhere along the way if she were that crazy for you, she surely would have mentioned it."

"This is a point of view I never conjured. I now have a new angle to direct the sorrow I have for her."

"You think about it. Or," Monique says unexpectedly, "your pipe must be something else."

After a short moment, the clarity of Monique's sexual statement hit Jason, prompting the response, "You're insane. Right now, honey, I'd like to rest my mind, possibly get some sleep."

"Please do; you have to be exhausted both mentally and physically. We can talk later."

"Thanks for listening. Now, I must bid you goodnight."

"Goodnight, love."

Jason hangs up the telephone pleased with the adjective Monique used to describe him.

TEN

Early the next morning Jason leaves for the station mentally exhausted from a night where his body slept but his mind soared with thoughts of his dilemma. However, his spirits somehow ride high having released some internal negative energy. As he directs his car onto the main road, sympathy for Crystin attempts to taint his mood, but a faint whisper of Monique's inspiring words warms his being like the sun on the morning dew.

Once inside the station Jason remembers the constant gloom that occupies most of the officers' faces and the thick, hazy air created by the cigarettes and tension. He finds himself bombarded with thousands of questions regarding his whereabouts over the past few weeks, especially the sarcastic, irritating remarks delivered by Detective McAllister.

"Been on a 007 mission, have we?" Detective McAllister questions sarcastically in his usual manner.

"How are you, and yes, I've been on a special assignment."

"What makes you so special?"

"Look, Chris, I'm not in the mood nor do I care to get into this today."

Jason walks past Chris heading for Captain's North's office. Chris grabs Jason's shoulder from behind, spinning him around. Jason reacts by knocking Chris' arm to the side, slide steps inches in front of Detective McAllister and seizes his genitals in his hand. Everyone witnesses the panic of Chris's face, knowing that the fate of his natural voice is within Jason's clutches.

"Okay, you two," Sgt. Austin interjects, "Enough!" as he separates and stands between them.

"You're awful touchy today, Jason," Detective McAllister states.

Jason's response isn't immediate; his eyes continue to peer not only at, but through Detective McAllister, as he raises a brow and replies, "Grow a dick."

Instantly, the room bursts into a loud roar of laughter leaving Detective McAllister's face a matching red color of the fire extinguisher. With all of the commotion, Captain North peeks down the hall to discover Jason in the building.

"Jerrard, in my office now," Captain North directs. "What's that all about?" Captain North questions as Jason sits opposite his desk.

"Nothing really. Chris was being Chris, so I embarrassed him."

"You guys are going to end your feud..what are you doing here anyway?"

"Don't you know?"

"I wouldn't ask such a silly ass question if I knew the answer to it."

"The Mayor didn't call you?"

"I haven't heard from the Mayor."

"Well, he decided to kiss and make up," Jason states too quickly.

"Kiss and make up, I thought someone was stalking his wife."

"It's a long story and confidential. In short, my assignment is over."

"Just between you and me, her figure could stop a truck. She has curves like…" He stops his words while trying to remember the woman's name his mind is envisioning. "…like…damn, she starred in the movie 'Monster's Ball.'"

Jason watches his superior struggle with his attempt at being hip until he notices the Captain's eyes widen.

"Halle Berry," Captain North says pleased with himself. "Definitely, Halle Berry, but on a taller frame. You've been watching her every move. Surely you've studied those marvelous curves she has," he says lustfully.

"Captain, believe me," Jason states as an internal devious smile warms him. "I know what you mean."

"Don't you ever tell anyone that I have the hots for the Mayor's wife."

"This is man's talk, and is automatically sacred."

"So, how is your shoulder?"

"Like new, no pain at all."

"Then, it's safe to say physically you are able to resume normal duties."

"There's nothing I'd welcome more."

"Good. I have something special for your talents."

"This sounds like trouble."

"It seems that we've had a spree of burglaries recently, and the ironic part is businesses and homes are not the primary target."

"Purse snatching," Jason suggests, stabbing in the dark.

"No...more like individuals at cash machines."

"That's a new twist...but one that had to eventually happen."

"So far they have been after dark, mostly late night."

"Any injuries?"

"Fortunately, none. Each victim reports that they did not resist."

"What more can you tell me?"

"It's all here in this folder," Captain North says while passing it to Jason. "Actually, there's not much to go on but give it your best effort."

"You got it." Jason smiles.

"No crazy antics."

"Captain, you know me," Jason replies as he exits the Captain's office.

Faint sounds of "that's what I'm afraid of" escape the closing door and fill Jason's ears.

"Jas, you have a call," says Sgt. Austin. "A lovely-sounding female," he adds.

Minor anxiety sets within Jason, fearing that the caller may be Crystin. "Jerrard, Sixteenth Precinct."

"Good morning, Jason," Monique recites.

The tension is magically lifted with the soothing tone of Monique's voice.

"Hello, dear, good morning. I didn't expect to hear from you."

"With the way you sounded last night, I'm calling to see how you are faring today."

"I'm fine, just a little tired from a restless night."

"I can imagine a lot went through your head."

"I'm pretty much under control today and I must say, it feels wonderful to be back to work acting like a real detective. Let's do lunch. We can have a small celebration."

"Sounds like a plan. I know you strive on being a detective and will be pleased to get cracking on a new case."

"I have one already," Jason boasts.

"Really! That was fast; anything interesting?"

"Robberies. It appears that several people have been held up at ATMs throughout the city."

The words "robberies" and "ATM" plummet Monique's thoughts to days past. Anxiety attacks Monique like a tidal wave on a small city causing her breathing to become broken, delaying a response to Jason's continuing conversation. After moments of silence, Jason becomes aware of the lack of Monique's mental presence.

"Hello, did I lose you?" Jason questions.

"No, I'm here," Monique replies noticeably different from moments earlier.

"What's wrong? You are not the same as you were in the beginning of this conversation."

"You struck a nerve, that's all."

"Let's not play a guessing game, so please tell me what has obviously rattled your nerves."

"Your case." Monique pauses. "I didn't want to tell you but," she hesitates once again, "I was robbed at an ATM recently."

"What! When?" Jason questions overly concerned. "Why didn't you tell me?"

"Jason, I didn't want to bother you because I wasn't harmed. They only took my money."

Somehow upon completing her sentence, Monique knows that her words will not make sense or even set well with Jason, but for the lack of anything better to say, she bows her head, waiting for Jason's response.

"So, when did this happen?"

"It happened the night before I came to the station."

"In all sincerity, you should have told me then."

"I know but..."

"Listen," Jason interrupts, "let's forget lunch and meet now. We need to talk. Can you make it to Rosalina's in an hour?"

"I can."

"Then, I'll see you soon...Monique?"

"Yes, Jason."

"I'm going to take care of you."

"I know you will," Monique replies feeling the comfort in Jason's words.

Jason leaves almost immediately for Rosalina's causing him to arrive minutes before opening hours. He knocks on the second set of double doors to be greeted by Alfredo.

"Ah, Jason, you must be extremely hungry this morning. You're quite early."

"I know. I am going to dine, but, actually I'm conducting official police business."

"Are you in need of another magical milkshake?" Alfredo asks.

A smile shows on Jason's face upon recognizing Alfredo's private joke. "No, this time I'm waiting for my guest to arrive."

"It must be of the utmost importance because your demeanor is not its usual friendly manner."

"I'm sorry, old friend, but it happens to involve someone I'm close to for a second time. I guess I'm a tad bit unnerved by the similarity."

"Can I assist you?"

"I don't know...have you been robbing people at the cash machines?"

"You know we criminals never tell on ourselves," Alfredo says humorously.

"Pity."

"I've read several stories in the paper about this over the last few weeks."

"Monique is a victim of this crime."

"She is the woman you had lunch with not too long ago."

"Your memory serves you well, friend."

"I'll be sure to direct her to your booth when she arrives and your coffee is on the way."

"Many thanks for your attentive service all of these years."

Alfredo simply smiles, nods his head and walks away knowing that Jason understands. Monique arrives at the double doors expecting to be greeted by Jason, especially since the doors are locked and the restaurant is empty. Alfredo approaches and presents her with a pleasing smile. Monique's not-so-natural return smile manages to light up the entrance foyer.

"Madam Monique," Alfredo greets, "Jason is already seated."

"Hello, Alfredo. He is in his booth, no doubt."

"Precisely."

"I'll make my way there if that's okay with you."

"Your coffee with Irish creamer is on its way."

"How nice of you to remember."

Monique stands at Jason's booth happy to be in his presence but uneasy about what she must reveal. Jason stands, administers an assuring hug before they sit. Her depiction of the events on the night in question sends her mind through an array of emotions, which her face profoundly reveals. The struggle to remain calm fails causing Jason to interrupt her re-enactment of the robbery.

"You should have told me sooner."

"I know...with all you've been through, I didn't want to involve you. Besides, I've functioned better not thinking about it."

"That's exactly why I wish you'd told me earlier, if nothing more than for peace of mind."

"They only took money. I wasn't harmed, scared shitless but health-wise okay."

"When can you go to the station to see the sketch artist?"

"I'm not positive it will do any good. Since that time I've tried blocking the entire episode out of my mind. And," she adds as an afterthought, "the lighting was very poor."

"It's worth a try; anything can help."

"All I'm certain of is that they were two Caucasian men."

"Monique," Jason states in another tone, another demeanor, a caring one that draws her attention. "Promise me not to repeat my past. Sasha stumbled onto the identity of the murderer I was looking for but for some reason, chose not to inform me and it probably cost her her life. Please no deja vu."

"Jason, I have no idea who the men are that robbed me, but I promise you, if I stumble onto any information, you'll be the first to know."

"Thanks, that will allow me the opportunity to do my job," Jason states in a manner which leaves Monique suspicious that he is not entirely convinced by her words.

"I will, I promise I will, so please don't worry."

"I have your word on that?"

"Yes, my Dear, you do."

"Good, I'd hate to start acting like a detective around you."

"Oh my, he's getting serious."

"I'd love for this to be a joking matter, but unfortunately, it isn't and yes, I...am... serious," Jason delivers slowly.

"I promise as soon as this lunch is over, I'll meet you at the station and provide a full report on what happened to me that night."

"Thank you, I'd appreciate that."

"Okay, now can we conclude this conversation?"

"Certainly, let's enjoy ourselves."

"Are you sure that you're okay?"

"Yes, I told you, I'm satisfied with your response."

"That's not exactly what I mean. Are you okay with what happened to you last night?"

"Hmm, that's not exactly what I meant, when I said, let's enjoy ourselves."

"I'm concerned about you."

"Thank you, Love, but I'm fine...even if I'm not, I know that in time I will be."

"So," Monique states as if she discovered something, "you're still bothered by the ordeal?"

"Please understand that I'm a bit apprehensive of women with guns."

A puzzled look occupies Monique's face.

"The last time a woman pulled a gun on me, I was shot," Jason continues.

"Sorry," Monique says while scrunching her face, "I forgot about that."

"It's pretty much put away, however, it is something I choose not to experience anytime soon."

"Okay," Monique says, sensing a change in subject matter is needed. "Let's enjoy ourselves."

The lunch moments transform into a less tenseful, happy occasion for both of them, concluding with Monique promising to keep her word to meet Jason at the station. After a long goodbye hug, which ended with a polite kiss on the lips, Jason sets out for the station with Monique following closely behind.

Jason logs an official report of Monique's robbery, escorts her to the sketch artist and leaves her in his care. Moments later, Jason returns to them and manages to slip her a note without the other officer being aware. Monique lowers her hands between her legs, reads the note which states that Jason will meet her later at her home. It makes her blush as it may have back in her adolescent years. The bashful smile remains apparent on her face as she addresses and apologizes to the officer for the intrusion. After she finishes detailing what little she remembers about the assailants that robbed her, she leaves the station without returning to Jason. In her car, before departing the station's grounds, she reads the note once more and a wide smile broadens her face as before.

ELEVEN

"When will we start our job for the Mayor?" Reggie asks.

"Probably tomorrow," Sly responds. "I'm in the mood for something more stimulating."

"Like what?"

"Well, I think when darkness falls, we should stake out more cash machines."

"Don't you think we're overdoing it? It's plastered all over the papers."

"I've seen it. The media is just trying to drum up another scare. Besides, I just want a few more hundred dollars, some pocket change, if you know what I mean."

"I haven't spent my cut from the last time."

"Maybe you're right," Sly states after more consideration. "Why take the chance of getting caught with one last fling. If our antics are being reported on TV now, surely the cops have some sort of investigation going on?"

"That's what I was thinking. It will be easy money following this woman Crystin and besides the Mayor seems eager for us to start."

"You're right. It makes better sense for us to take on the Mayor's task. We may have milked the ATM thing for all it's worth. We will be at the starting point first thing in the morning."

"That's what I'm talking about."

The following morning, Crystin leaves her home heading for the city. She directs her car into an alley, makes a right turn at the back of a building and parks her car facing a rear entrance of some establishment. She pauses a brief moment before exiting her vehicle, walks to the far end of a building and executes another right turn. Sly and Reggie slowly make the identical turn into the alley, carefully following Crystin. They make it to the end of the building just in time to see Crystin walking around the building's corner. Reggie remains seated with the engine running as Sly quickly exits the car and slowly proceeds to turn the same corner as Crystin. Crystin times his turn perfectly and greets Sly with a small-caliber handgun just a few centimeters from his nose. The startled Sly's eyes widen and his heart races, however his disguised turmoil is barely noticeable.

"Whoa!"

"Why in the fuck are you following me?" Crystin demands.

"Uhm, I don't know what you are talking about."

"Don't play dumb with me. You've been on my tail since I left my home and I want to know why?"

"Call it a coincidence but I'm not following you." Crystin's thumb brings back the hammer on her revolver. "Okay, okay!" Sly states. "It's your husband; he is paying me to follow you."

"Why?" Crystin demands. "And, it better be the truth."

"He knows about your affair with that detective."

"How could he possibly know? I haven't left any clues or given him any reason to be suspicious."

"Trust me, he knows."

Crystin continues with the gun focused squarely between his eyes. "That can't be," she states in disbelief. "So, how did my husband come to know you. I've never seen you before."

"We recently met and he thought I could be useful, so I'm following you."

"No way, you're lying. Anthony does not trust that easily. There's more," she states, this time tapping the gun against his forehead. "And you're going to tell me."

Sly deducts that he has more to gain than to lose by confessing all to Crystin, so, he conveys the entire scenario to her eager ears. Toward the end of his explanation, Crystin lowers the gun, tucking it neatly away in her purse. Sly's immediate inner thought is "gotcha," confident that his unique gift has served him well once more.

Crystin shakes her head in amazement before uttering, "You're wasting your time anyway. The son-of-a-bitch ended our affair."

"Oh," Sly states, sensing that there is something about the way Crystin delivered her last words.

Was it the flatter tone? The saddened expression that blanketed her face or the way her eyes darted away from his as she spoke, trying not to reveal the actual hurt that inundates her? It didn't matter; he is certain that she is bothered, and an opportunity like this is far too good to pass up.

"That Detective Jerrard is quite a character. It is none of my business, but, it's painfully obvious that he toyed with you."

The words enter Crystin's ears like a dagger through the heart. She closes her eyes, then opens them slowly to reveal a mixture of pain and revenge. Sly isn't able to distinguish which is more prominent. However, when she speaks her next words, he knows that continuing to feed on her weakness is his best move.

"He had the nerve," Crystin states with a shaken tone, "to tell me that I existed in his life because he hadn't faced the pain of losing someone."

"The old I didn't realize I was running trick. Player, player!"

"He thinks he can just sweep me away like trash. I'll get even with him," Crystin states with that all-too-familiar vengeful tone.

Sly raises an eyebrow. "We need to talk. Let's compare notes," Sly suggests.

Crystin ponders the idea for a brief moment, and then ultimately agrees to the meeting. By chance, they are behind a coffee shop. They continue their conversation inside in a more relaxed atmosphere.

"So you take pictures and follow people around. What else do you do?" asks Crystin.

"I'm an entrepreneur of many sorts but most profitable is the value-added services that my ladies do."

"You're a pimp?"

"Not exactly, I run a brothel on wheels." Crystin's face frowns, not understanding what he is referring to. "You've heard of the Mile High Club. Well, I provide the 175 miles-per-hour club to those who want it."

A dumbfounded Crystin states, "English, please."

"If you want to experience an orgasm on the ground traveling approximately 200 miles per hour, then I'm your man."

"Sounds dangerous."

"That's where the thrill comes in. It enhances the entire sexual experience."

"I see you're a man of many talents."

"I try to be versatile…you wouldn't be…?"

"Don't even think about it," Crystin interrupts even though deep down the idea intrigues her. "Well, let's get to the business at hand. How do you propose to get even with this Jason character?"

"I think we should first monitor his activities to better understand how to get under his skin and to see if he has any particular patterns."

"Seems logical. When do we proceed?"

"Since I won't be tailing you, I can concentrate my efforts on him. The part I have not figured out is what I'm going to tell your husband."

"Don't worry about him. I'll handle that situation. The best thing for me at this point is to come clean. If he doesn't understand, then so be it. Contrary to popular belief, I can make it on my own. Besides," she recites with a touch of humor, "he doesn't want too many waves during his election campaign."

"That's something I'm certain of."

Crystin receives a contact number for Sly, stating that she'll let him know how things went with her Mister, and Sly promises to start the initial surveillance of Jason as soon as possible. They depart in separate ways, each satisfied with the outcome of their strange encounter.

Crystin drives home conjuring up ways to approach her husband. After minutes of deliberation, she decides that the break-bad method will serve no real purpose and do more harm than good. Years of being his armpiece have taught her exactly how to handle this situation; she is suddenly sure of it. She arrives home and finds her husband in the study reading a book, wearing an embroidered bathrobe.

"Honey," Crystin interrupts, "can we talk for a few minutes?"

Mayor Blake lowers his head, looks at her over the top of his reading glasses, pauses, then replies, "Sure, Babe, what's on your mind?"

Crystin kneels beside his chair and strokes his face. "I want to talk about us...please...and calmly."

"Calmly, huh? It must be one of those conversations. What is bothering you?"

"Can we use this moment as a giant eraser and wipe away all the bad things we've done to each other?"

"I'm not following you?"

"Bluntly put," she says while making circular motions around one of his nipples with a finger. "I know about the person you have following me."

The Mayor is momentarily taken aback but decides to let her continue before responding.

"I know that you know about me and that detective."

An acknowledging mumble from the Mayor enters Crystin's ears.

"I know pretty much everything," Crystin recites while separating his robe near his penis. She fondles his member caringly, slowly, initiating a response from him.

"Do you know what you're doing now?" questions the Mayor.

"I'm fully aware of my actions."

She lowers her mouth onto his semi-erect manhood. The warm wet sensation springs the rest of him into action. She administers a few more strokes with her mouth, then grabs the shaft of his penis into one hand, making slow up-and-down motions. Crystin's plan seems to confuse the Mayor; he has difficulty determining which head he'd like to think with. On one hand, he can explode into her about her infidelity, but on the other hand, he can explode in ecstasy.

Crystin holds his member upright while pulling his skin downward, making him more sensitive to her next move. She lowers her mouth onto it once more, this time taking as much of his manhood as her mouth would allow and raises from him slowly while keeping the pressure administered on him.

"You may not know it but I also know..." She lowers her mouth onto him again and repeats the same upward maneuver as the previous. "...that you've had..." Crystin continues, "...many lovers since...we've been married. So, let's consider...ourselves even ...and start anew," she recites while pausing every few words to perform her maneuver.

The Mayor is not sure if her words are being intercepted by his ears. His only conscious thought is that he is so close to exploding. He wants her to continue talking with her mouth around his penis or finish him with her hand. It doesn't matter, he wants to be released.

"So, what do you think of my proposal?" Crystin states as she continues working him with her hand.

"Sounds reasonable, however, I can't truly concentrate in this excited state. Let's have a minor conversation about this in a few minutes after I regain all of my wits."

"And you'll come clean?"

"Yes, yes," he replies even more sedated by her hand movements.

Crystin lowers her mouth onto him, this time applying a swirling tongue around his member, then raises in the usual manner. Her hand triple times up and down his shaft. In a matter of seconds, he releases a loud cry of passion and explodes violently by her continuing movements. It leaves him sensitized to the simplest touch and causes his body to jerk. She leaves to retrieve a towel and returns to the Mayor who is still seemingly dazed. After a moment of awkward silence, the Mayor finally speaks.

"There has been a Lisa, an Allison on and off during our marriage, providing no significant value to me other than sex."

"Let's not forget your latest conquest, a woman named Mandy."

"Sorry, I forgot all about her," he states realizing that Crystin is actually acquainted with his extra activities.

"This Detective Jerrard has been my only moment of infidelity. Partly for payback and partly because I thought we had something special between us. I'm sorry and I apologize. I was wrong."

"This is a no-questions-asked conversation. With that, no apologies are required. By virtue of our confessions, all apologies are contained within."

"Agreed, but it is payback time."

"Excuse me?"

"Not with you but that Detective Jerrard. I have plans for him and I don't mean intimate plans."

"Don't do anything foolish. He is a professional, a damned good one at that."

"I won't be rash. I…we have a plan already in motion to embarrass the bastard."

"We…as in you and me?"

"No, we as in me and Sly. Actually, since I met Sly through you, then I guess *we*, as in the three of us."

"I will not be party to any foul play."

"Please don't patronize me. I may have been something pretty to show off in public but I can detail several of your," Crystin pauses for effect, "shall we say, foul balls."

"I seem to have underestimated you and possibly ignored a resourceful ally in you, so tell me about your plan."

Crystin goes through her conversation with Sly, detailing how they plan to dishonor the crown jewel of Virginia City. Maybe if the Mayor didn't feel beguiled by Jason, he could be objective and possibly talk Crystin out of her vengeful motive. But, lurking too fresh in his recent memory is Jason's betrayal of his confidence. He feels that Jason discarded the sincere concern over his wife's safety and purely lied unadulterated. Because of this, his decision to sit in the shadows and not actively participate in Jason's take-down sets well with him as long as neither she nor his name is in the media headlines.

Crystin loves it when a plan comes together. She gloats inside about how she easily smoothed the rough feathers of her marriage, virtually without retribution to herself. She also knows that part of her plan has been omitted. The Mayor is on a need-to-know basis and need not know that there is a second part to her plan, an altered version of the one that she and Sly agreed upon. She knows that she will have to keep Sly in the dark as well and is fully aware that she will have to deal with the consequences of her nondisclosure at a later time.

Shortly after her conversation ends with her husband, Crystin pages Sly to establish communications in order to tell him that all systems are go with their plan. After a conversation between the two, Sly advises Crystin that he will set things in motion.

TWELVE

J ason arrives at Monique's home relieved that the ordeal is over with Crystin but saddened that the situation caused her pain. He finds strength in knowing that Monique is in his corner, believing in the strength she has in him. He knocks on the door mindful that the experience gained from his relationship with Sasha will be the basis for a better life with Monique. She answers the door pleasingly surprised that Jason has called upon her.

Immediately Jason notices her excitement but becomes overwhelmed with the condition of her apartment. The cardboard boxes are stacked neatly in a corner. Tables, lamps, sofas and chairs are in the rightful places with the only thing seemingly remaining to accomplish is the hanging of the drapes over the balcony doors.

"Wow!" Jason states. "You work fast." Then it hits him like a ton of bricks. "I was supposed to help you with this."

"Yes, you were, lazy bones," Monique states harshly in her most upset tone. "Is this an example of how I can count on you?"

Jason stares through her searching for a response to her unexpected attitude.

"Don't look at me with that tone of voice," Monique continues.

"I...I," Jason replies unsure of what to say.

"Jason, my darling, I'm kidding, relax. Couldn't you tell that I was about to burst into laughter?"

"Obviously not," Jason responds with a half-disturbed smile.

"How quickly we forget…if you recall, I was somewhat of a jokester back in the day."

Jason sighs in relief. "I'll have to remember that you are somewhat like me."

"Do that, I want this relationship…" Monique pauses realizing that such a defining word may have been used prematurely.

"Continue," Jason urges.

"…to be fun," Monique concludes.

"Let's talk seriously for a moment."

Monique's defenses are raised, photon torpedoes armed, ready to fire with the serious overtures of Jason's statement, but as quickly as they jump to "red alert," they disengage as Jason continues.

"Will you tell me, why me? Why of all the promising men vying for your attention. Am I the chosen one?"

Monique's expression shows a bit of amazement with Jason's question, a perfect question, even if it's decades late. However, she entertains his question by replying, "My precious, Jason, we were on two separate ships that did more than pass in the night. We actually docked at the same port, but we never really came together as one. We've always been destined to be one. Our destiny is here, our destiny is now and if I have anything to do with it, our destiny will be all of our tomorrows."

Jason finds himself once again stunned by her words. Not so much by the content of them, but by the way they seem to be intercepted from his innermost thoughts and expressed by her.

"Okay," Monique states, "why the strange look this time?"

"Oh, nothing," Jason lies. "It is pleasing to know we're in sync…but, you still haven't answered my question of why me."

"You're intolerable, but I will comply. You see, I've always had men in search of me, wanting me, needing me, even back then. What makes me know that we are destined are the stolen glances we shared across a crowded room, and the way I am awed by your presence. To be near, breathing the same air as you, somehow filled my lungs with the essence of you. It does at this very moment. So tell me, how could I not know that you are the only one for me? Watching how differently you carried yourself from your peers was proof enough that you are unique."

"Unique. I've been called a lot of things; unique is a first."

"Jason," Monique states with heartfelt sincerity, "I love you."

Jason lowers his head, looks up with brightened eyes, attempting to conceal his sudden blush.

"I loved you back in high school; it simply never faded. You and I have had others in our lives. That hasn't changed the fact that our hearts are fated. Well, at least mine is for you. I accepted the knowledge many years ago that we will someday be together."

Monique's comments feel to Jason like a safety net of a flying trapeze act, hardly ever used but available if needed. Somehow they provide security, yet they sink into his being and touch a place he seldom visits.

"Do…" Jason pauses to carefully consider what he is about to deliver. "…or will you have the patience to see us through my getting over Sasha? I can't pretend that she or that situation is beyond me…for that matter, neither is Julie's ghost," Jason shamefully admits.

"My dearest, Jason, everything I just said is meaningless if that was not embedded in my feelings. If," Monique continues but really meaning *when*, "you let me. I intend to help you through it. So, what are your thoughts about us?"

Jason regards her with as much sincerity his scrambled feelings will allow. "I don't know where to begin, however, I will tell you, as I was knocking on your door, I was warmed by your strength in me…in us. I do know that the thought of you is as exhilarating as it was when we were younger. My heart seems synced with yours on a lot of things in this present time. Loving you, that's simple. I'll draw it from the secret place that it has been hiding all of this time and let it expand within me, lifting me from the ground. You see, my Angel, I…"

A broad smile illuminates across Monique's face, interrupting Jason's words, allowing her the needed pause to reply, "You are the first, last, and only person that has ever called me that. I've missed the subtle excitement in the way you use it."

"You have and always will be my Angel. Besides, I've loved others, some deeply, but now I somehow feel that my continued existence depends on loving you. I want to love you unconditionally, and not hold a sacred place for myself as I've done in the past."

"Jason," Monique cries. "Hold me, attack me, and ravage me. I want us now."

"I, too, share that sentiment but first, tell me what you like."

"What?" Monique responds, looking at him strangely. "I throw myself at you and you want to know what I like. I like what all women like…I'd like," Monique says boldly, "to feel you inside of me."

"I want that, too, more than you'll ever know, but, I must know what you like before any of it happens."

"Why not just wild, pent-up, frustrated sex?"

"Because, I want it to be magical, filled with all of the illusion of a perfect romantic encounter."

"Jason, no two people are like that, especially with the first sexual encounter."

"My point exactly. You see, most men enter a sexual encounter with a predetermined notion of a woman's desires. It stands to reason that very often they are off base, therefore, not really providing the woman with what she wants because each woman is different, with different wants, needs, and desires."

"You're serious about this, aren't you?" Monique questions with skepticism.

"Very. Like I said, each and every woman is different. Some differences are very minute but that minute difference can be what stands between being pleased or satisfied. Besides, what's the point of having an orgasm if the journey to that point is filled with misconceptions?"

"I somewhat agree with that question, but…"

"But," Jason intrudes, "you are going to tell me your weakest spot. The spot, when touched the right way, aids you in losing yourself…the one that makes you wet."

"Why don't you experiment; I'm sure you'll get to it."

"It's a waste of time because I could play touchy-feely with parts that you don't want touched."

Monique shakes her head side to side in awe. "After all of these years, this is what our intimacy has come to be."

"It has come to the place of no return. We can't retreat."

"And we shouldn't," Monique agrees. "Our relationship has to flourish beyond me telling you what I like sexually."

"It will," Jason assures. "I could ask you twenty-one questions, all leading to what I want you to disclose. However, you know better than me."

Monique pulls him into her beckoning arms, kissing him deep and hard while making sure it lasts for more than a few seconds. Jason welcomes the unexpected aggressive move. Actually it consumes him, warms and begins to change his being. Monique stops the kiss just long enough to gaze into his eyes with a strong passionate glare, revealing all of the emotions contained within her. Jason's senses catch all of the sentiment passed to him within the waves of her vision.

He removes her arms from around his neck and lowers them to his waist before removing his tie. Monique already feels herself weakened by his tender act. Jason corresponds with two softly spoken words delivered to her ears, "Trust me."

Screech! The brakes sound, the moment, the passion lost to instantaneous cold emotions. Beware of men who say, "Trust me"; her mother's words ring in her mind. Jason swears that he can sense the ever-so-slight apprehension filtering through her being. Nevertheless, he places the loop of the tie over her head, tightening it around her eyes with the knot of the tie in the rear.

"Too tight?"

"No," Monique replies while countering her mother's words with her own assuring thoughts of the stability in her trust of Jason. Her anxiety vanishes, completely consumed by the overpowering wrath of true love.

Another word is delivered evenly into Monique's ear—"relax"—causing her to let out a deep breath of air, seemingly conceding her will to Jason's strange game. He steps behind her while his hand descends to her waist, then up the back of her blouse to the hooks on her bra, all the while teasing her delicate skin with the gentle touch of his fingertips. His other hand is placed at the base of her neck, and then slowly moves upward into her hair, into a clutched fist that pulls her head back, allowing him to rub the base of his nose along the height of her neck. The subtle but aggressive move startles Monique's senses, awakening the sensuous desires caged within her. Jason creates a wet trail on her neck with his tongue and softly blows on the wetness with a warm breeze from his mouth. Chill bumps swarm Monique's body like an avalanche of snow running from her head to toe, enhanced by the feel of her nipples' freedom as her bra loosens from her breasts.

The tip of Jason's finger on her hardened nipple sends her senses into an electric overload, immediately soaking her womanhood. Her blouse is removed almost without her awareness. Jason administers tiny bites from her neck, down to her shoulder, and then gently kisses his way to her breasts. He bites one nipple through the bra, purposely soaking the fabric before using his nose to lift the garment from her skin, exposing her breast to his beckoning mouth.

Monique seizes Jason's manhood. Jason removes her hand, holds a nipple firmly between his teeth and issues a rule for his playful game, "No touching." Monique's arms fall frustratingly to her side, needing to feel, craving to touch any part of his being.

"Don't move," Jason instructs. "And, do not remove your blindfold."

Jason leaves for the kitchen to retrieve a few items and returns to the obedient Monique standing in place. He takes the first of three items and makes small circles at the base of her neck. The ice cube melts to an ever-increasing body temperature, sending a trail of water down the crevice of her back. The initial chill of the water contrasts with the hot, sultry sensations running through her veins. Fortunately for Jason, he is tall enough to be on his knees and reach her neck with the ice cube, allowing him to catch most of the water as its path funnels between her buttocks. Jason continues this until the ice cube is all but a small particle melting away in his hand.

Monique's knees weaken. Her hunger for his embrace coupled with her womanhood needing to be filled exasperates her lust for more. Jason's fingers pull downward at her waist, descending her panties in the process only to stop at her knees. He brings his hands together as in prayer, darts them between her thighs before spreading her legs as far as the panties will allow. He places the pointed end of the second item into her panties, aligns it parallel and directly under the design of her womanhood before standing behind her once again. He reaches around her and embraces a breast in each hand. The softness of Jason's palms surprises Monique in the sense that she is delighted that he has an inside job, one that keeps him from having the rough hands of a construction worker. Both hands slowly descend down the front of her to a destination Monique believes is her wetbox. Jason's fingers reach the smooth hairs of her womanhood causing Monique to brace herself for the insertion of one of his fingers into her. She sighs, holds her breath far too long in anticipation, only to be discouraged when Jason's hand maneuvers down her outer thigh in search of her panties. Jason senses her disappointment with the release of her breath. Nevertheless, to combat her frustration, he raises her panties ever so slowly with a pace that causes Monique to question his actions.

"Jason," Monique says, "I'm not one to tell you how to run things but, what are you doing? First, you show signs of removing my undergarments, then the reverse."

"I'm doing what I do best; relax and enjoy."

"How can I get enjoyment knowing that my panties will hinder what I want from you?"

"Be patient," Jason replies continuing the ascend of her panties.

"But," Monique responds just before experiencing a prickle from the teeth of the fork just above her clitoris. "What the…?" Monique questions before her words are cut off by Jason.

"Shhh, I won't hurt you," Jason counters while continuing the motion with her panties.

Monique finds herself inhaling, holding her breath as the stem of the fork separates and positions itself between her lower lips with the four prongs sticking into her pelvic area. Monique searches her emotions, unsure if the sensation is pleasure or pain.

Jason gives her a moment to become acquainted with what her senses are experiencing, and then whispers softly into her ear, "How does that feel?"

"It feels…"

"Walk with me," Jason interrupts.

He stands in front of her, holds both hands and guides her a few steps. Monique finds herself stimulated by the fork's presence. The slight pressure placed on her man-in-the-boat, coupled with the fork's teeth which seem to lower themselves dangerously close to her womanhood awaken a state of erotica within her that she has never known.

Jason stops, reaches behind her, digs what little fingernails he has into her buttocks, sending Monique's senses into frenzy, overloading them. Instantly, her body secretes natural juices on the stem of the fork, warming the slight chill of the metal object imposing on her.

"Are you okay?" Jason questions.

"I'm..." Monique replies, letting the word linger as if it will help return her heavy breathing back to normal. "Wet," she utters in an emotional tone which Jason is unaccustomed to.

"That has to be a good thing."

Jason turns her around and walks her back to the original location, causing her to be more sensitized in the area where the fork interacts with her lower area. He lowers her panties just enough to remove the fork without causing her discomfort and treats himself to the fork's stem housing her juices, devouring them before tossing it aside.

The third item is used on the lips of her womanhood, caressing them softly with a cushiony object for a few moments before separating them with gentle pressure. Once the entrance to her wetbox is located, he uses his middle finger to carefully slide what he has deemed a marshmallow surprise into her. He inserts it to where it can't be seen by the naked eye.

"We can finish this in the bedroom," Jason suggests.

"Do I get to remove the blindfold?"

"No, not just yet."

Jason escorts Monique bedside, removes her remaining clothes and lowers her to a sitting position on the bed. He attempts to lower her backward but senses a resistance from his subject.

"Jason," Monique questions with her abdominal muscles tight, holding her in a leaning position. "What kind of freaky shit are you into?"

Jason leans forward, kisses her cheek, then gently on the lips before taking a firm grip on her bottom lip and replies through his clinched teeth, "The next time someone asks you what you like, you might consider answering. Now, if you don't mind, I'd like to continue."

Monique descends to the bed without further comment as Jason immediately seeks his marshmallow surprise, diving face first into her concealing mechanism. His tongue skillfully searches for his prize, darting swiftly into her moisture, just reaching the marshmallow. He carefully retrieves her clitoris between his lips and softly caresses it with the top, tip, and bottom of his tongue causing her body to immediately gyrate. Monique exercises muscle control, squeezing her insides several times in an attempt to force the foreign object out of her. Being fairly successful with her unorthodox maneuver, it allows Jason to use his tongue to retrieve it from her. Jason crushes the marshmallow against the roof of his mouth, swallows, and then dives again into her wetness. This time inserting his tongue as far as he can into her womanhood, allowing the secretions from his mouth to add more fluid to her wetbox.

"Jason," Monique cries. "What is that? Why do I all of a sudden feel tingly?"

"You mean you like what I'm doing with my tongue?"

"Yes I do but, there is more. Something is stimulating me in a weird fantastic way."

"You'll be referring to the marshmallow."

"So, that's what you put in me, but a marshmallow would not awaken my senses down there. You must have something in your mouth."

"I believe because you are blinded, your other senses are more acute."

"That may have something to do with it, but there is definitely something else going on."

Jason doesn't respond verbally to her latest comment; instead he inserts the menthol drop into her with his tongue, then tackles her man-in-the-boat while it takes further effect. The menthol cough drop is successful in stimulating her insides in ways she's never experienced. Her sudden arousal is best described as vibrations without a vibrator, causing a numbing effect similar to a dentist's sedative.

"Jason, I need to feel you inside of me...now!" Monique cries.

As if Jason needed to do more to induce an orgasm out of her, he feels strongly that just the simple insertion of his finger into her womanhood will make her explode. He knows that she is primed, ready for their naked skin to caress each other, to be wrapped in his embrace...sharing a passion that synchronizes their souls, making them one. But, he is not finished. He wants to punish her for not speaking up, for not answering his question, so instead, he decides to perform his infamous Butterfly maneuver.

Jason inserts his tongue into her soaked womanhood, then lowers his head, placing the bridge of his nose into her opening. He slowly raises his head until he experiences her clit ride the base of his nose, across the tip, down to and between his closed lips. He inhales as deeply as possible, and then blows the air from his filled lungs between his lips causing them to flutter at a rapid pace. Even though it sounds to Monique like a balloon running out of air, Jason's soft lips vibrating against her immediately electrifies all within her. He repeats the process again and feels her leg muscles contract. The next time brings on quick gyrations in her womanhood. Maybe it is the erratic motion of his lips beating against her; maybe it is the stroke of his tongue on her clit between the maneuver; maybe it is the menthol drop working her insides or maybe she is just damned horny. Nevertheless, Monique explodes in a whirlwind of an orgasm. She lets out a cry fueled by heightened senses that seem to carry along with it her innermost feelings. It talks to him, calls his name and contains "I love you" in the way it is expressed.

Monique snatches off the blindfold, looks down at Jason who is blowing a warm breeze onto her, aiding her fantastic ride to a less sensitive state. Right after Monique finishes what she believes is her last quiver, Jason retrieves the menthol drop with his finger. The search initiates another cry from Monique's mouth, followed by an unexpected orgasm that produces tiny chill bumps all over her body.

"Stop it, damn you," Monique pleads, "I can't take anymore."

Jason places the menthol drop in his mouth, slowly makes his way to her face and kisses her deep, long, passionately. As the kiss ends, Jason transfers the menthol drop into her mouth.

I knew it, Monique's mind reflects while accepting Jason's gift. She pushes Jason over, attacking his clothes, yearning for his skin, needing the feel of his manhood inside of her. Jason is somewhat amazed at how quickly he finds himself standing naked in front of her. He also becomes amused with the anticipation Monique's eyes reveal as her vision passes his hardened member while she lowers his pants. As Monique helps him step out of his pants, Jason raises her to her feet and embraces her with a tight but tender hug before kissing her deeply. This kiss is free of the games, free of the foreplay, freely calling her, signaling that it is time to unite as one. He lifts her into his arms, lowers her to the bed and begins to position himself between her legs when a touch of reality strikes Monique.

"Don't you think we should use some form of protection?" asks Monique.

Jason's eyes gaze into hers without a reply.

"I haven't been sexually active so I'm not on anything," Monique continues.

"It appears that we have ourselves a dilemma."

"Yes, we're not trying to make babies here."

A look splashes across Jason's face so unfamiliar to Monique that it worries her. She has seen him cry, be troubled by things but something in his eyes lets loose, calling her attention.

Jason struggles to contain himself, struggles to keep his erection but he knows Monique's last words triggered something buried within. Monique rolls him over to his side, then duplicates his position, stroking his face gently.

"What is it?"

"I need to go to the beach."

"No," Monique firmly states. "I'm familiar with you using the beach to cleanse your mind, but today you can use me as your soap, your water, and your soothing waves."

"Maybe it is not such a good idea to be involved with someone who has as much baggage as I do."

"I'm not even going to entertain that because we all have baggage and skeletons in the closet. So, tell me what I saw in your face."

"Something about babies dove into me and uplifted a suppressed thought."

"You're referring to Sasha being pregnant?"

"Not only that, but more trickery Julie took me through."

"You want to talk about it?"

"Actually, no…"

"Actually, yes you should," Monique corrected. "Otherwise, it wouldn't pop up at such a delicate time."

Jason considers her words for a moment, and then lies on his back staring at the ceiling as if he is ashamed of what he is about to say.

"You know, I've always wanted children. During my marriage to Julie, I found out, painfully I might add, that she was taking birth control pills while leading me to believe that we were trying to have a baby."

"I'd imagine that deceitfulness was painful for you."

"Then she did the ultimate and had her tubes tied without giving me a say in the matter. At her request, I drove her to the hospital. It was the most difficult thing I've ever done. I pleaded, begged, tried to make her see that what she was about to do would be detrimental to our relationship, our marriage, detrimental to me. Nevertheless, everything I expressed was ignored or it simply didn't matter to her. I spent the rest of our time together pretty much a changed man. I used positive affirmations to keep me behaving like a married man; to keep my love for her strong...I still loved her but differently. I learned then and there that love does not conquer all."

Monique raises to an elbow with that comment and searches Jason's face to see what emotions are being displayed.

"What did you just say?"

"I said that loving someone unconditionally is not all it's cracked up to be."

"Surely, you don't believe that."

"Monique, I can't explain to you exactly what I mean. All I know is that the only thing that kept my sanity was this...excuse me..." Jason retrieves his pants from the floor and takes a tiny cutout picture out of his wallet. "...this. I look at it each time my hunger for a child tries to damage my spirit. This alone helped me get through my remaining time with Julie. Positive affirmations aided, too."

Monique takes the picture from Jason's hand. Jason continues to stare into his hand as if the picture were still there. It is a black and white of a child about thirteen months old, cute, smiling with curly hair. Boy or girl, Jason couldn't tell; it didn't matter to him. All that mattered is that his fabricated child soothed the pain that many times attacks him unexpectedly.

"You can't hide behind a picture all of your life."

"We survive by any means necessary. It's God's built-in survival tactic. Damn," Jason swears. "I've waited twenty-two years to be in bed naked with you only to ruin the moment with horror stories."

"I figured our first romantic encounter would be different but not quite like this. Am I upset? Of course not, because contrary to what you said or what you think you believe, love does conquer all. All that you've exposed to me is that Julie didn't love you in the same manner you loved her. That's where the pain lies, in that knowledge. You need to let that go, too."

"I'd like to believe that I'm beyond this…the pain, the sorrow of my relationship with Julie. I'm hoping that the seriousness of our relationship is what's exposing my hidden feelings."

"Jason, you know my son, Jason, is nearly twenty-three years old and I'm pushing forty-four. I submit to you that when things progress with us the way I know they will," Monique pauses for effect, "we will have a child."

Jason turns to his side and faces her. This time his face is unreadable. Monique finds it difficult to ascertain what thoughts were traveling through his mind.

"Are you okay, Jason?"

"I'm surprised…speechless."

"Don't be. When I love, it's unconditional and based on things you've expressed about your last two relationships, you do much the same."

"I suppose I do. Well, I will again," Jason assures.

"Besides," Monique continues, "deep down, I'd love to have another child. Your child."

Jason's mouth opens but no words leave it.

"Jason Jerrard," Monique recites with an unexpected excitement. "I love you."

Jason closes his eyes, inhales deeply as to add the essence of the words' meaning to his being, then slowly exhales, opens his eyes and regards her in a heartfelt way.

"I know you do."

After a momentary pause, Monique embraces Jason, thanking him mentally.

"Thank you," Jason says.

"No, thank you."

"Thank me, why?"

"For not being a typical man and respond with 'I love you' back, thinking that I wanted you to reciprocate my feelings."

"I'm pleased that you understand that. Although, I know you'd love to hear those words from me. I also know that you'd be more enhanced by them when I generate them from my own will and not induced by yours."

"Exactly. Be assured, there will be no pressure from me because when you do let those words reach my ears, they will contain everything I desire in them. Understood?"

"Understood."

"I don't think," Monique states, "that I'd be too far off base in saying that the mood for romance is gone. After all, you aren't a machine."

"I don't know...say something dirty."

"Okay, a white horse fell into the mud."

A silly laughter overtakes the room and settles itself as a smile on their faces.

"Can we start this evening from the beginning another day, say tomorrow?" Jason expresses.

Monique is fairly successful in disguising her mild disappointment. "Tomorrow is good. It will give me time to prepare for you."

"You don't have to do anything special."

"By the way, before I forget, you're lucky that I'd just taken a shower or all of those things you did would not have happened."

Jason raises a brow. "Who's the lucky one?"

"Well, me since I was on the receiving end, but all I'm trying to say is, I like to be fresh."

Jason shakes his head from side to side. "I have a suspicion that you're fresh all of the time."

"Tell me, Jason, does tomorrow mean that you have to leave tonight?"

"Unfortunately yes, I'd like to be one hundred percent. Do some soul searching, that kind of stuff. Hell, I might even take on the beach."

"I thought you were better."

"I am. I just want to stay that way. I don't know if you took me serious when I said that I don't like you seeing me this way, but it is very true."

"Okay then, tomorrow it is. You might want to plan staying the night," Monique replies.

"I'll do that," Jason responds to her leading remark.

Jason slowly and unwillingly puts his clothes back on, gives her a strong hug and softly whispers into her ear, "Thank you for being you."

Monique smiles and nods with acknowledgment, absent a verbal reply. Jason kisses her on the forehead, grabs his keys and leaves. Monique stands with her back against the door having her heart filled with love for him.

Jason elects not to take the three-hour drive to the beach. Instead he settles for second best. After he showers and retires to his bed, a quick push of a button produces a constant wave sound from a machine sitting on his nightstand. The last thing he remembers is the soothing sound that placed him in a comfortable sleep, allowing him to wake refreshed and ready to conquer the day ahead of him.

THIRTEEN

Driving to the station, he happens to be only two blocks away when the distress call comes across the police radio. It is just what the doctor ordered, something new and different to satisfy his yearning to perform true detective work. After all, his two-week investigation of the ATM robberies in the city has only produced one arrest which turned out to be what he considers an amateur. His description or methods didn't correspond with any previously reported cases or what Monique had described.

As he exits his car, his eyes glisten with anticipation. Immediately everything is familiar; old instincts seem to raise his investigative powers to a higher level. As if the case is already given to him, Jason takes charge of the crime scene. The victim is a fully clothed Caucasian male with an estimated age of 52. Apparent cause of death is a vicious beating. Bruises decorate his face as fashionably as the garments actors wear on award night. They are not to be overshadowed by the multitude of footprints imprinted on one side of his face. Highlighting and completing the ensemble are two black eyes and bleeding lips. Jason has the entire scene sectioned off with yellow tape and instructs a couple of officers to keep the gathering crowd a few feet from the tape's boundaries. Preparing for the arrival of the coroner and forensics team, he performs his initial examination of the body with thin rubber gloves.

Obviously, the person died from severe trauma to the head from the beating of a person or persons. Jason's immediate thought is more than one is involved with this crime. He is somewhat surprised that the John Doe has a wallet with identification still on him. He uses a piece of chalk to mark off potential tire marks but discards the idea based on indications that the body was thrown from a moving vehicle. Traces of blood and skin are discovered heading to the victim's final resting place. The forensics team arrives moments before the coroner and they negotiate the scene, recording all visible evidence. After the forensics team scans the body's surrounding area, the coroner reviews the body, discovering more wounds and bruises under the victim's shirt before the body is removed for what would appear to be a needless autopsy. Jason instructs the coroner to forward any unusual findings to him at the Sixteenth Precinct. Back at the station, Jason proceeds to Captain North's office to plead his case.

"Ah Jason," Captain North responds upon noticing him inside the door's threshold. "I was wondering where you were."

"Where I am in reference to my whereabouts or on the case I'm assigned?"

"Well, I was referring to the case but something tells me there's more to your question."

"It's just that hundreds of ATMs are spread all over this vast city. I've utilized every resource at my disposal, worked day, evening and nights looking for what? An organized unit or is it just some rare happenstance that seemed to occur together for a short period of time. It feels like you gave me this case just to give me something to do. Isn't it commonly referred to as," Jason raises both hands and performs the quotation mark maneuver with his fingers while completing his sentence, "keep-busy work?" In my opinion, it was a meager attempt to apologize for my assignment with the Mayor."

"No, that wasn't the case."

"Frankly, Sir…"

"Frank," Captain North interjects.

"Frank…my skills are being wasted. Wasted," Jason responds as an afterthought, "may be a bit strong so I'll change that to misused. I can serve this department and the city better in my normal capacity. And, might I add, my health is nearly one hundred percent."

"How long did you practice this speech?"

"I have not prepared anything. It happens to be the way I feel."

"I see," Captain North replies as he steps around the corner of his desk and begins pacing the floor behind Jason's chair. "That one arrest is all you've produced with your surveillance both day and night?"

"Yes, I've had myself and four additional units out well after dark, but we all seem to have been at the right place at the wrong time. As you know, a couple of robberies have occurred while my team was on patrol. Like I said, the city is vast."

"Yes, but this past week no reports of this type of activity have been reported here or at any of the neighboring precincts for that matter. Maybe your presence has been a deterring factor after all."

"That and the fact that every local station has carried the story should be a deterrent to most criminals."

"How do you propose we utilize your deductive skills if I take you off your current assignment?"

"Well," Jason starts with a smile, "I can start a homicide investigation of a murder victim I saw today. Truthfully, I've already started. Some poor guy," Jason replies while retrieving a note pad from his shirt pocket. "A Roy Darknight was apparently beaten to death. He got the living shit beat out of him. Also, I'm waiting on the complete details from the coroner. So you see, I'm already involved with a case which best suits my abilities."

"What can I say?"

"You can say yes and officially assign the case to me."

"Okay, Jason," Captain North states as he walks toward the door. "This one is yours. Let's see if we can get to the bottom of this before the media does. Speaking of which, you damn well better keep a low profile media-wise yourself. I do not, I repeat, I do not want a repeat of your last media publicity. I'm referring to the kind of recognition you received before the Mayor honored you. I will..." Captain North pauses long enough to grab Jason's attention further, "have your fucking badge. We understand each other?"

"Crystal clear."

"Okay then, get to work and give me your best effort."

Before Jason flashes his devilish smile, Captain North knows that he is asking for big trouble. Jason settles at his desk feeling rejuvenated with having a case worthy of his unique skills. After all, he is Super-Somebody, Virginia City's golden child. All within him tells him that he needs to be on the streets, ridding them of treacherous criminals that are involved in such violent acts he had seen earlier. He knows this case is the kick in the pants he needs to become his old self. First he runs Mr. Darknight's information through the computer, and finds no prior arrests, not even a parking ticket. On the surface, his John Doe is clean as a whistle.

Next comes the part of the job that he hates the most. The preliminary check discloses a Mrs. Darknight. He is now faced with the pleasure of telling Mrs. Darknight about her husband's death. The moment he picks up his keys to call on Mrs. Darknight, the telephone rings, stopping him in his tracks.

"Sixteenth Precinct, Jerrard."

"Detective Jerrard, this is Simms from the coroner's office. We've just completed the autopsy on Mr. Darknight."

"Anything unusual?"

"As we stated at the crime scene, trauma is the cause of his death. We believe that he was dead before being tossed out of whatever vehicle he was transported in. Simply put, the poor man was beaten to death."

"All of that could be ascertained without an autopsy. Anything in his blood? Drugs, alcohol or diseases?"

"Nothing, however, I did notice a flaky white substance on his penis which turned out to be his and a female's secretions. So, I checked his urethral tube and it revealed signs of him recently having an orgasm."

"Interesting...anything more to add?"

"Other than a couple of fractured ribs, that's about it."

"Thank you very much for your quick turnaround and please forward me an electronic copy of your report."

"As soon as it's entered into the computer, it will be there. What is your email address?"

"Defiantone@precinct16.org"

"That's different."

"I know, it best describes my actions at times. Thanks again."

"You're welcome, goodbye."

"Bye."

Jason isn't too alarmed with the report from the coroner; however, the talk of sex opens up a new avenue of motives. *Maybe a jealous husband*, he thinks. He isn't sure, but he knows that this will not be easy to trace with such scarce information. Forensics produced only a partial fingerprint. Something inside of him tells him that it will be a wasted effort but as a precautionary measure, he has the print run against the computer's database. While this is working, he sets out to talk with Mrs. Darknight.

It is midday. The sun warms him, somehow bathes his senses, making the dreadful ride bearable. It isn't that he is against being the bearer of bad news; after all, it is part of his job. Unfortunately, it's the part of his occupation that he has never gotten used to. He doesn't like having to steel himself for protection against the emotional outburst which immediately follows the tragic news. The physical abuse that sometimes accompanies the explosive emotions is easier to handle than the drain placed on his mental being.

He has experienced the same thing so many times to where he can envision the scene like a prediction. He will knock or ring the doorbell, introduce himself as a detective; then the initial startled response occurs. This is where he sees the person transform from cool and collective to a panic-stricken state, all before he delivers the dreadful news. He has always thought it to be along the lines of receiving an awakening telephone call in the middle of the night. In most cases it's bad news.

Jason thinks about his standard opening sentence, *I regret to inform you* and envisions the recipient's chest swelling with heavy breathing; the hyperventilating begins the process of them seemingly having a heart attack. The worst part occurs with the words, *that your husband, wife, son or daughter* has been *whatever.* This is when their outburst taints his steeled emotions. He feels that he can almost see a part of their soul being ripped from them. The soul pulls at his in search of a better place to hide, looking for comfort in a calmer being. Somewhere within their hysterically tormented emotions is a magnetic force that raises the hairs on his body, and claws at his mental stability. It is almost as if the process takes something away from him. At least that's what he believes because each time he reaffirms to himself that it doesn't.

He arrives at the Darknight home, located in a well-kept, middle-class neighborhood and knocks on the door of the two-story Colonial just short of hoping that no one will answer. Unfortunately, the call to the door is almost immediate. The troublesome expression on the woman's face is enough to make Jason pause before identifying himself. The woman is in her late forties or early fifties. She possesses an intellectual face, an average height, short blond hair and a body that's just beginning to show signs of aging. He holds up his badge, begins to introduce himself but is interrupted.

"It's my husband, isn't it?"

"Mrs. Darknight?"

"Yes, I am."

"I'm Detective Jerrard of the Sixteenth Precinct."

"Please forget the formalities. Is my husband okay?"

"Well, Ma'am, your husband has been…"

"Murdered," she cries, overlapping Jason's continuing word.

"…murdered."

Jason figures that the minute delay in her emotional outburst is her need to hear the dreadful words come from his mouth. As soon as Jason delivers the words, both of her hands cover her mouth as if all will change if she hadn't spoken first. She turns and runs around the corner leaving Jason standing at the door. Jason didn't have to guess where she might be. He knows that all he has to do is follow the sounds of her grief and fight his way through the loudness of her hysterical cry which seems to be riding on turbulent gale-forced winds, coming from the living room.

"Mrs. Darknight," Jason calls. He feels that it will be rather foolish to ask if she is okay but, as he finds her seated on the living room sofa, the words, "are you okay?" leave his mouth.

Jason wishes that he had Monique with him to console the distraught woman. But proper protocol dictates that the woman must be a female officer and not a civilian. Nevertheless, he is at Mrs. Darknight's home wishing Monique had answered her cell phone. He sits in a chair across from her and visualizes a steady mist being pulled from her as her spirit leaves her body. He watches the abolished pain dance across the room like bolts of electricity bouncing off walls, lamps, and every solid substance in its path. He feels his steel cage rattle as the vanquished emotions look for a new sanctuary.

After what seems like hours, the woman's eyes have dried and her breathing returns to normal. She speaks to Jason with a tone that indicates the aftermath of the trouble she went through. Her voice is somber, barely delivered loud enough for Jason's ears.

"I knew something was wrong when he didn't come home last night."

"My deepest condolences, Ma'am. My prayers are with you."

"Excuse my behavior earlier. I've been preparing myself for the worst. It seems that my preparation is flawed."

"No one is ever prepared for the loss of a loved one."

"How may I help you, Detective?"

"If you can answer a couple of questions for me, I will be on my way."

"I'll try."

"Do you know where your husband went last night?"

"He said that he was getting dinner at a restaurant named Rosalina's before taking in a nine o'clock movie. I'm sorry, Detective," she states as she brings her eyes to his for the first time. "I have to know, how my husband died?"

"It appears that he was beaten to death. He had identification but no money, so I suspect it was a robbery."

"Roy always carried money with him, too much for my likings. He couldn't have been broke. Where was he found?"

"He was found on the outskirts of town on the side of the road. He is now in the city morgue. We will need you to identify the body. Can you think of any enemies he may have?"

"To my knowledge, Roy was well liked by everyone. He runs..." She pauses. Her eyes swelled with tears, she continues. "I guess the proper term is... ran a successful accounting business. He also gets along with his partner, so honestly, I can't think of anyone who would have a motive or need to harm him."

"I won't trouble you further. May I call on you if I have additional questions?"

"Surely, anything to help. I'd like to see whoever is responsible for Roy's death caught."

"Given time, I'm sure we will find the person or persons. Please take my card. If I can be of further assistance to you, feel free to contact me anytime."

"Thank you for your concern…if I think of anything…"

"I understand."

Jason leaves Mrs. Darknight's home with sympathy for the woman who seems lost without her mate. He knew by the end of their conversation that her calm manner was temporary in nature indicated by the increasing tremor in her voice and the dark cloud which blanketed her with each passing moment. He feels guilty leaving her; after all, there are more questions that he would've liked to ask, personal ones involving their sex life. Starting with, "When was the last time you and your husband had sex?" He is aware that her answer hangs in the balance of his investigation. However, he didn't want such a leading question make him reveal his reasoning for asking. Her emotional valve was about to burst again and he didn't want to be part of the reason it exploded. Dealing with her onslaught of emotions is something he'd rather not experience again anytime soon.

Jason relives the conversation with Mrs. Darknight in his mind, extracting all useful information, separating it into a category of possible leads. He knows that he will check Mr. Darknight's insurance information, both personal and business, but his immediate attention will be diverted to talking with Mr. Darknight's business partner. He flips to his notes to recall the business address and the partner's name of Julian Stone.

The accounting business is actually located in a business park. It is a one-story suite with a tiny reception area, two small offices and a coed bathroom. After finding the correct building, Jason enters through a set of double doors and is greeted by a woman approximately ten years younger than he. She has a large frame and flattering curves considering her physical size.

She presents Jason with a warm gentle voice and an accompanying smile.

"Good afternoon," Jason says. "I'm here to see Mr. Julian Stone."

"Is he expecting you?"

"No, I don't have an appointment."

"Then may I ask whose calling?"

"Detective Jerrard, Sixteenth Precinct," Jason recites while exposing his badge.

A look of concern initially crosses the woman's face before she picks up the telephone to call Mr. Stone, however, from what Jason can ascertain, the concern is not revealed to her employer.

"He is in suite B," she says while pointing to the correct door.

"Thank you."

As Jason is about to knock on the office door, it opens with Mr. Stone greeting him.

"Julian Stone. Detective Jerrard, is it?"

"Yes."

"Please tell me you are here to talk taxes," he replies before continuing with, "and my illegal activities."

Jason smiles, ignores the humor attempt and goes directly to the business at hand.

"Actually, I'd like to ask you about your partner."

"Roy?" he interjects, cutting Jason off. "He's not in any kind of trouble is he, unless," he states while glancing at his watch, "being extremely late is a crime."

Jason is one who can appreciate humor but Mr. Stone's timing is wrong.

"He has been murdered."

"What!" Julian responds loudly, obviously taken by the information. The receptionist sneaks from her desk to listen to the commotion coming from the other side of the door. "When? I just talked to him last night at Rosalina's."

Julian sits in his chair hoping this action will help contain his rush of anxiety that has just about every one of his internal organs trembling.

"He was discovered early this morning."

"This can't be."

"Unfortunately, it's the truth. I know this news is shocking but was there anything unusual about your evening last night?"

"No...nothing that comes to mind. Tuesday nights are when we have our business dinner...well, this is what we called it, but it actually turns out to be the boys' night out. As usual, we had a few laughs and a couple of beers. We would normally take in a movie but I had a house guest arriving late evening so, shortly after I finished my meal, I excused myself and left him sitting at the table. I should have stayed with him," he sounds, shaking his head from side to side with it lowered.

"Don't go beating yourself up. How could you have known? Are you aware of any potential enemies of his?"

"Roy? You must be kidding. Mr. Congeniality, I doubt it."

"If you think of something that might be useful, even the oddest thing about last night..."

"Believe me," Julian says. "I will. I wish that I could be more helpful."

"You've been helpful and I thank you for your time. Oh, one more question if you don't mind. The two of you were close?"

"Very, why?"

"Has he ever mentioned anything about extramarital activities?"

Julian's face frowns, coinciding with his head shaking left to right, he says, "That type of conversation has never come up between us. Why do you ask?"

Jason ponders whether or not he should reveal the primary reason for asking. After a momentary pause, he states, "I'm just wondering if his beating is the result of a jealous husband."

"Roy cheating on his wife is unthinkable. He adored her."

"Not to switch things around but, if there is anything more I can do, please by all means contact me," Jason offers.

"Thank you, I surely will."

Jason leaves the accounting establishment close to the lunch hour. Figuring he can kill two birds with one stone, Rosalina's becomes the chosen place to settle his rumbling stomach.

He arrives at Rosalina's, greets Alfredo in his usual manner and proceeds to his booth. Even a blind man can see the luscious woman sitting at his customary seating. Being a creature of habit, he ponders a thousand ways to approach the woman and divert her to an empty table.

"Excuse me, Miss," Jason states. "I believe you've been incorrectly seated. This booth is usually reserved for me."

"Oh? Why should an entire booth be reserved for one man? Surely, there is room for us both. If not, maybe you're the one who should find alternate seating."

"What if I say that it is a private booth?"

"In such a public place...please," the woman replies with a hint of attitude.

"What do I have to say to get you to leave?"

"There's nothing you can say. I happen to know the owner," she boasts.

"What if I offered you a marshmallow surprise?"

Monique burst into laughter attempting to conceal her sudden embarrassment.

"I thought that would get you...what are you doing here?"

"I like it here and if you recall, I introduced you to this place."

"It's strange that you are here. I almost called you to have lunch with me, but since you didn't answer your cell phone earlier this morning..."

"You called me earlier?" she states somewhat surprised before retrieving her cell phone from her purse. A look of disappointment decorates her face as she reads the digital display advising her of one call missed. "So you did?"

"So, why are you here?"

"I just wanted to be close to you. I thought I could feel your presence by sitting in your seat. It has turned out much better than expected. You're here!" she states enthusiastically displaying a prominent smile.

"I'm sorry to ruin your moment of reflection."

"No, no," Monique interrupts. "You have nothing to apologize for. We've talked every night since the last time I saw you and you've explained things to me, so please don't feel sorry for doing your job."

"My job has prevented me from spending time with you."

"And...?" Monique says in a supporting manner. "For Pete's sake, you're a detective; detectives do that."

Jason gazes at her with amazement, filled with joy over her being so understanding.

"Where will you be for the rest of my life?" Jason caringly asks.

"Right here, with you, Jason."

Monique delivers those words so soothingly and comforting, Jason finds himself blushing.

"May I ask you something radical?" Jason states.

"It seems to me that radical may be an understatement or the improper word with that look on your face."

"Maybe my statement is forward or premature."

"It can't be that bad."

"I'd like us to live together," Jason recites with his attention directed to her eyes.

The words seem to pass through Monique; a blank unreadable expression cloaks her face.

"Excuse me?" Monique questions, not really needing to.

"I apologize...I must be out of line."

"No, you aren't. I just want to experience the sensation of that statement again. It makes my heart flutter."

"Would you like to share the same home with me?"

"Are you sure? I'm not trying to rush you into anything."

"I'm more than sure; I'm positive. Having you there will be my greatest joy."

"Yes," Monique responds barely containing the excitement within her. "I'd be delighted to. The question alone touches me deeply."

"Now, that the living together part is settled, where would you like to live? Your place, my place or we can get a neutral place if you'd like."

"Jason, I'm not concerned about my home belonging to you. Who cares what it says on paper? You would have to sell your home and my place is too small, so sharing your home with me is not a problem at all."

"Then it's settled?"

"Yes...well, I have to see about getting some of my money back."

"I thought you told me that you were renting monthly."

"True, but I paid for six months when I moved in."

"Well, you do what you need to do. If there is a penalty, then together, we'll handle the cost."

Monique's containment field breaks down. A huge smile dons her face, followed by a strong emotional hug which seems to trap Jason into her clutches. She manages to keep her bear-like grip around him and deliver a passionate kiss that transmits her joyous emotions to Jason.

"I'll take that as your signature," Jason responds.

"Sealed with a kiss."

"Angel, I don't want to spoil our moment, but, I need to ask Alfredo a few questions."

Monique believes that there is something more contained in his words; she is sure of it. There is some concern, which makes her believe that lunch isn't the only thing he hungers for from Rosalina's. As if Jason can read her thoughts, he delivers on queue.

"I'm lucky that you are here. I get to accomplish two tasks at once."

"You mean...you didn't come here for lunch?"

"Make that three birds. Actually, I'm investigating a murder. The victim had dinner here last night."

"Things have a strange way of working out for you, don't they?"

"The irony is eerie. Excuse me," Jason says in the process of standing. "I won't be long."

"Handle your business."

Jason walks to Alfredo who is making his usual scan over the establishment from the podium. After a quick exchange of words, Jason produces a picture of Mr. Darknight. Alfredo considers it carefully, but can't provide Jason with any knowledge of him. He recommends that Jason return during the evening hours to talk with the second-shift personnel. Afterwards, Jason returns to Monique, disappointed with no new information, but unmoved nonetheless.

"Well?" Monique asks.

"Nothing new, I sort of expected that. The upside is I'll have to return later. Care to join me for dinner?"

"It will be my pleasure."

"Then, I'll allow you to enjoy...my space," Jason amuses. "I'd like to get a head start on my report. This way we'll have dinner at a reasonable hour."

"Makes sense to me; besides, I'd better get back to the office myself. I'm about to start a new assignment."

"Anything interesting?"

"If you consider following a Mayoral candidate around interesting, to me it's the same old election BS."

Jason smiles reflecting on his last assignment. "Shall we rendezvous here at eight o'clock?"

"That works for me."

"Okay then, I'll see you soon."

Jason holds out his hand. Monique accepts his gesture for her to stand. He embraces her, gives a deep, attention-grabbing passionate kiss which leaves her feeling flush. He follows with a polite kiss on the cheek and vanishes as mysteriously as he came. The scene concludes with a small applause from a nearby table.

FOURTEEN

Craig Jones arguably holds the world record for coming out of a coma. He doesn't know how long he's been under, but he knows that he has been left for dead. Somehow, he believes that it is to his benefit. He is lucky to be alive, sprawled on the cold pavement, barely conscious, and bleeding from the mouth is better than not breathing at all. He feels that if he can get to his feet he'd be okay. He can find a way to flag down someone who'd assist him. As far as he can tell, his legs aren't broken, he can feel his toes and has movement in his arms, but he quickly discovers that any motion, even breathing, causes him pain. He quickly realizes that a rib bone infiltrating one of his lungs is the cause of his discomfort, limiting his movements.

The irony of the situation is that only a few moments ago his movements were limited in a different manner. The sensitivity of his post-orgasmic ejaculated penis made him plead with his lady for hire to cease her movements while it was lingering in her hot box.

He had ignored those types of messages for years, but the notation of a two-hundred-miles-an-hour club inscribed on the bathroom stall intrigued him. It was his fortieth birthday present to himself; it had been perfect. Speeding around the track at an excessive speed had added a special exhilaration to the explosion when he came. He even felt a little special when his partner washed him after the session, but his excellent start to his birthday celebration turned sour.

He remembers standing outside the vehicle paying for the rendered services, then being blindsided by a punch in the jaw that rocked his equilibrium. Before his weakened knees afforded him the pavement, the next thing he knew he was being lifted into the air at his rib cage in a tremendous bear hug. He recalls how quickly his breath escaped him, followed by the crackling sound of his ribs being crushed within. His own agonizing scream still rings between his ears.

As if that is not enough, he can feel the wetness of fresh blood flowing over the dried gash caused by the collision of his head on the pavement after literally being tossed away.

Still, he feels that if he can get to his feet or even roll over to his back, he stands a chance of living through the pain and suffering.

"And this too shall pass," he states weakly. "And this too," he grunts while turning his body over to his back, "shall pass."

He repeats the statement quickly several times in succession. Upon completing the maneuver, he lies on his back feeling that it is a form of success—short-lived nevertheless. Suddenly, a different kind of pressure begins building within, making him feel as though he is being pumped with air like a balloon. It is virtually impossible to breathe, his chest tightens, expanding to near explosion. Desperately he tries to exhale but only partially succeeds. He stops feeling his chest decreasing in size; instead, he finds himself struggling to regain the precious air he has let out. The pressure grows unbearable inside of him; his breathing transforms into quick short jerky breaths which barely provide him oxygen.

"This too shall pass, this too shall, this too…"

His eyes are half-closed, staring into the early night, not really focused on anything, just searching for something to relieve his pain. He catches what he thinks to be the tail end of a falling star. Coincidently, as the tail dances across the sky, disappearing across the horizon and slowly fading in the night, the pressure within him releases with one gigantic exhale that follows the heavenly phenomenon's course, taking his life force with it.

Following the tragic incident, Sandra is rattled by her job. An unnerving feeling fills her. After all, she has performed the same service countless times without ever experiencing any guilt or remorse over what she is doing or who she is doing it with. This time the difference scared her and she is haunted by what she has seen.

"Dakota went too far," she states loudly as if talking to herself will ease her nerves. "He should have left well enough alone. My client paid...even tipped me. Why did Dakota do it? He has never harmed anyone, at least not in my presence before. But tonight, the rumors of his activities gained substance. Damn it, he literally crushed a man with his bare arms."

Sandra Rhodes has never seen anyone die before, much less witness a brutal crime first-hand. She suddenly feels her own safety at risk. Dakota offering her a piece of the take didn't make things better. Murder is murder and not what she is hired to do.

Please my clients sexually, she thinks. *After all, flying around the track at high speeds is dangerous enough.*

Dakota alone decides to change the rules of the game, therefore, placing everyone's well-being at risk in the process. The two-hundred-miles-per-hour sex adventure is successful and is at the present time anonymous to any police activity. She works three to four times a week and receives three-hundred dollars for each trip in which she participates. It is easy money—money which certainly will be gone if Dakota's killings are somehow traced back to them. Sandra wonders if Sly knows of Dakota's viciousness. She knows that Dakota is Sly's closest friend and suspects that Dakota is jeopardizing that friendship if Sly is oblivious to Dakota's wrongdoings. She can't take the chance of asking Sly. The dilemma creates a two-fold problem: a headache and stomach cramp.

She feels ill, feels a need to talk with someone. She trusts her confidence with Delia Beardon, her dearest friend whom she introduced to the business. Delia isn't like the other girls. Sandra believes that she is classy, someone with a purpose and direction, knowing exactly why she is selling herself.

Delia is a thirty-two-year-old, divorced college sophomore who is paying her own way through school with the money she earns. She possesses a face years younger than her actual age and boasts a body that shames most teenage girls. It almost seems natural that she uses her greatest asset to her advantage. Unlike others, Delia never has sex without protection. Sandra finds humor as she reflects on Delia's personal motto, "If you don't top it off, you don't get it off." When she has to please her client with her mouth, she uses thin cellophane to cover the man's penis. On the rare occasions when her date for the moment wants to have-a-go at her peach, she insists on the use of the cellophane, even though experience from her personal life has taught her that she prefers oral sex performed on her without it. Sandra is sure that Delia will know what to do. She dials Delia's telephone number.

"Hello?"

"Delia, this is Sandra," she states obviously still shaken. "You got a minute."

"Girl, what's wrong with you? You always sound this way when one of your tricks rocks your world. How big was his thing this time?" Delia jokes.

"I wish that were the case; it's much more serious than that."

"So, why are you so frantic?" Delia questions with much concern.

"It's Dakota. He's lost it!" she blurts as if she couldn't contain the information any longer. "Tonight, Dakota killed my trick."

"What! You're lying."

"I'm not lying. I saw it with my own eyes. He had no cause to...just out of the blue he popped this guy, then simply crushed him in his arms." Sandra grows closer to tears; her words are barely acknowledgeable because of the tremor they contain. "He looked at me and asked if I had a problem...what was I to say?"

"You probably served yourself best by not saying anything. I can't believe he's taken to killing for a few extra bucks."

"Believe it, girl...what are we going to do?"

"We have to tell someone. Sly, he'll put an end to his activities."

"But Sly and him are boys; he may know about it already."

"I'm not sure about that. One of the things which helped me work for him is his no-violence approach to things."

"Girl, he may have been telling you what you needed to hear."

"I'm aware of that. Don't get me wrong. He speaks of nonviolence but with some of the other things he's into, he surely has to threaten violence. Besides, I'm not going to be a part of murder."

"So, you're saying we should talk to Sly?"

"I think we should. If I don't like what he's saying, I'm quitting."

"I've already quit. I'm not going back. My conscience is telling me to go to the police."

"Let's hear what Sly has to say. Quit if you feel you have to but involving the police can potentially put all of us behind bars."

"Not if I come clean," she states somewhat defiantly.

"Sandra, it's like being a little bit pregnant; you can't be. Murder, prostitution—they are both jailable crimes."

"Okay, I'll listen to what he has to say but I'm still quitting."

"You have every right to," Delia assures. "And besides, you and I are different. We're not desperate, strung out, or helpless without Sly. We will survive without making this quick and easy money, so let's calm ourselves so that we can talk with Sly intelligently."

"I'll make the call," Sandra suggests. "Give me a moment." Sandra clicks over to the three-way feature and dials Sly's pager, as if it were a direct call. Sly returns a call in record time. She greets him, and asks him to hold while she completes the three-way call. "Delia, Sly is on the line."

"Ladies," Sly says, "what do I owe the pleasure of hearing from my two favorite girls. Sandra, has someone rocked your world again?" the joking Sly utters. His hint of humor passes with a wave of silence. "Hmm, would someone mind telling me what's going on?"

Sandra bursts into a hysterical outpour, spilling out a wave of words that carries wind gusts. "It's your friend, Dakota; he has lost his fucking mind. He killed someone today!"

"What!" Sly blurts with more emotion than he'd like. Nevertheless, the news smacks him in the face, awakening his senses. "Ladies, it's too early for April Fools' jokes. Come on, what really happened?"

"I'm telling you the truth," Sandra blurts.

"Why would he do that? Was he provoked?"

"You'd do better asking him yourself. I'm afraid of him now."

"Sly," Delia interjects, "you need to find out what's going on. I believe her and we surely don't need to bring extra attention to ourselves."

"Agreed. I'll get to the bottom of this and make him stop whatever new shit he is into. The two-hundred-miles-per-hour club is going too well to be destroyed by such foolish actions. Sandra, when do you work again?"

"Probably never." Sandra pauses, waiting on Sly's reply. Delia anticipates a remark from him as well.

Sly halts the release of the first thing that popped in his mind: *Damn it, you fucking can't.* Instead he gathers his thoughts and evenly recites, "Let's talk over dinner tonight at Rosalina's. How about it?"

FIFTEEN

Sly has done exactly what he told Crystin he would do. Experience taught him to be extra careful when tailing people. Even though there is peace between he and Crystin, it truly bothers him that Crystin discovered him on the very first day. *Hell*, he thought, *she busted me after about twenty minutes.*

He understands that one successful tail of Jason doesn't make him an expert, so he chose to err on the side of caution to prevent a repeat mistake of getting caught. His cautious method served him well. He has discreetly tailed Jason for nearly two weeks straight while watching his every move in search of a pattern in Jason's daily routine. The effort is to discover who he comes in contact with, find out who he seems most familiar with and determine the best means to trouble Jason. He is determined to become Jason's thorn in the side, his nemesis, all in the name of ruining his popularity.

Somewhere buried within Sly is an agonizing thought of Jason's recognition. Maybe he is jealous, maybe envy taints him, or maybe it is the fact that he can't pass the Police Academy physical. After all, being born without the ability to exert himself isn't his fault. But, as far as he can remember the thought of his rare condition deeply bothers him. No sports, no hiking, nothing that accelerates his heart rate for prolonged periods. Of course, he can do all these things, but with a price of chest pains that feel like a ten-ton truck is parked on it.

The upside of not being a jock is that he learned to talk and has crafted a verbal dialogue that functions like a gift. It doesn't matter if he is talking with the high society or persons from the poorest ghettos, he always finds a way to persuade them to his way of thinking. He believes, in some ways, this is more rewarding than being an athlete. Therefore, he blocks his handicap out of his mind, ignoring it as if it doesn't exist and buries the pain it causes to the point where he can't speak its name.

Sly's observation lands him at Rosalina's where he becomes aware of Jason's unique relationship with Alfredo and easily notices Alfredo's roaming eyes and their deliberate attention to women. He knows that it is something that he can prey upon, making Alfredo an easy target to take advantage of to agitate Jason. And, he knows the perfect way to lure the insect into his tangling web. As an added bonus, Rosalina's presents him a chance to entertain and soothe Sandra's and Delia's nerves.

He doesn't like to call the women in his entourage a stable, but how else would you classify them? He makes a profit from their services and takes care of the needs of the weaker ones. Like clockwork, they all arrive outside of Rosalina's within seconds of each other. They exchange a cordial greeting before he and the ladies enter Rosalina's. A third woman named Debra is invited to the occasion because she is his companion. He knows that she will support him and help persuade Sandra and Delia to continue to serve him. Sandra, Delia, and Debra have the night off but even without their work attire and makeup-plastered faces, they are attractive, shapely, and definitely alluring. They stride gracefully through the second set of double doors with two of the ladies on one of his arms and the other decorating the other. All heads within their view turn, captured by their demanding demeanor. Alfredo catches himself staring, hopefully not too late as Jason's words, *don't be so obvious*, splash in his mind. The women appear Godly to him, perfect specimens of human beings, and it takes all restraint to keep his thoughts tuned on his work. For the first time, he wishes that he can be on the receiving end of "this way, please" as he escorts them to a vacant booth.

Standing at the podium, his casual glance over the restaurant seems to be more often than usual, and his attention to the booth with the three ladies continually draws his view like a moth to a flame. He hasn't taken one of his wonder pills for nearly a week but, just gazing at the signs of loveliness is enough to make his member twitch. He thanks himself for not being induced with Viagra; otherwise, he'd be confined to the podium as before.

Alfredo in a customary manner starts his rounds through the restaurant to inquire with the patrons if things are satisfactory. He structures his route so that the booth with the ladies is his last greeting. The anxiety of it all becomes nerve-wrecking. He knows that he has to remain cool and nonchalant, but, the closer he draws to the booth, the more excited he gets. He especially likes the woman with the short-styled hair; admiring how non-offensive both her tight top and short skirt reveal her figure, spewing her sexiness, calling unto him. She also favors his adolescent fantasy woman, reminding him of just how infatuated he was with this woman back then.

"Good evening," Alfredo states, "is everything adequate for you all?"

Sly is the first to speak up. "Excellent as always."

"I'm pleased to hear that...things are satisfactory for you ladies as well?"

Two of the ladies are chewing food, therefore, they acknowledge his question with a simple head nod. The other woman replies, "Things couldn't be better."

Alfredo catches her eyes as she delivers the reply and finds himself mesmerized by her beauty. *This one I like*, he thinks to himself. After a silence, which Alfredo becomes uncomfortable with, he releases his gaze, smiles and recites, "If I can be of more assistance, don't hesitate to call on me."

"Thank you for that," Sly responds.

Alfredo nods and walks away from the booth disappointed with himself. He knows that he is not as collected as he would have liked. He settles back at the podium, glances over the restaurant, wishing for a do-over with the woman that moves him. He watches what he believes to be a celebration and wishes he were a part of the joyous occasion. More importantly, the smile of the one he likes seems to have mystic powers. It glistens, calls his name while seemingly shining a glow on him.

The celebration ends with a serious conversation that appears to be unnerving to one of the ladies. Sly and his party of women leave the restaurant as elegantly as they arrived, but not before Sly excuses himself and backs away from his ladies to call someone on his cell phone. After rejoining the ladies, a devilish smile on Sly's face is more than apparent.

Alfredo notices Jason and Monique entering through the first set of double doors. Their sudden appearance presents him with only a small moment to regain his composure. In his best professional manner, he greets the couple, seats them and is pleased that Jason wasn't present to witness his earlier fascination of the women.

Jason takes the opportunity to individually question members of the evening shift about Mr. Darknight while their food is being prepared. Only one person recalls seeing Mr. Darknight, however, she reveals nothing earth-shattering or relevant to the case for that matter. He returns to Monique with their food already on the table.

"I was hoping that you wouldn't be much longer," Monique replies. "I didn't want to start without you."

"You should've, your food may be cold. As for me, I can eat mine either way."

"It would not have been the same without you here."

Jason smiles. Monique understands that Jason appreciates her gesture and proceeds to consume her meal. Jason mentally pushes away his case and begins enjoying Monique for who she is. The wonder of her character mellows his spirit. They laugh and joke during the entire meal, somehow bonding into the depths of one another.

"Before we retire to your place," Jason states, "how about a stroll through the park?"

"Grand Park?" Monique questions enthusiastically.

"Yes, unless you have something else in mind."

"No, Grand Park will be perfect. I've always wanted to ride the carriages there but, I've never had anyone special I'd like to share the moment with."

"Well, I'll try to make it as memorable as you've imagined it."

"I'm sure you will," Monique delivers in a devilish tone.

As always, the service as well as the food is excellent. Jason handles the tab and they leave for their rendezvous.

Arriving at Grand Park, as usual, there is a line of people waiting to take a carriage ride through the park. When they finally are next in line to ride,

Jason being a creature of habit, lets several couples ahead of them until he and Monique are next to ride his favorite Medieval carriage. The long process makes Monique wonder if Jason knows which carriage he is waiting for. So far, all of the carriages she has seen arrive are identical.

"Here it is," Jason says with excitement.

Monique thinks *finally*, but does not verbalize it. Her eyes catch the arriving carriage and instantly she appreciates Jason's zeal.

She smiles as she delivers, "So…you wanted a more private ride?"

A return smile equally as devious as Monique's decorates Jason's face.

"This one," Jason says as they step into the carriage, "is the only one like this out here."

Monique is pleased with the lavish interior and the oddness between it and the other carriages. As Monique familiarizes herself with the intricate details of the interior, Jason rests his back against the seat, tilts his head back and stares at the closed sunroof. Memories of his recent past invade his mind like a virus attacking a computer without protection.

Somehow, he hasn't anticipated the impact of this carriage on his mental being. He doesn't feel unnerved but if he closes his eyes, he can feel the presence of Sasha sitting across from him. The fond memories of his and Sasha's encounter in this carriage make him feel as though Monique is being used to recapture a lost part of his past. Jason finds it difficult to comprehend Sasha's ghost-like aura that pulls at him, forcing him to dig deep within to grab hold of his feelings for Monique. He knows that he has to in order to make tonight's stroll pleasurable for Monique. Jason has no way of telling if he'll succeed but, his conscious mind does recognize Monique's voice calling his name.

"Yes," Jason responds without releasing his glare at the sunroof.

"I seem to have lost you; are you okay?"

"I'm fine," he states while turning his head and eyes toward her.

Monique's head shakes from side to side as if she is signaling, "who are you trying to fool?"

"When are you going to learn," Monique says caringly, "that I can feel things, especially when it comes to you."

"Can you feel this?" Jason asks as his hand raises toward one of her breasts.

Monique intercepts his distraction attempt, interlocks their fingers and lowers their hands onto her lap. She places her other hand on top of his, caressing his skin with her fingertips. She provides him a look that captures Jason's full attention. She recites her next words in a tone which lets Jason know that she means business.

"What's wrong?"

"Nothing really. I'm having a hard time with this carriage today."

"Why is that?"

"This carriage and I have a history." Jason sees the immediate concern on her face and thinks best to leave Sasha out of his explanation. "One of the murders I investigated happened inside this very carriage. My mind flashed back to what I saw then."

"I knew something wasn't right. It is not like you to tune out like that. If it bothers you that much, we can head for my place."

"No, I'll be fine. This is my favorite carriage; therefore, I have to get beyond the awkwardness it brings. The downside is...it taints my mood for the pleasures I had in store for you."

"Jason Jerrard, as mouthwatering as that sounds, I wouldn't expect you to behave in an unnatural way. Having to force things out of your mind would cheapen the experience for me. As I've told you, I'm patient."

Jason cranks the sunroof back, places an arm around her shoulder, leans back with her and gazes out of the sunroof's opening into the night. Monique accepts the silence as his means of gathering himself, content with just being in his presence with their heads leaning against each other. Jason makes a few comments about how peaceful the stars look, otherwise, the silence is constant, interrupted only by an occasional kiss on her forehead. The ride ends almost without Jason noticing. He makes apologies about his actions and notes that he expects to be better once they arrive at her place.

"I feel as though we should go back to Rosalina's and start this evening over," Jason states.

"There is no need. I've never seen a murdered person, but I can sense what you might be going through. Besides," Monique says in a more humorous way, "Rosalina's is closed now. We did have to wait a while for the carriage," she jokes.

"You are correct. Had I known, I would have chosen another one. I…"

"No, you wouldn't have. I know you. Besides, there's no way you could have known. I'm not going to let you beat yourself up for being human."

Jason feels comfort in her words and becomes more relaxed during the ride to Monique's. However, lurking in the back of his thoughts are questions concerning his inability to separate business from pleasure or even better, pleasure from pleasure.

When they enter Monique's home, Jason feels more like himself and swears, based on his reaction inside the carriage, that he will be just that.

"So, what kind of nightcap do you want?" Monique asks.

"Are we in for the night?"

"I did say, prepare to spend the night."

Jason reaches into one of his pockets, produces a toothbrush and waves it playfully in front of her. Monique only shakes her head, but is pleased that Jason's warped personality is emerging.

"In that case," Jason states, "what types of wines do you have?"

Monique excuses herself to the kitchen and yells from the location of the refrigerator, "I only have some Asti. Is this okay?"

"Perfect and…" Jason pauses knowing that Monique will find the remaining part of the question strange. "Will you make a pot of coffee, too?"

"Coffee? At this hour, didn't you have enough at Rosalina's?"

"I have to feed the demons inside of me," Jason says humorously.

"You're going to be up all night."

"Now, who said anything about sleeping?"

Monique smiles inwardly, pours Jason a glass of champagne then prepares the coffee and escapes to the bedroom while it is brewing. Jason enjoys the flavor of her chosen brand of beverage. He savors it, as he does being in her presence. He sits wallowing in his joy, letting the essence of time escape him. He unconsciously finishes the glass of champagne and begins thinking back to their relationship of years ago when the aroma of the coffee invades his senses, bringing him back from the past.

"You okay in there?" Jason yells.

He is about to repeat the question when Monique enters the living area wearing a deep-red silk robe. It harnesses an embroidered dragon on the back. The intricate detail of the embroidery indicates that the garment might have cost her a pretty penny.

"You look wonderful," Jason responds. Just that quick, the short length of the robe has enticed him. It complements her long legs, exciting him in a manner that makes his pants bulge. "Do I get to see what's underneath?"

"Depends. What is your imagination telling you?"

"In this case, using my imagination would be a waste of energy."

"How so?"

"I've already painted what I envision is under that inviting robe on my eyelids. All I have to do is close my eyes and see all that I need to."

"Very interesting. So, my psychic friend, what do you see?"

Jason closes his eyes and inhales deeply. "I see a cream-colored lace bra, sheer control-top hose and a pair of matching heels to accent your near nakedness."

"You simply described your favorite look on a woman, but you're way off. Open your eyes and look at my feet."

Jason obeys the command, and realizes that her bare feet indicate that he can only be partially right. Monique lowers the robe off of her shoulders.

"Way off base," Jason says. "Hell, I'm not even in the same ball park."

Her breasts seem to be supported by a clinging red halter-top with white dots.

"You wear that nicely," Jason confesses.

"Stand up and close your eyes again." Without hesitation, Jason heeds to her instruction. Monique walks within arm's reach of him and commands, "Touch my breasts."

Jason raises his hands slowly above his head, descending them to each side of her neck. He massages her neck for a moment before continuing to travel down the front of her shoulders, bringing them together in the middle of her body where her cleavage begins. His fingertips are stimulated by her silky skin and her accompanying fragrance invites him, nearly forcing his eyes open. He maneuvers the index and middle finger of each hand down her breast toward her nipples. His senses instantly are aware that her breasts aren't covered by a fabric; instead it feels like rubber or plastic. He touches the substance with all of his fingers and determines that he has no clue as to what he is feeling.

"You can open your eyes now."

Jason's eyes open, directed to her breasts.

"It's liquid vinyl, a form of body paint; you like?"

"Very nice…you just painted this?"

"Yes, it dries fast."

"I like your makeshift halter, red with white hearts."

Jason closes his eyes once more and caresses her breasts. He will swear under oath that the silky substance feels as natural as her skin. His convincing factor is that he senses that through the body paint, Monique is receptive to his actions.

"What does this feel like through the body paint?"

"I can feel your fingers' presence but it lacks…I mean, through the paint that is."

Jason responds, "You could've fooled me."

He has an idea of what she means. His mind tells him that it is similar to him wearing a condom. The sensation is pleasurable but lacks the added surreal feeling of the wetness that surrounds his tool. He uses his thumb and index finger of each hand to seize the middle of two hearts, which happens to be painted over the nipples of her breasts. Applying slight pressure, one of her brows raises, followed by a tense look that signals to Jason, it is a good thing. He glides his fingers along the silky surface to the top of her halter and slowly peels it away from her skin. Jason watches her skin pull, then release from the paint. He carefully tugs on the substance until it is a few centimeters from her nipples. Jason swiftly snatches the remaining material as if he is a magician removing a tablecloth from a table while leaving the glasses standing. The substance tears away jagged but is removed cleanly from her skin with little to no residue.

Monique moans because of Jason's actions. He is unable to determine if the cry is one of pleasure or pain. Suddenly and unexpectedly, Monique wraps her arms around him, gives him an aggressive passionate kiss and then and only then, he knows that she finds enjoyment in his rough act.

Monique concludes the kiss by whispering softly into Jason's ears, "My nipples are stinging, but I have to admit that it was a rush."

"You've gotten freaky in your old age."

"I know Mr. Fork user is not calling me freaky."

"So, I am." Jason confesses. "Shall we continue in your bedroom?"

Monique answers yes by grabbing his hand and walking them toward the pleasure haven. She is happy that she is leading; this way he can't see the overzealous smile on her face.

SIXTEEN

Alfredo exits the entrance set of the double doors of Rosalina's. He stretches as if his day has been tiring, which is partially true, but, his mind soars with thoughts of the stimuli he experienced earlier. The pictures of the alluring women are imprinted in his mind like a face on a coin. He envisions them as if they were standing inches away from him. It taunts and teases him, seducing him to swallow one of his wonder pills just a few moments before he walks out of the door.

Alfredo's plan is simple: take one now and enjoy the effects of it later. He knows that Viagra takes about one hour to take effect. By that time he'll be walking into an empty house that provides him the comfort and privacy to partake in what he refers to as the upper cable channels. They consist of the Playboy, Spice and Hot Network adult channels. It doesn't matter which; all he seeks is to let a sexy specimen entice him.

He understands the rules of engagement quite well and knows that the wonder pills extremely increase the chances of a man his age securing a full erection. He never forgets maybe the most important caveat when taking the pill. "Be motivated," or as he comprehends the medical claims, be seduced or turned on. He understands that he can't simply take the pill and *wham*, his penis will rise to the occasion. Therefore, the upper channels provide him enough stimulation to make his member work effectively in conjunction with the pills. It isn't like he has plans for the erection. Taking matters in his own hands is out of the question in his mind. He is simply elated that his member responds the way it does under the effects of the wonder pills. The last time, however, proved to be painful. It isn't that he forgot about his stiffened physical state; he simply rolled over onto it while attempting to sleep. He recalls the pain being awful, but he smiles to himself knowing that one day he will put it to good use.

He steps off the bottom step onto the sidewalk. At a distance he notices a human silhouette a few yards away. One quick glimpse of the silhouette's stride helps him determine it to be a woman's frame. Alfredo slows his pace to allow their intersection to occur in the most illuminated area that the moon and streetlights provide. He doesn't know why or how but he finds himself loitering in the light waiting for the woman to approach him. When the woman speaks to him, he suddenly realizes that he is stationary, but her words elude his ears because his eyes are transfixed on what he is seeing. She wears a light-green coat which hangs open loosely. It reveals her luscious firm breasts that are supported by a lacey push-up bra coupled with a pair of extremely short hot pants that display an impression of her womanhood, even in less than adequate lighting. A pair of pumps, matching the color of her trench coat, completes her saucy outfit. The woman repeats herself.

"You work here, don't you?"

This time Alfredo manages to release his gaze, confronts the woman's eyes with his, and sounds, "Yes, I'm the maitre d'."

"I thought so. My name is Azuri, and I may have what the doctor ordered."

Alfredo knows just by looking at her that he doesn't need any medical advice on this, but he wrinkles his face in a manner of informing the woman that he is clueless about what she is referring to.

"I know something about you…you don't know that I know," the woman continues.

Alfredo's facial expression coincides with the verbal words, "Oh really. I'm almost afraid to ask."

But, he isn't afraid. Fear never enters his mind; fascination yes. He is pleased that a woman of her caliber is addressing him. He enjoys her look, the sexy way she dresses and even the sound of her voice. All of this puts him at ease, allowing him to enjoy their conversation.

"Do you like what you see?" the woman asks.

Duh? Alfredo thinks to himself, *Didn't you see the drool running down my chin when you first approached?*

He desperately wants to verbalize his thoughts but decides to let the odd question pass him by.

Azuri continues, "How about the three women you lusted over earlier?"

His eyes dart away from her while his mind contemplates a thousand scenarios of how she is knowledgeable of his earlier activity. He returns his eyes to her; immediately she senses all of the curiosity his being contains.

"It's my job to know these things. Otherwise, how could I promote my unique services?"

"Exactly, what are they?" He knows that it is a rhetorical question. However, he wants to hear her spoken words.

"I," she announces evenly, "can arrange for you to relive times past. Sensual times, which you may feel are long gone…that is, if all of your bodily functions still perform adequately."

Alfredo is appalled with the accusation and blurts in defense, "Of course, it does!"

"Well then, we may be able to arrange something."

"I do not pay for sexual favors," Alfredo states.

His tone reflects defiance, his posture supports it as well, but his eyes encompass all of her, and defeat any conviction in his words.

"Most men believe that paying to be pleased is disgusting, but those same men will rent or pay to see an X-rated movie, jerk themselves off, all for the simple pleasure of saying that they don't pay for sex. I don't see the difference."

Alfredo conjures the similarities between him and what just invaded his ears. Her words taunt him, torment him and make him realize that a good use of his planned erection can be in the foreseeable future.

That will not happen, his mind tells him. He is sure of it. He thinks. This is before his eyes view the woman's body like a computer scanner from head to toe, registering every detail of her physical being through his eyes. He barely recognizes what he's said, powered by the twitch in his member, when the words, "how much?" leave his mouth.

"Just what I like...a man who knows how to seize the moment. For a mere four-hundred dollars, you can have the ride of your life."

The cost jolts his senses. It is quite a step for a simple piece of ass, his rational side thinks. But the woman has already enticed him. His member is in ahead of him; it is semi-hard.

He sighs and gulps before pronouncing, "That's acceptable."

"Wonderful, you will not be disappointed."

"So, where do we do this?"

"Slow your roll, my reacquired virgin friend, I'm not—even though I'd like to be—the one who will serve you."

Alfredo feels cheated. His mind races with thoughts of walking away.

"You get to choose a woman from the three you admired so dearly," Azuri adds.

The disappointment fades; an enthusiasm overwhelms him. Like a cat being offered catnip, he loses his usual containment and becomes giddy with thoughts of having the one he adores.

"So, which one of the lovely ladies is it?"

"I didn't get that formal with any one of them."

"Then, describe her to me."

"The celebrity look-a-like."

"Ah, I know exactly who you are referring to. You're going to love her," Azuri assures.

"Again, when and where will this happen?"

He is eager and excited. But most importantly, he is on the clock. By his mental calculations, he has about thirty minutes before his wonder pill is in full effect.

"She will be here in fifteen minutes. All it takes is a phone call. Shall I proceed?"

"By all means."

The woman retrieves a cell phone out of her coat pocket, backs away to a less lighted area and begins a brief conversation. In a relatively short time, she approaches Alfredo.

"It's all set," she states with a comforting smile. "Within the next half an hour, you'll be getting your rocks off."

She emphasizes her words by tenderly grabbing his penis into her hand. The maneuver shocks him, but he enjoys it nonetheless.

"I'm to wait here?" Alfredo asks, trying to contain the butterflies within him.

"Yes."

"When do I pay?"

"After services are rendered."

Alfredo nods.

"Have fun," she states while executing a well-timed turn. She uses an exaggerated body motion to cause her coat to partially expose her rear. The maneuver literally makes his mouth water. As if she has to do more to sexually seduce him, she lifts the coat above her waist and starts a proud stride down the sidewalk away from him. The hot-pants she sports expose half of each well-rounded firm cheek. Alfredo eyes how magnificent they look until they are well beyond visible recognition. As she fades into the darkness and the silhouette turns the corner, he hopes and prays that her assessment of his chosen woman is correct. He admires Azuri's body but the physical attributes of his choice in a sex partner are far better.

The images of her dancing vividly throughout his mind cause him to dash into Rosalina's to retrieve extra money needed to complete his fee. He then waits in the landing of the double doors, semi-concealed in the shadows by the brick-wall extension for the doors. Alfredo fights with himself, perplexed by the fact that he is actually going to go through with the arrangement. His mind toys with the idea of walking away. Financially he hasn't lost anything and physically as well.

That's it, he thinks.

He hasn't lost the sensation in his member since seeing Azuri's rear strut away from him. He realizes that the wonder pill has his member in a half-awakened state. It isn't fully awake but conscious enough to be aware of things around it.

"It has been such a long time since I've touched a woman," he announces aloud in an attempt to dismiss the nervousness that suddenly taints him. "To smell a woman's fragrance...to hold a woman's hand...to hold her up close and feel her tenderness will be..."

His thoughts are interrupted by the arrival of a huge vehicle pulling to the curb. An instant wave of anxiety sweeps him. The sports utility type vehicle is larger than most. It has tinted windows and according to Alfredo's memory, it sits lower than most. Nevertheless, he expects to see his woman approach from afar in the fashion of Azuri but the passenger door opens and a woman steps onto the sidewalk. She looks around as if she is waiting for someone. Her vision scans left and right before residing to rest her back on the vehicle and wait.

Alfredo's anxiety is in full effect. His stomach churns and the butterflies he is experiencing seem to be several decades old. Part of him feels as if he is about to experience a blind date, and a need to make a good first impression swarms over him.

Nonsense, he thinks.

He knows very well that he is paying for the romantic encounter and shakes his head from side to side as a means of correcting his own thoughts. Alfredo steps into full view, centered on the cement platform of Rosalina's. He sighs, maneuvers the first step and thinks, *you only live once.*

The woman pushes away from the vehicle with her rear, takes a few steps and settles in the same-lighted area as Azuri. Alfredo still feeling somewhat apprehensive closes in on the woman with his hands behind his back with two fingers crossed. He doesn't know why they are crossed; they just are. He appears to be twice her age plus a few years to boot. It doesn't matter because upon closer inspection he knows.

It's her, his mind dances.

The pleasing thought produces a brilliant smile on his face. Likewise, the woman returns one equally as welcomed.

"Hi," she says, extending a hand. "I'm Delia. Have you been waiting long?"

Alfredo's response isn't immediate because when he eases her hand into his, his thoughts scramble like an old-model radar gun being jammed by aluminum foil. For the moment, he is living his fantasy. His childhood dream suddenly materializes in front of him. It is her, but it isn't her. She is a younger version but a remarkable look-a-like. It doesn't matter. At this point Alfredo is too far drawn into this dream of his to be rational.

"They should call you Eartha," Alfredo blurts, breaking his silence.

Another smile decorates the woman's face. This time though, the closeness, the full effect of it convinces him that he is actually envisioning Eartha Kitt. Alfredo grew up in her era of stardom. He admired her work, he admired her, and as foolish as it sounded back then, he swore he'd marry her one day. He is so enthralled with the essence of the look-a-like, his mind actually tricks his ears into believing that her words, "Are you okay?" intercepted by his ears, sound like the real Eartha Kitt.

"Excuse me?" Alfredo states while trying to regain his composure.

"Are you okay?"

"Yes, Ma'am, I'm fine."

"I'm sorry…I didn't get your name."

"Alfredo," he says, apparently still not himself. I'm sorry…you have a remarkable resemblance to Eartha Kitt."

"I should. She is my mother, you know."

Alfredo's eyes widen with glee. They speak to her and make her realize that her attempt at humor may be plummeting him deeper away.

"Breathe," she states jokingly. "I was just trying to loosen you up. Eartha Kitt is not my mother, however, I get commented on the similarity a lot…your reaction to it is certainly different than most."

"I apologize if I've been inappropriate…a wave of emotions overwhelmed me."

"I just hope that was a good thing."

"Trust me, it is."

Delia's attire is different from earlier in the restaurant. Her clinging dress is replaced with similar clothing as Azuri's, but baby blue in color. Alfredo has already noticed this. He recognizes the same styled trench coat and wishes that hers hung loosely as did her predecessor's.

"So, how do we proceed?"

"Azuri has worked out the particulars with you…the fee, I'm referring to?"

"Yes, those terms are acceptable…I'd imagine you have a hotel or motel somewhere."

"Not exactly. You don't know what's in store for you?"

"Ma'am, I'm not sure. I'm following you."

Delia hooks Alfredo's arm at the elbow and guides him to the back of the vehicle. Alfredo notes that all of the identifying markings of the vehicle are removed, but the body is unmistakable. This huge sports utility vehicle is a Ford Excursion. With her free hand, she carefully opens one door, swinging it to the left; then the other, swinging it to the right. To Alfredo's surprise, the interior of the vehicle is outfitted with a single bed centered in the cargo area. The rear seats have been removed to accommodate it and other lavish furnishings. The bed has a silk comforter, folded back to reveal matching sheets and pillowcases with lace-embroidered sleeves. There are two handcrafted towels folded neatly on a mounted brass holder. The black tinted windows disguise the interior from the outside and the half-height sheer curtains adorning each window decorate the inside. On the opposite side are two tiny sinks with a brass faucet and an unknown water source. The plush environment is somewhat pleasing to Alfredo, although he wishes that the elegance was on non-mobile means.

"Azuri did mention a thrill ride, didn't she?"

"Surely, you didn't expect me to take her literally?"

"Maybe, she should have been clearer."

"So, what does this entail?"

Delia is sensitive to Alfredo's inquisitiveness. She embraces him differently, replacing the arm lock with them holding hands. His fingers are clammy intertwined with hers. She feels his strong tender grip, almost as if it speaks to her. She feels his apprehension, feels his excitement and is ecstatic with the thought of breaking in the Pope himself. But there is something more; she just hasn't put her finger on it.

Unlike the younger men she has in mind, Alfredo is patient, the non-aggressive type. Yet, she understands his hesitancy. She swings her arm around in a manner that moves Alfredo from her side and positions him in front of her. Delia kisses him politely on the lips, Alfredo's eyes close and she uses that gesture as means to proceed more passionately. Her lips press harder against his. He responds favorably by parting his lips; slowly he inserts his tongue into her mouth. Alfredo savors the feel of their tongues' interaction while enjoying the flavor of her minty mouth. He pushes hungrily as if to wipe away all of the lost forgotten years with one single kiss. He stops.

"I'm sorry for my roughness," Alfredo apologetically states after a deep exhale. "It's been so…"

"There is no need to explain," she says. "I understand."

Alfredo feels comfort with her words. He thinks maybe it is her duty to patronize him or it is simply something polite to say.

No, he tells himself.

He closes his eyes as if to banish both negative thoughts. Alfredo is reacting to what he felt in the restaurant and she is feeding off of it. He is sure of this; at least, this is what he is forcing himself to believe.

Her hands travel behind his back and clutch the underpart of his buttocks. She stares into his eyes and watches his timid expression as she begins slowly pulling their beings together. Alfredo willingly allows himself to be transfixed by her spell. He doesn't know why, he only knows that he wants it. When their middle sections meet, Alfredo feels the softness of her body. It makes his member twinge and a bewildered expression decorates his face.

Delia smiles before saying, "There is more to follow." She kisses him softly on the neck. "Shall we continue?"

"Nothing will please me more," Alfredo replies exasperatedly.

Alfredo helps Delia into the vehicle, follows directly behind and settles on the right side of her. Delia motions for him to pull the door nearest to him shut. He adheres to her wishes and she closes the other door. The process leaves them sitting on the foot of the bed with their heads inches apart. Their eyes lock in silence which neither understands why. Delia releases the glance first, slides one foot to the other in the narrow walk space until she reaches the inside tinted sliding glass that separates the driver's cabin from the living area. With the palm of her hand she taps on the glass three times; like magic, the vehicle begins to move. She executes the same awkward walking maneuver to rejoin Alfredo who is now sitting on a wooden box in one of the cabin's corners. She takes the twin box in the opposite corner.

"Are you ready to begin?"

"If I'm allowed the leeway," Alfredo confesses. "I was ready for you when I first laid eyes on you inside of the restaurant."

"That's sweet."

"Sweet, but true," Alfredo counters.

"Name your poison. Which would you prefer: to undress me or me undress me?"

Alfredo looks at her almost in disbelief. He is close to her, close to fulfilling a longtime desire, yet, the questions presented to him are baffling. He decides that he didn't care which; he takes his first bold step and falls to his knees in front of her. She sits with her legs shoulder-width apart and the trench coat that is buttoned only to her waist allows the perfect tease to his eyes. He finds the bottom button, closes his eyes and releases it.

Delia thinks that it's strange that he doesn't wish to watch but says nothing and lets him open his prize as he desires. Alfredo proceeds with the remaining three buttons, releasing each as if he is handling delicate pearls. He touches her shoulders while deliberately ignoring her breasts. He gently pushes the garment away from her shoulders. As if he doesn't want to miss a magical transformation, he opens his eyes to witness the coat's descent.

Delia watches his eyes open, they glisten and contain a supple amount of passion that she unknowingly feels erotic. His eyes lock with hers; immediately she understands her strange client's motives. She feels the desires of a thousand years being conveyed in a simple glare. She senses his longing for a warm woman's body to help him continue to function as a man and be counted once again, active like a man. She can almost feel his natural instinct of wanting to cohabitate with the opposite gender.

She also understands his craving to be released, how the natural act will somehow complete him. His gaze is many things: passionate, sad, confused, trusting, and all combined into his last plea for sanctuary of his manhood. She knows and feels that this is more than a simple fuck.

She smiles pleasantly. "Are you okay?"

"I'm just amazed at how wonderful you look."

With that she places one of his hands on her breast. The silky lacy garment provokes his fingers and sends tiny sparks of electricity through each fingertip that carry throughout his being. The simple touch of her bra awakens his member. Alfredo isn't sure how he did it, but a finger slips through the center of the lacey garment and it springs open and her breasts release from their containment.

Alfredo assumes that gravity will take place and her supple breasts will fall. He is awed when they only fall a centimeter or two and bounce jiggly-like in place, standing firm as if they are still a prisoner of the bra. He touches her nipple with the tip of a finger as if he is afraid he'd damage the immaculate breast.

"Really touch them," she announces. "And," she adds boastfully, "they are real...so don't be afraid."

Real or not, Alfredo is afraid. He feels as though all the past years have evaporated, making it seem like he is about to re-experience his first sexual encounter. He initially stumbles through the process of fondling her breasts, pauses, and then begins gently caressing them. The softness of her breasts calls to him like a newborn's sense of its mother's breasts. He leans forward, opens his mouth, and closes it around her larger than average hardened nipple. Delia hadn't anticipated the warmth of his wet mouth to be so pleasing. She finds herself holding her breath as he repeats the maneuver again and again. He sucks softly for a while, like a baby on a bottle, and then proceeds to make circular motions around the nipple with his tongue. She has encountered this technique countless times, but in her recent memory, she can't recall being stimulated to this degree.

Alfredo loses himself and nibbles on her nipple with too much pressure. A faint cry from Delia catches his attention. The gesture isn't too hard for Delia, nor is it too soft; actually she believes that it is damn near perfect. But it reminds her that she is the one doing the pleasing. With that, she calls his name while using her best interpretation of Eartha Kitt's voice, deliberately rolling the "r" in his name. Her new dialect breaks his focused attention on her breast. Alfred lifts his head to be greeted by a smile and revealing eyes that speak "your turn." She excuses herself as she sits on the edge of the bed, centered in the middle. Delia slowly lowers to her back, raises her knees above her breasts, tilts her hips and removes her hot-pants with one continuous motion. Her smile darns him with a slight giggle as the garment is tossed toward his face. The hot-pants slide down his face and hang in midair. Alfredo smiles the best he can with his teeth clinched, holding the thrown garment between them. She pulls him by the hand, positioning him in front of her. Alfredo stands slumped with his shoulder blades pressed against the top of the vehicle. Her hand caressing his member through his pants is overshadowing the awkward position. As a diversion, she bites on him through the pants while her hands successfully release his belt buckle. The fastening button and the zipper are partially lowered before he realizes what's going on. Alfredo gasps, his mind counts the years, ten…fifteen…he loses track of the count when he feels her hands on his penis. He looks down and is pleased that his wonder pills are working. His mind quickly reflects that this is by far the most hardened state that he has experienced, even while viewing the upper channels.

She strokes his member softly as if it is a delicate object, fragile to the touch. Alfredo is so startled when he feels a warm breeze being blown from her mouth, he jumps. She masterfully strokes him with one hand, leans over and up just enough to reach the wooden box to her right. She lifts the lid, retrieves a piece of cellophane precut to handle the largest man's penis. She places the material in the palm of her hand and positions the center of it at the top of his throbbing member. She makes an "OK" sign with her thumb and middle finger and smoothly proceeds to apply the material around the shaft with a motion that takes her hand away from her down toward his body. Alfredo realizes that times have changed; therefore he doesn't question the protection. He wouldn't have cared if she had wrapped it with duct tape; his anticipation is massive, almost unbearable. Immediately, when he feels her warm mouth encompass his erection, his knees weaken. It forces him to support himself with the palm of one hand on the ceiling of the vehicle.

She savors her Popsicle, tasting his shaft as if she is losing precious juices from it melting. She teases his head with a swirling maneuver of her tongue around the rim and caresses his testicles in the process. Alfredo enjoys her; he tells himself that he loves what she is doing and tells himself that he loves her. She continues to please him until she senses his breathing change. She actually feels the air leaving his nostrils because Alfredo is breathing hard and forceful. Long deep inhales are followed by equally strong exhales. She is very sure that he wants to be released; however, her professional instincts tell her that this isn't how he envisions his first orgasm in eons. She stops her movements abruptly. Alfredo opens his eyes; sweat darns his forehead, his breathing is erratic and his mind wonders "why."

"Relax," Delia states smoothly and comforting. "We're going to change positions."

She directs Alfredo to the bed and suggests that he lie on his back. She manages to remove his clothing with minimal effort. After ridding him of the cellophane, she revisits the magic wooden box, this time retrieving a ribbed lubricated condom. Alfredo watches how simply, second nature-like, she places it on him. What happens next, he really doesn't expect, but she straddles and lowers herself onto him. Her apparent wetness makes her cowboy move easy.

Is she turned on, too? Alfredo questions himself.

His thoughts are distracted when she leans forward, placing her perfect breasts at his mouth. He pushes them together with his palms, bringing both nipples a short distance apart and devours them with his hungry mouth.

She seems to be into it, he thinks, *into me. Naw, she's a professional,* the logical side of him counters. *Just enjoy,* Alfredo forces himself to think.

Alfredo is elated that his enjoyment is so great. The price that he is going to pay for her services, he can't consciously remember. It doesn't matter. After so many years without a female, he will mortgage his home to experience the marvel of this woman's touch. When she rises, her breasts are removed from his mouth. Alfredo's eyes remain closed and his lips smack, still tasting her supple breasts. She leans backwards; her hands support her weight from behind. She begins waving her body, moving it perfectly, precisely timing the fluid motion. Alfredo watches her body seemingly ripple upward from where his manhood enters her womanhood to the top of her head. Alfredo gazes at her in awe, sedated by the way she makes him feel. He feels whole, he feels human and he feels like a man again.

"Oh shit!" his mind echoes.

He feels himself coming. Maybe it is all of the excitement, maybe it is the Viagra or the thousand years since his last explosion but he erupts with the force of a raging bull. Delia catches the panic look in his eyes and shifts her movements into another gear to enhance his orgasm. After all, she hasn't received what she wants to hear. She wants to achieve her own personal goal, and she isn't about to let him off the hook or ruin her successful streak. She moves on him faster and faster, seemingly bucking her bronco, caring less about an orgasm of her own. All she wants is to make him cry out in ecstasy. Thus far, he has only grunted; this is unacceptable in her mind. The friction between them grows greater; both bodies are soaked with sweat. Her heart races as her hips tire from the rapid pace. She wins. Alfredo screams with a loud roar that echoes throughout their haven with vibrations. Delia smiles to herself as she lowers her exhausted body onto his. The next few silent moments are spent gathering their composures, letting their body temperatures return to normal. Once Alfredo resumes his normal breathing, he becomes aware of how wonderful her breasts pressed against his chest feel. He strokes the top of her head with a hand as in "thank you"; as in "thank you very much."

Her head tilts in search of his eyes. She wants to see the calm pleased expression first-hand, but all that she finds is a chin. However, she knows that her trick is very much satisfied. His scream told her all she needed to know. She is pleased with herself...she is disappointed. Delia enjoys this particular trick more than any other and finds herself somewhat sad that the session is coming to an end.

She thinks, *most men make it to the track and last until the high-banking curves before they lose their cool. Oh well.* She internally shrugs.

She raises on her hands, shifts herself forward and is about to tap on the sliding glass, customary to indicate that she or any other woman has concluded her business.

"What are you doing?" Alfredo asks.

"I'm about to signal and have you returned to where we picked you up."

"What for?"

Maybe it's the Viagra or the thousand years between the recent excitement and his last explosion or maybe he is just plain horny. Alfredo has rebounded, rising to the occasion like a superstar making the final shot at the last possible second in a championship game. She shifts back to her sitting position to catch his words as well as his gaze. To her surprise, she feels his hardened member beneath her. The surprise makes it to her face because Alfredo smiles, acknowledging the fact to her.

"Aren't you full of yourself," Delia states delightedly. "My, my."

"My…my," Alfredo returns, "my turn," he announces in a manner that is not only a statement but also a demand.

Alfredo politely places a hand on the outside of her shoulder, pushes gently and she follows his indication to roll off of him. She cooperatively settles next to him on her side. He then removes the used condom, wipes himself clean with a nearby towel, pauses and gazes at her. She reads his eyes that are filled with purpose, illuminating his desires that draw her deeper into his trance. He positions himself between her legs with his gaze affixed on his childhood dream.

Delia attempts to recommend the use of another condom, but, the strangest thing happens: Alfredo kisses her. She'd kissed him before entering the vehicle as a means to jumpstart the bashful gentleman. This kiss, however, startles her in an engulfing manner. It moves her. She cannot move. With that simple act, their entire encounter miraculously is romantic. She closes her eyes, accepts his kiss openly while her mind attempts to rationalize what she is truly feeling. She becomes nervous and conjures reasons why she shouldn't be enjoying it. Alfredo continues the everlasting kiss for what feels like hours, but she is unable to pull herself away. She loves what he is doing; she loves him. Alfredo chews, swallows her whole and spits out remnants of what his perfect woman is. The re-creation is the same, yet it's different. He interrupts the kiss, glimpses her caringly, lovingly, pouring all of his emotions through a simple glass called vision. She receives his emotions that enter her being through her eyes. They transfix themselves within her, arranging, rearranging feelings and beliefs, providing her a coziness that she seldom feels.

Alfredo enters her moist-box almost without her being conscious of it. *Oh no!* her mind rivets.

It is far too late. Her motto is all but a faint whisper between her ears. The internal transformation she'd undergone is nearing completion. Her resistance is futile, a senseless effort to reject the fact that she is into him. Therefore, she releases the negative notions and begins to enjoy his stride.

Alfredo feels that all he needs to do is to regain the rhythm he had long ago. He wants desperately to transform the vivid memories of his glory days into something tangible, and then, the rest will be like riding a bike. His strokes are slow, deep and well timed. One after the other, one as slow as the other, they all intoxicate her more. She begins tilting her pelvis at the end of each slow endless thrust. Alfredo helps himself to one of her breasts, caressing it with the exact precision as he is applying to her womanhood. Delia isn't aware how, nor does she understand why, but she finds herself being more stimulated by his slow move than the banging thrust she's accustomed to.

Delia thinks about the kiss, the fact that no other had the insight to do that before and wonders if her response would've been the same. She has no definitive answer, but she is fully aware that the kiss, his kiss, emotionally touches her. Delia also enjoys his delicate patient touch and feels that the expertise of a true gentleman is rare and welcomed.

Alfredo continues to gaze at her with every stroke of his hardened member. He loses himself in the act itself, belonging to it while possessing it at the same time. Delia wants to free herself of their moment. She needs to reclaim her senses but the hypnotic eye contact will not release her. To her it feels like the pull of a spacial anomaly that keeps her suspended in an intricate weave of emotions, joining them, mending their hearts. She calls his name; the sensual words enter his ears and dance throughout his being with the energy of a Spanish dance, synchronizing all within them. He feels trembles in her womanhood, she feels his manhood expand, and they both know that the moment is near. Delia's body is shaking in anticipation with the desire to have a real orgasm. She has faked so many that she often convinces herself that the fake ones are real. This one can't be stopped. It's like a freight train traveling at a high speed with faulty breaks, destined for ecstasy.

Even near explosion, Alfredo's rhythm is flawless, perfectly timed…constant. He calls her name. His words light her internal fuse. It burns rapidly to her stick of dynamite called an orgasm. She screams as her body releases like a violent storm, blanketing the interior of the vehicle with vibrations of thunder. Her passionate cry carries to the driver. He turns down the radio and applies less pressure to the accelerator to listen for signs of trouble. What he hears is Alfredo's release and chuckles to himself, amused by the words, "Oh God, I'm coming."

Alfredo gazes at her. She tilts her head to the side not willing to let him know what she is feeling. She doesn't want him to know that their sexual act has become more than what she is being paid to do. It has gone beyond sex, beyond intimacy; she feels as though they have just made love. Alfredo needs more than a profile of her; he will not settle for less. He raises her eyes back to his with his fingertips on the side of her chin and kisses her once more, causing her arms to embrace him in a smothering hug. With their tender embrace, they understand that their magical night is something tangible.

Delia releases her hug, shifts forward, taps on the glass and they both feel the vehicle lower in speed and leave the track. Delia reaches in the sink, washes Alfredo with a cloth, then herself and suggests that they get dressed.

SEVENTEEN

The vehicle drives to its usual secluded location where they conclude the business transaction. Delia and Alfredo stand behind the vehicle engaged in an uncomfortable silence as Alfredo pays the fee for the services rendered. Quietly, Dakota slowly creeps behind Alfredo. Delia develops a new type of anxiety as she notices Dakota. Alfredo's pleasant smile vanishes when Delia's face becomes panic-stricken. He turns just in time to see a gigantic fist thrashing upon him. The blow catches him on the top of his forehead; he blacks out. Before Alfredo's nimble body hits the ground, Dakota wraps his massive arms around Alfredo's frame and lifts him in a crushing bear hug. Delia screams as she runs toward Dakota and begins pounding on his back to no avail. She begs and pleads for him to stop hurting Alfredo. Dakota releases Alfredo. His lifeless body falls to the ground, sounding like a loud smack as his body contacts with it.

"What do you care?" Dakota asks.

"I don't care to see you injure innocent people."

"He is not innocent," Dakota snaps. "He's just another lonely soul trying to buy companionship."

"This man didn't do anything wrong, he…"

Dakota cut her words off. "He is how I make my living."

He raises his foot and stomps onto Alfredo's upper body as if he is trying to break boards. His ears catch a last pocket of air escaping Alfredo's lungs.

"Pathetic," Dakota states in a matter-of-fact manner.

Delia's scream echoes though the night, failing to find someone to give it meaning.

"Check him," Dakota says.

"What?"

"Check to see if he's breathing."

"I won't participate in your criminal activities," Delia states defiantly.

"You will," Dakota demands with mannerisms that instantly control her.

She lowers to her knees, touches his neck, and then places an ear on Alfredo's chest. "He is not breathing," Delia says in sorrow. "You fucking killed him!" she screams.

As if her emotional words pass his ears, Dakota searches her purse, finds a compact makeup case and holds the mirror part under Alfredo's nostrils.

"I told you," Delia states shocked by Dakota's untrusting of her, "he isn't breathing."

"I can't trust a woman who seemingly has fallen for her old-ass trick."

"What in the hell are you talking about?"

"I heard your scream. It was different, not like any of the others I've had the pleasure of hearing."

Delia is lost for words. She finds it difficult to believe that Dakota is jealous of a man that she is being paid to have sex with. After a satisfying moment, Dakota removes the mirror from Alfredo's nose and tosses it at Delia. He then takes the remaining money from Alfredo's wallet, stands and questions.

"Are you coming?

Delia hasn't realized that she is standing. She's surprised how nonchalantly Dakota takes the matter. She hears the driver's door slam shut, jumps into the back of the vehicle emotionally disturbed and cries endlessly.

Alfredo's body lies motionless on the ground as the vehicle leaves the crime scene unnoticed. When it is safe and the wheels of the vehicle can no longer be heard, Alfredo releases his breath. He heavily and carefully inhales more precious air. He remembers little about the incident that places him in his current predicament but he recalls hearing Delia say that he isn't breathing.

Must have been just after I regained my senses, he thinks.

Even in his battered condition, he realizes that Delia is trying to protect him and decides at that moment to play along until it is safe. The condition of his body helps tremendously. It pains him to inhale, it pains him to exhale, and it pains him to hold his breath as he did, but he knows that the latter is what kept him alive. He finds minor amusement with being right. Alfredo pictures Delia's face in his mind before the pain his body is experiencing forces him to pass out again.

During the drive back to Delia's apartment, she yells emotional obscenities at Dakota, promising that she will tell Sly. Dakota's "do what you have to," unemotional remark is unsettling and makes her feel like throwing up. He ignores her from that point and finishes the drive in silence. Delia silently weeps, vowing to quit this business. Although her nerves talk about quitting, she hasn't convinced herself entirely because her chosen profession provides means for easy money. This fact alone makes it difficult to be definitive about quitting. Her heart suddenly races, jumpstarted by Dakota's whispering words intercepting her ears.

This can't be, she thinks. Anxiety blankets her like morning dew on autumn grass. She is suddenly fearful of her life. For the first time she consciously feels herself shaking. For the first time, all doubt about quitting the business is removed. *Control yourself*, she demands her being. *Just make it home.*

She ignores the notion to jump into Dakota's case and find out who he is talking to on his cell phone. The little rational side she has left forces her to say nothing. She feels the vehicle stop and steps out of the back. Delia delivers a rude goodbye to Dakota and walks briskly to her apartment building even though fear is willing her to run. Knowing that the containment of her apartment can easily be compromised, she somehow feels a little safer inside. She lets the door close and falls back against it before verbalizing the words that haunt her: "It's done." Those words climb through her with the swiftness of a cheetah, unnerving each strand of her DNA. She sits on the sofa feeling sorry for Alfredo, feeling sorry for herself.

EIGHTEEN

Finally, Jason thinks when all of the liquid vinyl is removed from Monique's body. After all of their necking, the teasing, the games, the time has arrived for intimacy between them. The eons that passed between their first aspirations for each other seem like a forgotten moment. Time has changed many things around them except their unspoken words of love and a bond that unknowingly united them through the years. They both knew that all of the things they used to make their encounter special is unnecessary, primarily because everything they need is already occupying spaces in their hearts.

Jason lays her on her back and she is proud to have her nakedness whet his appetite. She wants him more than ever and in just a few seconds, she'll have her wish. Jason seductively makes his way between her legs. He is on all fours gazing down at her, fighting the temptation to ravage her like a hungry beast. He leans forward and kisses her politely on the lips. The peck sounds sweet to Monique's ears; it makes her blush inside. She spends a few seconds hoping that Jason can't detect the impact it has on her. Jason admires what Monique's eyes portray; they warm him. He knows that the time is right. He starts the descent to place his manhood where it wants to be, where it needs to be. Just being near her wet-box, he can feel the heat radiating from her desire.

Everything around them is perfect. The time is right and he knows it…he knows when the vibration from his pager causes it to fall from the nightstand to the floor, that the right time suddenly is the wrong time.

Jason raises a brow hoping that Monique will sense what he is thinking. Monique smiles, and then closes her eyes to conceal the anxiety that sweeps her. She reads his expression, perfectly as a matter of fact; it disappoints her and makes her feel as though a carpet has been yanked from under her feet.

She is patient and understanding, but *damn*, she thinks. *I actually felt his cock touch my opening.*

Her warming thoughts make her realize that a simple forward thrust will electrify her in a thousand ways. She opens her eyes, despair apparent in them. Jason doesn't have to guess what her expression means. He possesses sympathy for her. However, when she wraps her legs around him, crossed at his butt, Jason understands, and takes a moment to reflect on the fact that her move surprised him.

"Must you answer that?" Monique questions, knowing the response.

"Unfortunately," Jason responds somberly. "My love, you know I do." Jason feels his midsection being drawn near by her contracting legs. "You're asking for trouble."

"Please trouble me," Monique states from the bottom of her desire.

"Two things, one...only work and family have my pager number. Therefore, I have to assume that the caller has some sort of emergency. Two," Jason states more as a benefit for himself, "I'd love to wet my whistle, if you know what I mean, but, I'd never leave if I did. And," Jason adds as an afterthought, "I'm not into quickies. That's an easy habit to start and I'd imagine an even harder one to break."

"I understand," Monique conveys with as much conviction she can muster, even though it's eating her up inside to be understanding.

Her leg lock releases and her legs fall into the position one has while delivering a baby. Jason shifts his weight up and to the side, reaches across her to the floor to retrieve the pager. In the process his hardened manhood slides across her skin and travels from her haven to her stomach. Monique's insides fry, fuse and go into a frenzy. All of her senses become aware of every inch of Jason's frame. She is sensitized to every pore of his skin, every strand of hair he possesses and feels her natural juices increase and escape her womanhood. She no longer wants to be a nice girl; for the moment she doesn't feel the need for politeness, and she recites exactly what she is thinking.

"My pussy is so wet. It's lubricating the outside of me."

Her words are like a drug to Jason. They make his penis twitch and make him dream of the endless possibilities that being inside of her joy will bring. Her nasty words are the catalyst that makes him use two of his fingers and gently swipe the lips of her soaked box. He feels the sweet nectar moisten his fingers. He lowers to kiss her but when their lips are about to touch, he places the two fingers into her mouth and directly follows with his tongue separating the fingers. He enjoys the taste of her and embellishes in the fact that she doesn't squirm when tasting her own. Jason removes his fingers and continues the kiss passionately. It is a long heated kiss that drives Monique wild. She is so ready and extremely horny; she entertains thoughts of ripping his thing off and ramming herself with it.

Monique breaks the kiss because she isn't far from being overly aggressive and taking the man that she loves. She wants him; there is no hiding that. She cannot hide aspiration even if she wants to; neither can Jason. The passion in their eyes tells all.

Jason shakes his head and sighs, glances at the pager and states, "It's the station."

"I figured as much, duty calls."

"Are you sure that you want to be involved with a person that can be snatched away at any moment?" Jason asks after sensing a degree of disappointment concealed within her words.

"I'm fully aware of what I'm getting myself into. Besides, you getting called away will not always happen at such a delicate time."

Jason gazes at her with compassion and is amazed at the wonder of her. "You are incredible," Jason states with a decorated smile.

"I am what I am...now, get dressed and handle your business."

Again, Jason strokes her with his eyes in awe. He knows that she has stated those words for his benefit. He knows that she is aware that he knows and finds wonder with the fact the Monique has the courage to recite them despite this fact. Nevertheless, he follows her instructions immediately. He dresses, sits on the side of the bed and places a call to his precinct. By the look on Jason's face, Monique instantly knows that he is the receiver of bad news. His head lowers as he places the telephone receiver back in its holder.

"Honey, what is it?" Monique questions with concern.

"Something has happened to Alfredo."

"What? You're kidding me."

"I'm afraid not and I don't mean a piece of string."

Monique appreciates the fact that Jason attempts to lift his spirits with a bit of humor. She smiles and responds, "Sometimes your humor hangs on that very string. Is he…"

"No, he isn't dead. My life comes full circle again. He is hospitalized, unconscious."

"Coma?"

"I'm not sure."

"Are you okay?"

"I'm fine. It's just that Alfredo is like family to me."

"Yes, I'm aware that the two of you are very close. I wonder who could harm such a gentle man."

"The world is full of people who like to prey on the kindness of others."

"Sadly, I have to agree with you."

"I must leave your pleasant company."

"I understand. You need to get to the station."

"Actually, I'm headed to the hospital."

"Do you want me to accompany you?"

"Thanks for offering, but, I'm going to need all of my faculties when I get there."

"Well, you know where to find me."

"I know where I want to find you."

Monique's expression tells Jason that she is unclear of his meaning.

"After I leave the hospital," Jason continues, "I'm going to the station to start piecing all of this together. So, take these keys, and in the morning get a duplicate set made for you. And, I'll see you at home."

A smile darns Monique's face.

"Don't be surprised. We have to see if you like living with me."

"We both know that that will not be a problem."

"I don't know…you may not like seeing my pants hanging on the bedpost."

"I'll adapt."

"Remember, I told you that it will be our place, so if it is a real problem, we can talk about it."

"You worry too much. As I've stated before, go handle your business."

NINETEEN

J ason arrives at the hospital, locates Alfredo's room and is pleased to learn that he isn't housed in intensive care. He is in awe yet pleased with the fact that Dr. Bodou is the attending physician checking Alfredo's vitals.

"Greetings, Doctor," Jason states. "Do you ever sleep?"

"Very little," Dr. Bodou responds professionally. "I happen to like what I do. I'm not the least bit surprised to see you."

"Oh? Why?"

"It seems that you know most of the people I treat."

"Believe me, this isn't something I'm proud of."

"I surely understand."

"So, what's his story?"

"He was brought here just like you see him. We cleaned him up some. Our initial examination reveals a couple of broken ribs and several badly bruised ones. If there is an upside, there are no internal organ injuries."

"Thank goodness for that."

"For a person his age, his bones are strong."

"Has he been conscious at all?"

"Not yet, but his pulse is steady."

"So, he is not in a coma?"

"I seriously doubt it. His condition is similar to yours when you were a guest in our facility. He'll wake eventually, out of the blue just as you did."

"Anything more to add?"

"Nothing in medical terms…the ole boy seemed to have had a good time before his serious beating."

"I'm not following you."

"Well, to put it bluntly, he recently had an orgasm."

"You're kidding," Jason announces before his facial expression turns into one of serious thought. "It is interesting that you say that."

Dr. Bodou initially didn't make the connection between the broken ribs and an orgasm. A few seconds pass, and then his face frowns as he states, "A jealous husband."

"That would be my first thought, however, the orgasm thing relates to at least two other cases that I know of. If anything changes with him, you know how to reach me."

"Consider it done, Sir."

Jason leaves the hospital determined more than ever to connect the similarities between Alfredo and the two murder victims. He races through the darkness, driven by an instinct that he loves to have possess him. He settles at his desk, pulls out the other two related case files and systematically reviews every detail of the three cases. He writes the common points on sticky notes and places them on his computer monitor.

"Alfredo, you old fox," Jason verbalizes. "It seems that Viagra got the best of you. Now tell me," he states while looking at his picture, "what is your connection to the not-so-lucky victims? Talk to me…the whole thing is too odd."

Jason studies the common facts: all were male, beaten and seemingly engaged in sex before their attack. He wants to have forensics visit the crime scene and make imprints of any tire prints. He makes a note to himself to have the teenaged couple's car tires imprinted to rule out their vehicle.

After all, Jason read, it was their attempt at making out that brought them to the secluded area to discover Alfredo. Jason also notes that Mr. Darknight was last seen at Rosalina's. His gut feeling tells him that someone or possibly something made the initial contact. Jason knows enough about his dear friend to believe that Alfredo wouldn't have troubled himself with the prostitution area of town.

Alfredo has too much pride for that, he thinks.

Jason doesn't look forward to telling the people at Rosalina's that their icon is injured. It's clear that he'll have to continue his investigation at Rosalina's. He strangely feels that all will reveal itself as clearly as the post-it notes are to his eyes. He jots down a few more things that he wants to rehash later after a couple of hours' sleep and places the folder in his desk drawer. He locks the drawer and proceeds home for the rest his body is asking for.

Normally, driving home at this late hour, the ride is usually short, but tonight's trip ends even quicker. Jason finds himself sitting in his driveway continuing to compute and process all of the evidence at hand. The one thing that he is fairly certain of is that the same person or persons are responsible for the beatings. The sex part is what baffles him the most. Immediately, Jason realizes that every escort service listed in the Yellow Pages is a suspect in the crimes. He thinks of the massage parlors; they alone multiply the list by three. He rules out a jealous lover primarily because it's highly unlikely that the three victimized men are involved with the same woman.

Jason exits his car and uncommonly starts removing his tie before entering his home. He notices his partially unbuttoned shirt and views his shirttail which is pulled out of his pants. He shrugs his shoulders upon realizing that he doesn't recall taking these actions. He opens the front door to his home, takes a few steps inside and a voice calls to him.

"Come to me and push my buttons."

"No, no, pick me," another voice addresses him. "You know you'll like my taste."

Jason ignores the cries of the remote control and the coffee pot and proceeds directly upstairs to the bedroom. He places his pistol harness, shirt, and pants on one of the tall posts at the foot of the bed, then dashes into the bathroom for his pre-bedtime teeth brushing. A short moment later, he walks his nude frame to the bed, slides under the comforter and drapes his arm around Monique's naked body.

She grabs his hand, drawing him nearer to her. When Jason's chest makes contact with Monique's back, she curls her knees slightly in front of her and Jason places his knees into the puzzle piece directly behind hers. She experiences an immediate secure, comforting feeling cradled in Jason's embrace.

"Are you all right?" Monique asks in a mellow tone.

"Yes," Jason replies equally as melodious.

"Alfredo?"

"He is stable. His injuries are not too serious but he hasn't awakened yet."

It isn't that Jason sounds worried, but the way that he delivers the sentence makes Monique's brow raise.

"He'll be fine," Monique states after detecting a hint of concern in Jason's words.

"I'm sure he will be. So, this is a most welcomed surprise," Jason states more delightfully.

"I just wanted to be here when you got here. Woman's intuition told me that you might need me."

"Thanks. Where is your car?"

"In your garage."

"If I had the patience to wait for the garage door to open, I would have known you were here earlier. Imagine my surprise when I saw a body in my bed."

"Do you mind, Dear?"

The "woman, please" expression that Jason's face displays is hidden from Monique because of their cradling position. However, the chosen words that leave his mouth are far different.

"I hope you like your new home," Jason announces softly. "Our home."

Monique's eyes remain closed, but a smile forms on her face.

"Sweetheart," Jason continues, "do you think our son will object to us living together?"

Monique's eyes slowly rise to an open state. She turns, faces him and nearly loses herself to the effect that the shadows have on Jason's features. She stares at him for a moment, pleased with his eyes embracing her.

"Jason knows..." she replies in a comforting tone, "my true feelings about you. He will be fine with our decision to live together. Surely, you aren't nervous about meeting him?"

"Surprisingly…yes. I feel that there's a certain expectation I have to live up to."

"Don't feel that way. This is not a test."

"I can't help it. I know that you raised him in my image, to be like me, but how could you? We didn't spend that much time together. The kind of time which would help you define who I am."

"My dearest Jason…" Monique pauses, uncertain of how to proceed. "I know you more than you think. I know that you are a kind person with a good heart. I know you like attention, borderline demand it…but not over-bearing," she adds, realizing that she is about to get interrupted. "There is so much more I can add, but I'll summarize with what's most important by saying this…" Monique pauses again, this time sure and confident with what she is feeling. She looks Jason directly into his eyes and captures his full attention. "I know the things that define the character of your soul. I know every fiber of your being, down to the intricate strands of your DNA. Everything that makes you; you is embedded into me. Our past time together gave me this and this is what makes me love you."

There is a brief awkward silence while Jason searches himself for a comeback or rebuttal, something which will indicate that he has not been emotionally violated. Knowing her precious Jason, Monique is armed, ready, patiently waiting and welcoming anything he may utter.

"Of course," Monique breaks the silence, "your sense of humor can be a bit corny. Dry may best describe it."

Jason doesn't really have a comment. For the first time he is truly speech-less. He has no comeback, no quick wit to get him out of this jam. Nothing comes to mind because deep down he knows that her words are true. *My sense of humor is much better than dry*, he thinks to himself.

He is aware that Monique, the one woman that his heart never banished, understands him. He knows that he doesn't understand why and he knows that he loves her. He tries telling her, but the words will not leave his lips. He fights deep, hard, and searches his heart for the valve that can release those words. What he finds is Sasha standing next to it, seemingly protecting her interest, her own sanctuary within his heart. His heart smiles as he approaches her. All within him is overwhelmed by seeing her. His arms spread wide eagerly wanting to embrace her.

Sasha unexpectedly turns; her back faces Jason. His arms fall to the side in disappointment. Sasha reaches for the valve as Jason positions himself beside her. She seeks Jason's eyes with hers and her hands holding the over-sized valve.

"Together...we shall do this," a voice in Sasha's likeness tells him.

Jason's hands seize the valve, turn it counterclockwise, but it doesn't move. He sees Sasha reposition herself to obtain a better grip. Jason follows her lead and gathers more leverage for the next try. Sasha applies pressure first; Jason notices the muscles tightening in her forearms and administers his added force to the valve. The valve resists as long as it can, but proves to be no match to the combined will and determination of Jason and Sasha. It squeaks as the seal breaks and slowly becomes easier to turn. Once the task of turning the valve can be handled by one person, Sasha stops her motion and gazes at Jason again. He suddenly feels a need to remove his hands, which he does and Sasha then continues opening the valve.

"I know you love me," Sasha's voice tells him.

Jason doesn't know why he is hearing her. He is sure that her lips aren't moving but her voice is as clear as spoken words.

"To love me is to love her," Sasha's voice recites with a gaze fixed into Jason's eyes. "Love her, I'm part of that...love us freely."

At the end of that sentence, the valve is open to its fullest capacity. With it is an understanding so clear, it virtually feels tangible.

Jason hears the last words of advice in Sasha's likeness: "Remember my words."

Monique's face appears to him. It contains a puzzled expression.

"I lost you there," Monique states with concern. "You look like you had a revelation."

"I think I did," Jason responds in a soft tone.

"So, you just had a talk with God."

"Something like that."

"Are you going to leave me in the dark?"

"I'm going to ask you to turn back over so we can sleep."

Monique is mystified with Jason's evasive maneuver but doesn't question it because of the tone it carries. She complies and rolls over. Jason cradles her again, strong and tight. He squeezes her as if to combine their bodies and releases her with thoughts of Sasha's words. Monique quickly feels sleepy again, intoxicated by his comforting presence.

"I love you," Jason states softly.

Monique's eyes quickly open as if seeing in the darkness will help her believe what just passed her ears.

"I love you," Jason conveys a little louder but with the same emotional tone.

This time the clarity in his words fill her, bringing joy to her being. The exuberance spreads like the plague, wonderfully contaminating each vein, each artery of her body until it reaches her heart and possesses it.

"I love you, too," she returns as silent tears fall from her eyes. "That must have been some revelation you experienced."

"It truly was," he replies before kissing her on the back of the neck.

During the next few moments, silence fills the air. Each of them draws strength from a love that can't be forged or ignored. A short moment later, both Jason and Monique have the sandman knocking at their door.

"If you plan to sleep tonight," Monique announces out of the blue, "you'd better calm your friend down."

Jason is unaware of his throbbing member. Monique turns to him with a desire provoked by what she is feeling. Jason feeds off the same desire and is suddenly aware of his member playing soldier, standing at attention.

"You know how they say, a mind is a terrible thing to waste," Monique asks.

"I've heard that a time or two."

"Well," she continues, partially joking but mostly serious, "wasting a hard-on is even worse."

Jason flashes a smile at her, understanding exactly what she wants. He knows why.

"My love," Jason responds. "We've been through so much. We've waited so long for our special moment, let's refrain until…"

Disappointment closes Monique's eyes. She wishes that she can turn off her ears to prevent them from hearing his distressing words.

"…you're Mrs. Jerrard."

"Say that again!"

"In layman's terms, please be my bride, my wife, the mother of..." Jason stops his sentence, realizing that he is getting ahead of himself.

Monique, knowing him so well, finishes what Jason has started. "I'd love to be the mother of your...child; children might be a bit much for me at my age."

"Monique, please marry me," Jason responds with his heart overflowing with emotion.

"I will, Jason. Any time, any day, or any place."

"Let me know if you think I'm rushing things, but I'd like to marry shortly after this case is over."

"Sweetheart, you tell me when and where to be; I'll be there with bells and whistles. If it's tomorrow or ten years from now, I'll be there."

"I love you," Jason repeats over and over, each followed by a peck on her lips.

Monique is too overwhelmed with joy to do anything more than accept his graces.

"Let's get our positions straight," Jason comments.

"I thought that we were going to wait."

"Nasty person, not our sexual positions. We have plenty of time to get those kinds of things worked out. I'm referring to sleeping ones. Let's call the cradling position number one and the one with your head resting on my chest number two."

"Done, anything else?'

"No. Baby, lay your head on my chest."

Monique shakes her head at Jason's humor and finds a comfortable position resting on Jason. She can hardly contain her emotions but the constant beat of his heart relaxes her. It helps her fall into a deep slumber. Jason has already found his calm and fallen asleep ahead of her.

TWENTY

The next morning Jason starts his day visiting the site where Alfredo was discovered. Even though the area is sectioned off, the location as a whole appears to be compromised. What he finds hard to determine is whether or not the crime scene was violated before or after the police tape was put in place. He examines the immediate area where Alfredo's markings are. The huge secluded dirt area contains several sets of footprints, one of which is Alfredo's. His task is to determine which of the remaining ones can be associated with the other victims.

"That will help me determine if the criminals have a special place where they harm the victims," he announces out loud.

He follows the tire tracks to where they appear to have stopped and locates a set of footprints originating from the left side of the vehicle. Logic deduces that these are the driver's prints. The driver's prints track to the back of the vehicle and mesh with several other sets with one much smaller than the other. The footprints gather a few feet beyond the rear tire tracks and dance in confusion with each other.

"This doesn't make sense," he announces loudly. "A blind man can clearly see that the driver's prints return to the vehicle from the same spot where they originate. The other sets seem to appear out of thin air."

Jason carefully circles the tire tracks, making sure his footprints are far enough away not to be confused with the ones from the crime scene. His footprints encompass the entire area in question but his effort doesn't provide means of determining where the other prints originated. He stands a few feet away, staring at the scene as if he is trying to determine the missing ingredient from something he cooked. He mentally notes that the vehicle must have some sort of rear entrance. Nevertheless, he orders cast moldings of the tire tracks and footprints. He strongly believes that at least one of them will match the imprints from the two related deaths. He leaves the scene for Rosalina's and orders a constant surveillance of the area as a precautionary measure.

Jason, being a creature of habit, arrives at Rosalina's a few minutes before the lunch hour. He enters the second set of double doors. He feels eerie not seeing Alfredo standing at his usual spot behind the podium. He braces himself as he is greeted by Loretta Silverstone, the restaurant's assistant manager. She is an elderly woman who sports her silver hair in a short tapered style, far too young for her age. Her face displays wrinkles of wisdom.

"I take it," she says, "that again your early arrival has something to do with police business."

"For the most part, it does. However, I will have something to eat while I'm here."

"Please pardon my memory, but I can't recall what your meal is. I do know that it is always the same thing. Alfredo would normally place your order but he hasn't arrived yet."

"He won't today," Jason states in a leading tone.

"Something has happened to him; I know it," she states abruptly. "He is never late and he has not phoned in."

"Alfredo is in Memorial Hospital. He has been attacked."

"What!" She sounds loud enough and with concern that a couple of cooks peer through the small window of the kitchen entrance door. "I said police business but I'd never dream it would involve Alfredo."

"Unfortunately, it does."

"Is he okay?"

"The doctors advise that he'll be fine…although he has been beaten pretty badly."

"Who would do such a thing?"

"This is what I aim to discover. I'll start by asking you and others a few questions."

"Anything to help."

Jason questions Mrs. Silverstone as well as the other personnel about the previous night and Alfredo's other recent activities. As suspected, the restaurant is Alfredo's life; no one can provide any pertinent information about his life outside of the job. Because of this, Jason's investigation with everyone he speaks with is fairly brief. He concludes the questioning and decides that maybe additional inquiries may come to him while he eats his meal.

He takes the initiative and advises the cooks that he'd have his usual meal before returning to his favorite seating. Mrs. Silverstone apparently remembers that Jason is fond of coffee. A large pot is waiting for him at the booth. He fills the cup, savors the robust flavor of the first cup as his thoughts switch back and forth between Monique and Alfredo. While he drinks a second cup, everything within tells him that he is in the right place. A connection between Alfredo and the other victims is lurking, seemingly hidden, too obvious to be noticed. As Mrs. Silverstone approaches with his meal, the entire scene feels as awkward as him trying to bat right-handed. Something about the swing feels unnatural.

For years Alfredo has served him; seeing her in his familiar role seems to provide added stimuli to unravel the mystery of his attack. Jason consumes his meal in his usual lustful manner and finishes in record time. It is always prepared flawlessly, dating back years. He also realizes that he has emptied the pot of coffee during the process. He wipes his mouth in conclusion, places the napkin on the empty plate as the multiple cups of coffee command his bladder. He walks toward the bathroom in an unusually fast pace, ignoring his patented smooth glide through the restaurant.

Jason, unlike most men, proceeds directly to a stall to do a number-one because he is extra careful after relieving himself due to his lack of underwear. Toilet paper and a lot of shaking are involved to prevent wet spots from appearing on his pants. He stands in front of the toilet doing a dance familiar to both men and women. He had begun marching rapidly on his toes in place, hoping to contain the dramatic pressure of his bladder. He releases his belt, unbuttons his pants and lowers his zipper. He leans forward with one hand extended to the back wall, and his head hangs down with his eyes closed. His closed eyes ascend to an open position in direct correlation with his emptying bladder. He sighs in relief after the initial rush passes and thinks about his stance. It reminds him of the picture he once saw of a father at the Vietnam Memorial. The father is in a similar position and a reflection of his fallen son appears on the wall. The soldier's palm touches the very place where the father's rests. His open eyes focus on his hand at the back wall as if he is trying to visualize the soldier's hand. Located between his thumb and pointer finger is a telephone number inscribed on the wall. He disregards the number for the most part but while he is performing the keep-dry ritual, he glances back to where his hand was. He reads the caption describing the number and stares at it as if it is one of the great wonders of the world.

Jason fixes his clothes, reaches behind him, opens the stall door and backs out of it like he is being forced to leave. After the door closes, he holds it shut at the top and uses a quarter to lock it from the outside with the designed slit on the opposite side of the locking knob. He literally runs from the bathroom to Mrs. Silverstone, returns with a pencil, cellophane tape and a pair of scissors. Jason snatches a paper towel from the dispenser, places it on the countertop and uses the scissors to shave lead from the sharpened pencil onto it. Mrs. Silverstone joins Jason in the men's room. She primes her mouth to ask Jason, *what's the cause of the sudden excitement?* But before the thoughts materialize into words, Jason asks if she can get her hands on a makeup brush or cotton balls.

She excuses herself, returns in a short moment with a bag of cotton balls. She watches Jason shave more pencil lead, walk into the stall, dip a cotton ball into the pencil shavings and lightly apply it to the general area where the telephone number is written. She suspects that Jason is looking for fingerprints on a wall that without the small section of graffiti is flawless. She thinks, *I certainly hope that he is going to clean up after himself.*

Jason draws closer to the painted area and with a strong breath he blows on his masterpiece. The area appears only a little cleaner, however, the change is adequate for his needs. He places several pieces of tape over the area and uses another cotton ball to apply light pressure to each piece before turning to Mrs. Silverstone.

"I'll require your assistance again, please."

"What is it this time?" she states in a tone that reflects her discontent with the wall.

"May I borrow an empty tall clear glass?"

She nods, leaves the restroom irritated, as if Jason hasn't noticed her patience growing thin, but she soon returns with the item he requested.

Jason carefully lifts each piece of tape, affixing them carefully to the glass. He holds the glass to the light and a smile decorates his face upon noticing the makings of fingerprints.

"I'm afraid," Jason states, "I'm going to have to close this stall from public usage. It has officially become part of a police investigation."

"You're kidding?"

"I'm very serious. Just keep it closed until I receive the result from the fingerprint comparison. I'm aware that you have a business to think about, so I will not have it sectioned off with police tape. But, I will require you to lock it from the outside and place an 'out of order' sign on the door. This should prevent the customers from getting alarmed."

Her eyes dart to the ceiling and return to Jason as if she is still in thought. "That's an acceptable compromise," she announces somewhat arrogantly.

Jason gazes at her in a manner that suggests, as if you have a choice.

"I will let you know something as soon as I receive the results."

Mrs. Silverstone returns her familiar nod as Jason takes up a quick pace to his vehicle. He enters the vehicle and is pleased that his subconscious mind directed him to take the police cruiser. Immediately after the car starts, flashing red and blue lights decorate the front grille. In the rear window, matching lights dance much the same. Both are seemingly being overshadowed by the siren as he races to the police station.

Before he reports to Captain North, Jason gives the glass to forensics for print analysis with the other recent victims. Everything about it tells him that Alfredo's prints are among the ones lifted from the wall.

Jason advises his superior of his findings as well as his suspicions.

"Don't you think," Captain North asks, "that you are reaching a bit? After all, millions of men perform that dance every day and find themselves in the same position you were in."

Jason thinks to himself that he may have been too detailed when telling how he stumbled on the telephone number. He feels belittled, though he doesn't express it. However, in defiance he states strongly, "No! If we didn't have two people last seen at Rosalina's, both beaten, both showing signs of an orgasm, then I'd feel as though I'm reaching. Captain, my instincts tell me something good is about to happen."

"I hope you are right. Not that I doubt you, but part of my job is to be objective."

"Understood."

"Now, I've asked you this once before but, has this case evolved into a personal vendetta?"

Jason cut his eyes at his Captain. He knows fully what the Captain is insinuating. The last time, a loved one was in the middle of his investigation. It became personal. He also knows that it'll be personal to his superior if the shoe was on the other foot. He wants to express the sudden anger that sweeps him, but he maintains his cool and lets his piercing eyes tell all.

"Jason, if you recall, your last confrontation was not executed by the book. You escaped prosecution by the skin of your teeth...and, how much skin is on your teeth?"

"I get your point. Things will be different this time."

Jason has more to say on the matter but their conversation is disturbed by a knock on the Captain's door.

"Jason," Sgt. Austin states. "Forensics dropped this package on your desk. I thought you might want to have it immediately."

"Kevin, you thought correctly."

Jason opens the package, bounces his head up and down as he reads the findings of the tire prints.

"Interesting," he announces aloud.

"What is?" Captain North questions.

"That the tire tracks lifted are common to just about all makes of SUVs. These are standard tires for the Ford Explorer and the Dodge Durango as well as many other vehicles."

"With so many vehicles using this tire, it will be almost impossible to identify the criminal vehicle."

Captain North watches Jason's expression move from coy to disappointment as the results of the fingerprint analysis appear to his eyes.

"Jason, I know you expected one of the prints to match your close friend Alfredo's, but looking at you, I can surmise that it didn't happen. It was an ingenious thought though, nice try."

Jason's head shifts from side to side as he states in anguish, "Alfredo's prints are not among these. I would have bet money on it."

"As I said, it was a nice college try."

"Captain," Jason announces with a half-smile. "I do have a match with the second victim, Craig Jones."

"I agree now, this is interesting, but we have no proof that he dialed the number in the bathroom stall. It is purely circumstantial."

This time Jason gazes at his superior as if he'd lost his mind. "Captain, I can take a forensics team to Rosalina's and have them dust the place from head to toe but that is unnecessary. You know as well as I that a break like this is more than enough to go on. Hell, I've gone on much less before."

"Knowing you, I bet you have."

"Surely, you're not going to have me justify my police instinct."

"No, I'm not. I just wanted to make sure that you feel strongly about what you discovered. It seems that the pre-accident Jason has submerged. Proceed by the book, call the number and see where it leads."

Jason's mind only acknowledges "call the number." "Yes, Sir" leaves his lips as he stands to leave Captain North's office.

"I mean it, Jason," the Captain states firmly. "I want this one by the numbers."

"Captain, I'll give it my best."

"Make sure your best is by the book."

"My best will produce results," Jason conveys as he exits the office.

Jason sits at his desk circling the telephone number with a pencil. Finally, he picks up the handset, presses a number for an outside line. The tone sounds in his ear for a few seconds. Suddenly, he holds the handset away from his ear and stares oddly at it. Caution sweeps him. He rises from his desk, exits the building and stands outside the station.

He dials the tempting number with his cellular phone. When the ring registers in his ears, he starts a stride away from the familiar sounds of the police station. He thinks to himself, *well now* when a sultry woman's voice leaves the earpiece.

"Thrill Adventures," she states.

"Hi," Jason responds enthusiastically. "Will you tell me how your services work?"

"I'd be delighted to...whom am I addressing?"

"My name is Tyrone," Jason lies.

"Tyrone, huh, you sound like one, wink...wink."

"You know how it is."

She replies with laughter in her voice, "You're just like everyone else. The thrill ride is the ultimate sexual experience."

"How so?"

"Ever heard of the Mile High Club?"

"Who hasn't?"

"Well, the thrill ride is the equivalent of that but on the ground. Imagine yourself having an orgasmic experience traveling in excess of one hundred miles per hour. Furthermore, to add the adrenaline rush, picture yourself exploding on a high-bank curve. Trust me, there is nothing like it. Sound intriguing?"

"I must admit, it does but...what about the woman?"

"All guaranteed to be clean and disease free. Some of the most gorgeous women you've even seen. To prove it, you get to pick the one that's most exciting to you."

"Pictures can be deceitful."

"Agreed, that's why we've gone one step further. You get to see a video clip, full body and all, with audio."

"The most gorgeous women in an enticing message?"

"Truly, I'm not bad myself and they make me envious."

"Yeah but, how much does this experience cost?"

"You are in time for our special; the works will cost you a mere three twenty-five."

A quiet overtakes the airwaves, and the few silent moments are a telltale sign that her potential client isn't completely convinced.

"I can lose my job for this, but would two hundred-fifty help your decision?"

For effect, Jason takes his time to respond, "Two hundred-fifty, I can manage that."

"I promise that you won't be disappointed."

"What do we do now?"

"We need to meet so you can pick the lovely lady that suits your fancy."

"Sounds reasonable."

"By the way, how do you know about our service?"

"I'd imagine one of your satisfied customers became so eager to share the experience, he put an enticing message in a bathroom stall."

"That should be proof enough. Mostly word of mouth brings business. So, now that all of the formalities are settled, when would you like to experience this thrill ride?"

"I'd like to choose my girl today because it'll take me a day or so to get the money together."

"We accept plastic."

"I'd prefer not to use my credit card. This sort of thing I'd like to keep undercover."

"Most of our customers do."

"Where do you normally meet your clients?"

"We are fairly flexible as long as it's not too far out of the way."

"You know where La Magnifique is?"

"The French restaurant, yes, it's well known."

"Let's meet there later this evening. Say, seven-thirty."

"That should…" she says as Jason actually hears the turning pages of what his mind deems an appointment book. "…be fine. I'll be traveling in a black Ford Excursion and I'll be carrying a laptop."

They conclude their conversation seconds after her last sentence. Almost as quickly as their goodbyes, Captain North's words of wisdom invade his mind.

By the book, he thinks.

The words taunt him for several minutes. He knows what he must do. He must live by a code of ethics embedded in him for years. A code that defines a book, *his* book. He hopes, finalizing his thoughts, that the results he will achieve will satisfy his Captain's request for straight and narrow. Jason shrugs his shoulders while thinking, *excuse me while I dance*, ignoring his conscience, following his gut, thereby eluding proper police protocol with his own thought. However, he does go back to the station to get forensics to check to see if any of the tire tracks can be linked to a Ford Excursion.

The afternoon hours turn into evening; the evening hours slowly drift into moments before his scheduled rendezvous. He finds himself waiting in the parking lot of La Magnifique a few minutes early. As he is watching for the vehicle to arrive, he questions himself whether subconsciously he chose this particular restaurant because of Crystin. He scans the parking lot for her car and keeps one eye focused on the front door for her. Out of nowhere, a faint whisper of "to love her is to love me" rides through his thought patterns. As if he forgot why he is peering at the door, his head shakes from side to side and his full attention is diverted to carefully watching for the expected vehicle.

A short moment later, the vehicle enters the parking lot from the main road. He marvels at the size difference between it and the smaller Ford Expedition. The vehicle parks somewhat in the middle of the nearly empty parking lot. From Jason's vantage point, he can visibly see the rear of the vehicle. He observes the passenger-side door open, watches Azuri as she exits the truck and stands near the rear doors. She shifts her head in Jason's direction upon hearing his car door shut and pats the case containing the laptop computer as he approaches her.

Jason thinks, *what a shame*, as he gazes at her work attire. The same thought possesses him upon realizing just how beautiful she really is. As he reaches out to shake her hand, her hand holding the laptop falls to her side; the other extends forward opening her trench coat. Her body is revealed to his eyes. Jason literally freezes like a statue. His hand is extended but not as inviting as the gesture should be, more like a lawn ornament that's missing a pail of water. He finds himself taken by her physical appearance and feels somewhat embarrassed by his reaction to her. He begins watching her in a childlike way as if his mental age is set back a couple of decades. His hands are fidgety, unable to find a suitable resting place. His feet accompany his hands by kicking and scuffing all over the pavement. Azuri is amused with his reaction to her.

"Hi, I'm Azuri," she states, breaking the awkward silence. "Mr. Tyrone, I presume."

"Yes, yes…Tyrone," Jason utters after remembering his pet name. "Azuri is a name suited for a woman as beautiful as you are. You are…" Jason's eyes dart to the early P.M. sky, "…not a slouch."

Azuri smiles, realizing what he is referring to. "As I said, wait until you see my girls."

"Unexpectedly, I can't wait."

"Well, let's sit down and have a look-see."

Azuri steps away from the truck, opens one door, then the other and motions for him to sit in the opening. Jason obeys and she follows by sitting very near to him.

Immediately, her fragrance wraps him in a comfortable shell. For a small instance, he wishes that the undertones of being in her presence were not business. The laptop is powered up and ready to preview her girls in record time. Jason senses that she can perform this part of her duties with her eyes closed and the commentary that accompanies each four-minute video has been rehearsed to perfection.

For the most part, he discards her words, letting the pictures speak for themselves. Only two of the twelve women he views are particularly unattractive to him. Of the remaining ten, one moves him in a way that provokes the thought, *just the ones I like.*

Jason's standard reply when asked what kind of women he likes is, "I like all women but just the ones I like." The comment refers to race, creed, color and a smile warms him as he recalls how he finishes this thought to one of his colleagues: *She can be blue with zebra stripes and have a horn sticking out of her head. If I like her, then nothing else matters.*

"She suits," Jason states lustfully, "my fancy."

Azuri nods before stating, "Just like her name, Sharon—simple but elegant. She is one of the favorites; I'm positive you'll love her."

Jason carries the scene further by requesting that he see Sharon's video again. For effect, he watches it with his mouth parted. He sees Azuri's smile as he gleams at the video and feels confident that things are going as planned. Unfortunately, he doesn't have a plan beyond this meeting. Not one that consists of proper protocol. He has come too far to turn back; any retreat now will go against his grain. He somehow needs to find a way to satisfy his Captain and remain true to himself. After a short moment, his eyes turn away from the computer screen and catch Azuri's glance.

"What do we do now?"

"From my point of view, everything is settled except when you'd be able to pay. After seeing these wonderful women, will you still need a day or so to get the money together?"

Jason smiles, scratches under his chin with a pointer finger as if he is giving it serious consideration.

"Well, maybe not a couple of days. I'll have to wait until tomorrow though…tomorrow afternoon I'll have cash."

"Tomorrow it is then. Try to sleep; don't let your anticipation keep you awake."

"It will be hard but I'll manage somehow."

Azuri manages to get the laptop back in its case as smoothly as she produced it. She slides forward and stands tall facing Jason.

"What if…" Jason states standing in her magnificence, "I changed my mind about my chosen sexpert?"

"What about it?"

"What if I choose you?"

"Me!" she replies with a brilliant smile. "I haven't taken the ride since… well, since I can remember. I'm flattered but I'd have to turn you down. But, if this was even as little as a couple of years ago, you'd be on."

"Just wondering."

Azuri closes the right door and Jason assists her by closing the left. Azuri walks into his space pretending to whisper something into his ear. As Jason leans forward to retrieve her words, he feels her soft hand seize his and place his fingers against her womanhood.

"Enjoy yourself tomorrow," she whispers.

Jason exercises great concentration while his fingers bathe in the warmth radiating from her womanhood. He literally wills them to remain still.

"I can't wait," Jason replies as she releases his hand.

Their goodbye is brief. Jason remains stationary as she walks to the right of the vehicle and enters the passenger-side door. Simultaneously as the sound of the closing door registers in his ears, the vehicle's engine starts. Instinct causes him to look forward, glaring into the driver's side mirror. The vehicle pulls away and turns onto the main road before Jason moves a muscle. After he is certain that he can no longer be seen, he reaches into his shirt pocket and produces a small notepad.

His method was risky, however, he didn't want to raise any suspicions by being seen writing. Instead he acted nervous when they first met, thereby allowing him to code the vehicle's license plate number on the pavement with the leather sole of his shoes. To anyone else, it will appear to be bad abstract art, but he coded it in a way that makes it easy for him to decipher. Jason leaves the parking lot and heads for the station to write his preliminary report while it is fresh in his mind.

Late that evening, Jason returns home and smiles to himself upon recognizing Monique's car. He pairs his car with hers, thinking "perfect" as he exits his vehicle. He reflects on how near perfect his life is since she's been a serious consideration in his life. Somehow, he gains a sense of confidence he has never experienced before. He knows it is right and yearns to make things right with her. Therefore, he vows to keep his word and make her his wife soon after he finishes his current case. He enters his home to silence and near darkness. The small light source provided by the base of one of the oriental lamps in the living room is his guiding light to the kitchen. He finds a note taped on the refrigerator stating that dinner is in the microwave.

"I can get used to this," Jason states aloud. "But what would happen to Rosalina's? I'd hate to lose my privileges there."

Jason shrugs his shoulders, decides to worry about it later and finds Monique sleeping comfortably under the sheets. He lays his footsteps softly on the carpet, stops at the bed and hangs his pistol holster on one of the tall bedposts. He removes and decorates the other bedpost with his shirt, using it as a hanger. He stops short of the bathroom's entrance and removes his shoes to prevent the metal heel plates from sounding on the marble floor.

Jason washes his hands, then his face and studies Monique as he brushes his teeth. He hangs his pants on top of his shirt and chooses the side of the bed with the most room to ease under the sheets. Almost immediately, Monique's arms embrace him tightly, then one of Monique's legs swings across him. Jason is at ease with her actions. He believes that she is finding a comfortable resting place, but when she starts grinding her midsection against his leg, he gazes at her. To his surprise, her eyes are shut and her breathing is heavy.

"I love the way you feel inside of me," Monique states in a sexually excited manner.

Jason smiles in awe, realizing by her comment that she is having a sexciting dream.

"I knew that it would be like this," she cries in Jason's ear.

Her hips grind hard and hurriedly against his leg until her breathing becomes heavy pants that accompany each thrust. The pace of her movement multiplies frantically before suddenly and oddly stopping.

"Oh God!" she screams. "Fuck, I didn't want to come so soon!" she states as her hips pick up their rapid pace once more.

Jason squints and closes his eyes as the words delivered directly into his ear pain him. As oddly and abruptly as she ceases her grinding before the orgasm, she pushes away from him and makes a one-hundred-eighty-degree turn. She tosses the sheets to the side, stands glaring down at Jason.

"Holy shit," she echoes with her hands covering her eyes to conceal her embarrassment. It is too late; her embarrassment radiates from her like the orange glow of a hot oven coil. "Honey, I'm so sorry."

Jason smiles as he delivers, "I just hope that I can compete with the man in your dream."

"The man is you...somehow, I think you know this already."

Monique sits on the side of the bed with her back toward Jason. Her elbows rest on her thighs with both hands cradling her face for a small silent moment. She turns toward Jason.

"This is all your fault."

"Mine." Jason chuckles. "How so?"

"Yes, yours...I've only spent a couple of nights here and have already lost control of myself."

"I still don't see how you having wet dreams is my fault. I..."

"Because," she interrupts in her defense, "you poke me until you fall asleep."

"I poke...I see," he says with a huge smile. "Well, you feel good in my arms."

"And, I feel good under your embrace, but, while you're stabbing me I just want to roll over and have my way with you."

"Is this a roundabout way of stating that it is dangerous being in the same bed with me?"

"That's not what I'm saying, but your statement is true."

Monique slides back under the sheets with her back to Jason. She is too ashamed to look him directly in the eyes.

Jason immediately cradles her, positioning them in the center of the bed. He kisses her politely on the back of the neck before whispering, "Forgive me," into her ear. The words "for what?" are about to trail off Monique's lips, but when he moves the arm that's hugging her just below the breast to and between the back of her thighs, she realizes that her question is about to be answered. Her eyes widen as she feels his hand slowly crawling toward her wetbox. Everything within wants her to stand firm, clamp her legs shut, but her wet desire summons his touch with greater control. Monique moans as he carefully slides two fingers into her juices, makes a walking movement with them and removes them as delicately as they were inserted.

Jason tastes her juices as if he is extracting nectar from a peach and savors her sweet treat until the only remnants of her juices is a memory of him inserting his fingers into his mouth.

"You're so nasty," intercepts Jason's ears.

"Someone once told me that a hard-on is a terrible thing to waste. Well, I believe wasting fruit juice is a greater sin."

"You're still nasty."

He kisses her on the back of the neck once more before replying, "Tell me something I don't know."

"You must know that I want you and frankly...waiting until we're married is," she rolls over to her other side, locking her gaze into his, "in my honest but humble opinion, a waste of time."

Jason smiles as means to conceal the fact that he believes her words to be true.

"Angel, my love, though realizing my adolescent dream will just about complete my existence, I'd prefer to wait. For once in my life, I'd like to do something morally right."

Monique is startled with his words, but somewhere within them she finds compassion, a certain serenity that overshadows the disappointment she feels. Therefore, she nods in agreement, reluctantly. She holds him in a tight embrace, softly kisses his lips and rolls back to her other side. In an automatic fashion, Jason assumes their number-one position. Silence fills the air with both of them attempting to sleep. Suddenly, Monique removes the pillow from beneath her head and places it between their bodies at the waist.

"Sorry," fills Monique's ears.

Her reply is a silent shaking of the head.

TWENTY ONE

Azuri states to the driver of the vehicle, "Now, that's an interesting trick. He seems as refined as they come, but I know that he had trouble controlling his excitement. He was trying to be so cool it almost became comical. Sharon is going to rock his world. You know what?" she asks when Reggie appears to be in deep thought.

"What?" Reggie responds without looking at her.

"He actually asked if I would take the ride. I guess I still have it."

"Still!" he replies as if her words surprised him. "You haven't lost a thing. If anything you've gotten better like a fine wine…wiser, all of these are positives."

"Thank you for your kind words. That's the nicest thing you've ever said to me."

"It's true. I remember when you women were required to wear those traditional ceremonial oriental gowns. You drove me…" He pauses briefly. "Damn it!" he yells loud enough to startle Azuri. "Oh shit…oh shit, this is bad!"

"Reggie, calm yourself and tell me what's going on?"

"I thought that I recognized him when I saw him in the outside rear mirror."

"You know him? This guy I just met…Tyrone."

"Tyrone, my ass; that guy is a detective named Jason Jerrard. Sly is going to shit a brick."

"Are you sure that it's the same person?"

"Hell yeah, I'm sure."

Reggie makes no further comment and proceeds to press "recall," then the number three on his cell phone. When Sly's number appears on the display, he presses "send" and waits anxiously for the call to connect.

"Sly!" he shouts overly excited. "You won't believe what I'm going to tell you."

Reggie's comments are rushed, childlike in nature. The erratic way he attempts to talk to Sly is flustering enough to make Sly interrupt and wait until they are face to face. Sly does comprehend the general idea of what Reggie is telling him. His mind is already working on a plan, something diabolical that will keep him out of jail, save his business and satisfy Crystin's need for revenge at the same time.

✳✳✳

The nightmare that Crystin has the previous night is repetitive. It has swept her dreams for many days, becoming a pest to her conscious being. She isn't a victim of a crime, a haunting, or a stalker. She isn't threatened in any way. Her nightmare is the result of her mind's continuing fight of telling her heart that she hasn't fallen deeply for Jason. Her heart's constant attempt to convince her mind that it is in denial typically has her lying in the bed, staring into the darkness, wanting him near. It pains her to think that she surrendered all of herself to him. It pains her to know that Jason can simply turn off his emotions like a water faucet, never again to shower her being with his.

"The fucker," she announces loudly, "doesn't have the decency to call to see how I'm doing. He knows I've been hurting since he broke it off. The way I responded to his news should have told him that."

It seems like eons since she has seen him. The time apart would normally serve as a buffer, a healing device for her emotions. Instead, her disappointment in him grows into anger, the anger grows to hatred and the hatred controls her to the point of wanting to take revenge. She doesn't know how, but she knows she'll have to talk Sly into doing more than just embarrassing Jason.

"The fool does not realize that a woman scorned is the worst enemy a man can have," she states aloud in search of Sly's telephone number.

✳✳✳

Delia has been trying for close to a day to reach Sandra. Her phone just rings. The answering machine is full with calls from her and has stopped recording messages. It worries her that Sandra hasn't returned her calls or any pages. After so long, her fear of leaving the apartment fades to a serious caution, a strong form of self-preservation. She isn't sure that Dakota is responsible for Sandra's disappearance, but she knows that she will not wait idly for him to find her locked in her haven, falsely secure. The problem is, she has no place special to go. Therefore, she lies on the bed with her hands clasped behind her head, eyes focused on the pale ceiling without décor, as are her thoughts. She desperately seeks a refuge away from harm's way, an unlikely place that will elude her business associate's thoughts. Her eyes widen, staring firmly at the nothingness of the ceiling. She jumps up frantic in nature, and stuffs a few days' supply of clothes into an overnight bag. She dashes into her bedroom, places makeup and other necessities into the overnight bag for an extended stay away from home.

Delia finds herself lurking around Alfredo's hospital room for nearly two days. During her captive stay at the hospital she uses their restroom facilities to freshen up before changing clothes. She waits and checks on him as if he is one of her closest relatives. Dr. Bodou becomes so accustomed to seeing her that he starts delivering condition reports to her. Of all the crowds of people visiting Alfredo, she is the one person who remains, the one constant companion very much concerned with his condition. And then there is Jason.

Before reporting to work, his relationship with Alfredo forces him to check on his dear friend prior to starting his day. He arrives at the hospital sometime around six a.m. in the morning and walks into the room with Delia sleeping in a chair. Jason's footsteps bring her out of the uncomfortable slumber. She wipes the sleep from her eyes, looks at Jason and bows her head. As she always does, she excuses herself without an introduction when others enter. Jason is left alone with Alfredo.

"You don't have to leave because of me," Jason states as she is walking away.

His words are apparently ignored, determined by her constant footsteps. Nevertheless, he sits at Alfredo's bedside and talks to him as if he is conscious. Jason continues his one-way conversation while rehashing some of the memorable times they shared together. To Jason's dismay, he realizes that all of their special moments have been related to Rosalina's. This fact saddens him and he vows that once Alfredo is healthy enough, their bond will continue beyond Rosalina's.

As always, Jason uses Alfredo's silence as a time to reflect on the case. He believes, although he hasn't completely convinced himself, that it all makes sense. He feels strongly that the answer to Alfredo's situation will smack him directly in the face. Jason stares hard at him for a moment, and then shoots a glance out the door.

Jason leans over and whispers into Alfredo's ear, "You're nasty."

Jason has a strong sense that those responsible for Alfredo's hospital stay will soon be brought to justice. He exits the room, sees the mysterious woman waiting in an area outside of the room and takes her into his gaze. Without a word, she turns her head away. Jason sits in the chair next to her, pauses for a small moment before saying, "Delia?"

Her head slowly turns toward Jason's with a puzzled expression.

"Isn't your name Delia?" Jason repeats.

"Yes," she replies, "but I'm not sure that we've ever met."

"We haven't. But I've seen you somewhere before. I spend a lot of time at Rosalina's and if you are visiting my friend in there, this might be the place."

"It is a possibility. I dined there recently."

"How is he?"

Delia's head veers toward Alfredo's room. "He's sleeping peacefully."

"Are you a relative of his?"

"No, we just recently met, but I'd like to think that I'm someone special to him."

"Don't be alarmed, but I'm the detective investigating his case. I also know who you are and what you do, but the part that I don't know is, how did he come to this conclusion?"

Delia's eyes widen; initial panic sweeps her face. She stares at the floor for a long while without saying a word. Jason places a hand on her chin and slowly moves her head around, bringing her eyes into his.

"I'm not here to arrest you. I just want to know what happened to my friend."

As her mouth opens, the panic leaves her face, rises above her head and dissolves into thousands of tiny pieces.

"He started out being just another trick. But somewhere, in the process he…we found something in the experience. I believe with all my heart that we formed an unspoken…" She pauses, uncertain how Jason will accept what she is about to say. "…love for each other."

"Very interesting," Jason comments with his head nodding in agreement. "I can believe that. My name is Detective Jason Jerrard and I've met Azuri." A surprising look dances across her face. "I'm to meet with Sharon later today for the thrill ride."

"So you are telling the truth," Delia states, conceding to Jason's knowledge of her activities.

"Azuri nor any one of the women I saw on video are capable of administering this kind of punishment to Alfredo. I'd like you to tell me who this person is."

"His name is Dakota and I saw him do it."

"You'd be willing to testify under oath to this fact?"

"Detective Jerrard, for the last couple of days or so, I've been camping here at the hospital, fearful of my life. I may be paranoid, but I have a certain gut feeling that I'm no longer safe in my apartment."

"It's better to err on the side of caution."

Delia removes her gaze away from Jason, stands and walks into Alfredo's room. Jason follows her lead, joining her at Alfredo's bedside. She catches Jason's gaze and points at Alfredo as she picks up her conversation.

"For this man, I'll surely testify. You know, we barely spoke the night that we were together. Us being together was much more than just having sex. It was intimate, passionate, a uniting of sorts. I can't explain it, but every-thing inside of me tells me that he feels the same way." Delia tenderly caresses Alfredo's forehead. "I just know he does," she delivers with compassion. "I'm going to be here to let him know my feelings when he wakes."

"Why would this Dakota character want to harm you?"

"Jealousy, I guess. He probably picked up on the vibes Alfredo and I were having. He has truly been acting strange lately…you know this is not the first time that he attacked someone. Another girl in the group told me she saw him attack someone else a few days before he attacked Alfredo."

"If we are talking about the same person, I already know of two other cases. It's highly unlikely that he'll look for you here, but you can't remain here forever."

"I'm aware of this…I just want to be here when he wakes. The remainder of my life depends on what's in his heart."

Jason finds himself in a strange dilemma. He has at his disposal a material witness that can bring this case to an immediate close. Proper procedures tell him that he should be marching down to the station with her in tow, yet he is about to leave such an important witness at Alfredo's bedside. Thoughts of her disappearance ring in his consciousness, but he has fallen for the conviction that she displays in her last sentence. His instinct tells him that she will not run, coupled with the fact that he finds more anxiety with the sight in front of him. Alfredo's condition shapes what he must do. It hampers the protocol he swears to uphold. He suggests that she remain at Alfredo's side and gives her his pager number just in case his condition changes.

Jason leaves the hospital en route to the station to retrieve the money needed for the thrill ride. He reports to Captain North after having the money in his possession and details a complete plan to his superior on how he is going to carry out the scheduled arrangement. With a couple of minor changes suggested by his superior, he receives orders to proceed as planned. Jason conveniently forgets to mention Delia because he knows that he'll be ordered to bring her in and take a team to wherever she thinks Dakota might be. The burning inside of him—driven by the picture of Alfredo lying in the hospital like a mannequin and the rehashed memories it produces of Sasha in a similar fashion—assures him that he'll face Dakota. It will be man to man, no matter what the consequences might be.

TWENTY TWO

Jason calls Azuri with the final outcome being a scheduled meeting during the early evening hours at Rosalina's. After a late lunch at Rosalina's, Jason waits with mixed emotions for his scheduled rendezvous. As hard as he fights the notion to proceed as planned, the underlining tones of his character dictate differently. The demanding need is nearly as strong as it had been when having to face Sasha's nemesis. It controls his will and all of the genes that make him do the right thing. After all, Alfredo is like family to him and harming family is in his eyes the same as harming him. As a precautionary measure, Jason writes the details of his altered plan down on a piece of paper, places it in an envelope and passes it to Mrs. Silverstone. Her instruction is that if he isn't back by nine p.m. to call Detective Austin at the Sixteenth Precinct to come retrieve the envelope. Mrs. Silverstone reluctantly accepts the instructions.

Later that evening, Jason stands on Rosalina's steps much in the same fashion as Alfredo had. At the scheduled time, the SUV pulls to the side of the road and flashes its lights capturing Jason's attention. He starts down the sidewalk toward the vehicle. Sharon exits the passenger-side door and meets Jason on the sidewalk near the vehicle. Jason thinks to himself that she is twice as beautiful in person as in her video. Face to face, Jason gets a chance to examine her up close and personal and finds himself admiring her distinct Native American features. Her long silky hair, high cheekbones and a smile that is near angelic have a calming effect on him. Just in that quick moment, he ascertains that she is a girl with Southern ways and values. Oddly, he wonders if she is a great cook. However, she isn't the person that he is after. Bringing Dakota to justice drives him, and he just has to pass the time until something happens.

"I'm here, I'm ready...I think. I've never done anything like this," Jason confesses.

"Well, you don't have anything to worry about," she announces in a failing attempt to disguise her Southern tone. "This won't be painful. I promise."

Jason smiles as if to say, "If you only knew."

"Shall we get started?"

"Most definitely."

Jason walks by the passenger-side door while following Sharon to the rear of the vehicle. He looks into the window but the vehicle's limousine-tinted windows prevent him from seeing anything useful. Sharon opens the left rear door and Jason follows suit as he did with Azuri, opening the adjacent door.

"Welcome, Detective," Sly states.

Jason freezes in his tracks with having a pistol pointed at him.

"Sly, what's going on here?" Sharon states startled.

"Sharon, don't bother yourself with matters that don't concern you. Get back into the front of the vehicle and be quiet."

Sly's aggressive tone easily influences Sharon to ask no further questions. She quietly gets back into the passenger seat and closes her eyes. Jason may have been more alarmed, but the sight of Crystin stepping out of the vehicle proves to be more amazing than having a pistol pointed at him.

"Just like we discussed," Sly blurts, "frisk him. He may have been on to us all the time."

Crystin stands inches from Jason with her eyes peering through him. Jason finds it hard to believe that a woman, who is considered eye candy, can distort her facial features to what is best described as tasting sour fruit.

"I told you that I'd get even with you," Crystin angrily states low enough to prevent her words from reaching Sly's ears.

Her hands slide up his sides, then under his arms. She stoops down in front of him, pats him along the outside of his legs. She pats the inside of his legs as high as his crotch and fights off the urge to punch him in it. Crystin stands, this time closer to Jason. As she rises, her breasts travel up his thighs, across his stomach and settle at his chest. She concludes her unorthodox maneuver by pressing her breasts against him firmer.

"All of this was yours," she speaks softly to Jason. She turns her head toward Sly and states, "He's clean."

"Step into the vehicle nice and easy," directs Sly.

Jason follows his instructions mentally tormented. He expected something to happen but not this soon. Protocol laughs through his being. After stepping completely inside the vehicle and being forced to sit across from Sly, Jason receives a hostile instruction from Crystin, barely recognizing her tainted voice.

"Sit your ass down," Crystin demands as she snatches the pistol from Sly.

Jason looks at the couple sitting across from him bewildered that Crystin can hold this type of anger. He senses that there is more but he isn't able to ascertain her true intentions. Sly taps on the glass twice; almost instantly the vehicle begins to move.

"What are you doing here?" Jason questions Crystin.

"I'm here because…"

"Why are you here is what I should ask?" Jason interrupts. "Surely, you've had ample time to…get even with me."

"You are in no position to ask any questions, but you should know that you hurt me deeply, like never before. That should explain it all. It took a while but I'm going to have you," she states with a brow raised. "And then, you'll be hurt as badly as you hurt me."

"You're out to get even after all of this time," Jason states in dismay. "But what is your relationship with this character?"

"I have other issues with you," Sly interrupts.

"Okay, I'll bite," states Jason, too sarcastic for a person in his predicament. "What kind of injustice have I done to you?"

"Don't you worry about me…I'll be part of the hurt she just talked about. At that time, I'll spill my guts just like they do in the movies, right before you reach your doom. You're so predictable, the city's golden boy, I knew that you could not resist the temptation of playing hero once again. No gun, no wire, no backup, and you call yourself a good detective."

"I was good enough to find out about your operation, but I had not figured Mrs. Mayor would be caught up in a sex scam."

"I'm not part of anything," Crystin defends, "but a weird turn of events happened to work things out this way. You know, I've been in so much pain since you discarded me. You can't imagine the anguish I've gone through. All I ever did was to try to...love you," she says while turning her head away. "But no," she continues with her eyes affixed on him. "Mister High Almighty dumps me because he is hurting. How dare you? Everyone hurts at some time in their lives."

"Crystin, I explained my position as honestly and truthfully as I could."

"Well, since we are being honest with each other, I'll return the favor. As I told you, I will have you, well not you exactly, but your child. You see since our last sexual encounter, I've had my IUD removed. My doctor says that I'm as susceptible to pregnancy as I was in my twenties. Add a fertility injection that I had yesterday and my chances of becoming pregnant increase one-thousand-fold.

"As I said, a strange turn of events offered me this sex mobile to complete my plan. As for you, the hurt you will suffer from the humility of letting Virginia City, hell, the entire United States for all that matter, see us create this offspring of mine will destroy you. What he has in store for you...let's just say, I'm not going to be around for that. I'll be long gone with the tape of our sexual act."

"Aren't you forgetting someone?"

"My husband? Please. He'll be wondering what happened to me. I have enough of his money put away to last me for a lifetime."

Jason observes the way she speaks her words and desperately tries to find something in their delivery. He replays them back in his mind looking for a flaw in her poker-face that will identify it as a threat, but all that he sees is a wave of mixed emotions that are diluted and misguided by a scorned heart.

"So you see, I'll be raising Jason Junior or…" She pauses, grabs his attention with her eyes. "I'll name her Sasha, if it's a girl."

Jason's heart skips a beat as the thought *twisted* swims through his mind.

"Isn't that the bitch's name you used to end our relationship?"

"My, my, my," Sly states, "what a tangled web we weave."

The seriousness of Jason's predetermined fate seems all but a wicked dream until Crystin's words bring him back to reality.

"Tie him up," she instructs Sly.

"You heard the lady; lay your ass down on the bed."

Crystin motions the pistol as an incentive for Jason to cooperate.

Jason gazes at her with concern. He started the thrill ride without a real plan other than to confront Alfredo's attacker. Somehow, he doesn't believe that Sly is the one behind Alfredo's condition. He notices that Crystin is careful in not mentioning Sly's name. He needs to know and a thought materializes that is the catalyst that triggers a fly-by-the-seat-of-his pants move.

"Crystin," Jason states, "you still have the chance to get out of this fairly free, but, Dakota there," he continues with his eyes on Sly. "He is the one I'm after."

Sly laughs before replying, "You have the wrong guy. I'm the brains, not the brawn. You see, I knew that Alfredo would be a means to bring you to me. I've been studying both of you for some time."

"Why would you single out such a kind man like Alfredo?"

"He is…a victim of your circumstance. I've nothing personal against him. He is simply a pawn to flush you out."

Jason wants to recite his true feelings about the contempt he has for all parties involved with Alfredo's condition, but the better part of him forces the rage to remain controlled.

"I've done nothing to you because I'm sure that we've never met."

"You…"

"Guys," Crystin interrupts. "I enjoy the foray between the two of you, but, the first part of this is going to be all about me."

You're right, Jason thinks, *this is about you*. With that Jason's fly-by-the-seat-of-his-pants continues.

By this time, Sly has Jason's legs and arms tied to the pedestals of the mattress frame with a silky fabric. Jason tilts his head toward Crystin, giving her a vision of somberness.

"I can't believe you're doing this," he states to Crystin.

"Believe it."

"You can't be doing this, this way."

"Doing what…what way?"

"Having a baby without me."

"No, it will be with you."

"That's not what I mean and you know it. You know I told you how desperately I wanted to have a child and you drive a stake completely through my heart with your scheme."

Crystin lays her body on top of Jason's, sniffs his scent and replies, "Did I hurt your precious little heart? Welcome to the club."

She kisses his neck, bites the tip of his ear and starts a hand toward his member.

"This is going to be easy. I already feel you wanting me."

"Don't be so sure."

"Jason," she whispers into his ear. "You're the one who got an erection with a gun pointed at your thing." She turns her head toward Sly. "I think you can break out the video camera now."

Sly has the camera out and recording almost instantly. His job as cameraman is to record their sex act and make sure that there are vivid pictures of Jason engaged with Crystin. The same rule applies for Crystin with the exception of showing her face. He will then post portions of the video on the Internet and sell the full video to the news station. In a perverted kind of way, he finds the ordeal stimulating.

Crystin unbuttons Jason's shirt, flings it open a little too eager for her own good and claws at his chest. She finds pleasure watching his skin whelp from her forceful ways.

"You like that, don't you?"

Before giving him a chance to reply, she takes one of his nipples into her mouth and expertly nibbles on the very end. Jason's resistance is, well…he doesn't have any. All of his efforts to contain his erection never generate more than a faint glimpse of a rebellious thought. His only recourse is to remind himself of his fly-by-the-seat-of-his-pants move.

Crystin returns to his neck with her tongue, this time tasting it as if it's an ice cream cone. Jason whispers words.

"What was that?" she asks while continuing to enjoy her dessert.

"I said," Jason announces a little louder, "why are you fooling yourself?"

"Me fooling myself…it's you that refuses to believe that you'll get hard enough for me to take your dick ride."

"I'm not a machine nor are my senses. You'll accomplish your mission eventually. But, it's you who believes that raising my child will satisfy your desire to have me. You know you want me there changing diapers, washing bottles and listening for the first spoken words. I want to be there, to be a real father."

For a quick moment, he feels her chest freeze. The expanding, contracting motion halts to where he is actually feeling the thump of her heart. She releases her breath and continues with him.

"Sounds appealing, but at this moment you'll say anything to stop me."

"You spent enough time with me to know that I only say what I feel. Tell me something, why during our relationship didn't you ever mention that you wanted us? Not once did you offer any indication of us being together without your husband in the picture."

"I…" She stops her words while tilting her head to the side. Jason sees her reflecting on their past time together. "I felt it," she continues defiantly. "You should have known…you're the detective. Why didn't you detect that?"

Jason gives her a "nice try" look before responding, "I'm not a mind reader. So, did you think of a time when you spoke of us? You can't deny that you didn't. In other words," Jason continues remorsefully, "I'm supposed to open my heart completely to you with no direction for it?"

She finds his words to be like daylight to a vampire after searching her inner self. However, she makes no further comment and directs her attention to his nipples.

"It's ready now," Jason recites.

"What's ready?"

Crystin is so lost in reminiscing about how she used to please him, she hasn't noticed his hardened member.

"So, you are," she says, "just remember who got you there and who will get you off. Of course, you won't enjoy this as much as you have in the past."

"I think that's going to be you."

"How so?"

"It seems your plan for vengeance has aided you in forgetting the feeling of my arms around you. You're the one who will miss the strong embrace they provide and how comforting you used to tell me it was. Unless, that's something you've forgotten."

"I still remember, but I don't need your embrace to do what I need to do."

"You need to have my arms tenderly holding you, gently caressing your skin. I want to hold you like that. If I'm to be forced to a climactic state, hell, I might as well enjoy it myself."

Crystin is surprised that Jason has turned so quickly; for that matter, she didn't expect him to roll over to her side at all. She wonders if their naked tops swimming against each other is rekindling the flame in him as it has in her. Deep down she wishes for their past times to be current times, and the current times to manifest into future times. She searches her soul and realizes that her anger toward him is derived from a love for him. A love rejected by him, but one alive with vigor. She wonders if there is a remote chance that his words contain truth.

"Kiss me," Jason states.

During the entire time of working him to an erection, the desire to let their lips unite calls her like the scent of an animal in heat, willing her into the dangers of the flesh.

"Kiss me," invades her ears again.

This time his words explode within her, controlling the very thing she doesn't want controlled...her will. She leans forward, places her lips against his, looks into his eyes and sees everything her aching heart yearns for.

She presses harder against his lips, forces her tongue into his mouth as if it will provide more life-force to her being. Crystin closes her eyes, savors their closeness and welcomes the danger of untying his arms. Jason responds favorably to her eagerness while he reminds himself that he is playing thespian. The quirkiness of his personality runs thoughts of the perks of his occupation through his mind.

Crystin removes her remaining clothes and manages to get Jason's pants down to his tied ankles. She straddles him, lowers onto him, gasping as he fills her.

"I've missed this so much," Crystin confesses.

She lowers her breasts onto Jason's nakedness, pressing them firmly against his hairy chest.

Jason whispers, "It feels good to be inside of you once again. I…" He pauses to let Crystin's eyes catch his. "…need to touch you."

Crystin raises her upper body from his, gazes down at him with an emotion that displays passion, confusion and a distorted judgment that flings her into not only remembering the past, but living in her past. Her hand slowly creeps to the silky tie.

Sly tilts his head to the side away from the camera's viewfinder. "What are you doing?" he questions.

As if his question defies her authority, she swings the arm with the gun toward him hostilely. Sly's eyes widen, but he remains still.

"I want to be with you," Jason states with as much emotion as possible, using the window of opportunity to his advantage.

"Woman, can't you see that he is playing with your emotions?" Sly yells bewilderingly.

"All I see is you interfering with matters of the heart."

"Wake up, woman!" Sly yells. "Before you take all of us down."

"No!" she snaps. "He is serious about us this time. I know it!"

By this time, Crystin has released one of Jason's hands, thereby, accelerating Sly's anxiety.

"I never told him how badly I wanted us. That was my mistake…my fault, but now he knows and has opened his heart to me again. This is my last chance to cure the dreadful pain that poisons me. I will not," she emphasizes, "let it slip away."

Jason unexpectedly seizes Crystin's wrist that's holding the gun. He lowers her hand and positions the barrel against his heart.

"I'm willing to die for us," Jason states with a tone that matches the caring expression decorating his face. "Pull the trigger now, if you believe my words are deceitful."

Crystin snatches the weapon away, cradles it near her heart before stating, "I won't do it; I know that you love me."

"Crystin!" Sly yells while pouncing toward her.

Crystin's arm swings around with the swiftness of an adrenaline-added will. The gun fires, and the blast connects with Sly's chest, sending him flying backward to a seated position. Both Jason and Crystin watch his body slowly topple to its side…lifeless.

"I didn't mean," she cries while tossing the gun to the floor. "It just went off, honest," she explains defensively. "I only wanted to scare him."

"Untie my other hand so we can get him to the hospital," Jason suggests.

Crystin follows his instructions. She removes herself from Jason's manhood and sits on the side of the bed with her face enclosed in her hands. After releasing the restraints from his ankles, Jason pulls his pants up, buttons his shirt before checking Sly's neck for a pulse. Not even a faint whisper is felt.

"I truly didn't mean it," Crystin weeps.

"I saw what happened. We'll work this out."

As if a second personality emerges, Crystin's tone and attitude switches to another demeanor.

"Oh honey, I know that we will," she states while kissing him all over the face. "I've missed you so badly. I love you, I love you, I love you."

"I love you, too," Jason states without really thinking about what he is saying. Sly's lifeless body brings caution to his words. "But, we're not out of the woods yet. This guy obviously is not the one that's been hurting and killing people. The one I'm looking for will have to be physically more frightening."

Jason cuts his words short after realizing that the vehicle has stopped.

"Sly?" Dakota announces from the rear of the vehicle. "What's going on in there?"

Jason picks the gun up from the cabin floor, checks the revolver and finds it strange that the only bullet the revolver contained was the fatal one. He tosses it back to the cabin's floor.

"You stay here until it is safe," Jason states.

"Please be careful, honey."

Jason opens the left door slowly. When no one is in his initial line of sight, he pushes open the door completely with more force. From his vantage point, he is unaware of who is calling Sly; then the monster of a man steps into view standing a few yards away from the vehicle.

Jason scans him for a few seconds, and then states with assurance, "So, you're the one called Dakota."

Dakota is a tall muscular burly man with a baritone voice as intimidating as his physical being.

"I am and you're Detective Jerrard. Now, that the formalities are out of the way, what now?"

"You're under arrest for…"

Dakota's laughter swims over Jason's words like a heavy wind, erasing their substance from the air.

"You should not find prison so amusing."

"Little man, what planet are you from?"

"Xavier…third moon of Jupiter."

Jason's quick response, delivered in a serious manner, throws Dakota off to where he nearly didn't finish his sentence.

"Sly is obviously injured or dead. The girls will be too frightened to talk, so that leaves you against me, mano y mano."

Jason assesses the situation. Without further study, he deduces that Dakota's overpowering stature is able to inflict the damage Alfredo suffered.

"Yes, this may be true. But, my advantage is, you don't know what you are."

"I am three times the man you are. I'm much stronger and relentless with the kill."

"Like I said and your words alone, justify my thoughts. You simply don't know what you are."

Dakota is both amused and mystified by Jason's arrogance.

"You seem to think that you know me better than I know myself. What am I?"

"Overconfident," Jason snaps crisp and clear.

"Bring it on, punk."

Out of the infinite possibilities of how to confront Dakota's massive being, Jason thinks only of the tale of David and Goliath, and he knows which one he is. However, his version of the Biblical tale sends his thoughts to many years ago when he gains the upper hand while being ambushed by three thugs. This however, is not in his teenage years; in retrospect, the whole idea amazes him to think that twenty-five plus years later that he can successfully execute that stunt again.

Jason's heart tells him to think of other means to take down his adversary, but his mind has already calculated the distance between them. Just like the old days, he has enough room to run and get into the air. His feet began their pace.

Not now, he tells himself. *A little closer…now!* he thinks as his legs spring him from the ground. Just like the old days, he soars through the air in a brilliant flying knife kick. His right leg is tucked under his body with his left leg straight as an arrow. His forward foot is tilted to the side, executing a perfect blade. But, his age has taken its toll; his leg muscles pain him to remain straight and his toes cramp while his foot shapes the simulated knife blade. Dakota sidesteps out of Jason's flight path and snatches him from the air like he's a piece of paper floating aimlessly. His massive right arm seizes Jason around the upper body. Jason's momentum forces a dance. Their romantic lovers' waltz grants Dakota the chance to complete a bear hug with his left arm. They twirl a few times and cover a span of about six feet with Jason suspended in the air. In a matter of seconds after Dakota's feet stop moving, Jason feels the hydraulic pressure of Dakota's steel-like arms forcing his precious air from his lungs.

Dakota contracts his arms in a short, painful, air-freeing, unyielding way that provides no relief between squeezes. Jason's head falls back, and his mouth releases a violent roar as his internal bones begin feeling as though they are breaking from their cartilage. Panic strikes him. The plan that his mind conceives from years past is a futile attempt against a worthy opponent. The situation is different but it's the same. Jason knows his life hangs in the balance of the next few seconds. Oddly, a picture of Sasha appears in his mind, followed by Monique's smiling portrait. Uncommon with the theme of two beautiful women is an image of an unknown teenage boy with bloody eyes. He has always heard that in near-death situations, one's life passes before them, but never has the tale been told where the images are the means for continued survival.

It all comes back to him—the daring, damaging part of why he flew through the air. Jason rolls his head forward, steels himself against the incredible pain that all but destroys him. He catches Dakota's facial expression. It is intense, his eyes are closed and his face is deformed as if distorting it provides him additional strength. Jason's hands rise above his head, arms spread wide like seeking heaven's blessing. Suddenly, with his remaining breath and dying strength, his arms arch with cupped hands. They swiftly cut through the air and land soundly against Dakota's ears. Dakota's knees wobble, his grip loosens but doesn't break. Jason repeats the maneuver, this time Dakota's grasp releases completely as they tumble to the pavement.

Jason snaps out of it and brings his thoughts back to the present. Not only is the harmful vision he quickly experiences a real possibility, it is too close to reality as he reflects on the fatality of the other victims, and Alfredo's condition. He acknowledges that he has attempted some foolish things in his life, but oddly, his premonition strikes him as stupid. Somewhere, in the tangled cobweb of how to confront this particular foe, he consciously reflects that while executing a flying sidekick, his top leg isn't fully extended until just before impact to be the most effective. "Plan B" flashes through his mind as means to restrain the fear that wants to consume him.

Jason's sight ventures beyond Dakota, plants itself on Crystin who is sneaking up behind him. Somehow, Dakota senses something astray and turns just as she is about to hit him on the back of the head with the empty pistol. He catches her downward thrust in one of his massive hands. In a quick movement, he swings her around to a position with one of his biceps clutched around her throat.

"What the fuck are you doing?" Dakota asks. Before she responds, he continues, "You're supposed to be on my side."

"I can't let you harm him," Crystin blurts.

"It seems to me, you need to reevaluate your allies."

"She is not a part of this," Jason states as he slowly walks toward him.

"She is now. The moment she tried to steal me, she became my enemy. So, what are you going to do?"

"As I said, she is not part of my beef with you. The one that's important to me has already been harmed by you."

"So, you know what I'm capable of and you still challenge me?"

"Jason!" Crystin shouts, "What are you saying?"

"I'm simply stating that there is no need to hurt you to get back at me. The damage has already been done."

"That is not what you meant," Crystin states emotionally. Her eyes swell with tears. "You said that I'm not important to you. What about all you said just a few moments ago?"

"Damn it, Crystin!" Jason shouts out of frustration, "just zip it for a minute. Now is not the time."

"You're yelling at me." She cries as tears fall from her eyes.

"This really is touching but neither of you are reacting rationally. I'm your trouble," Dakota states.

"You're nothing more than a mild nuisance," Jason confidently says. "More like a speed bump in the middle of the road."

"You have a lot of balls for a person who is about to be broken."

"I said, don't harm him," Crystin defends.

She stamps one of her feet on top of his foot, but not nearly forceful enough to cause anything more than a mild discomfort.

"I'll deal with you later," Dakota states before unleashing a powerful blow on the side of her face.

Crystin's body falls limp into his grasp. He releases her to fall heavily onto the pavement. Jason's eyes twitch as her body sounds on impact.

"Are you going to make a move or are you just going to stare off into space like you did last time?"

"I'm going to arrest you, then see how you hold up in prison."

"Little man," Dakota bellows with his deep voice, "I will not go back to the dorm."

"That is cute…referring to prison in such a nice way."

Jason starts circling him; Dakota follows. The yin and yang feed off each other until Jason is comfortable with making the first move. He flinches at Dakota; instantly a left hook flies toward him. Jason leans back in the fashion of a boxer out of harm's way. He begins the chuck-wagon move again. He flinches at Dakota and moves away once again just in time to avoid bodily harm.

"So, you're going to play this cat and mouse game?" Dakota says in frustration.

"Not exactly. Let me enlighten you. First I'm going to charge you with a jab, followed by an uppercut, then another jab. After the jab weakens you, I'll take you down with a final blow on the chin."

"Sounds like a plan, bring it on."

Jason's motive is to get Dakota's timing down. Therefore, he flinches at Dakota for the third time and surmises that Dakota has a fair amount of quickness for a man as burly as he is. Jason shuffles his feet before starting the circle in the opposite direction. He flinches at Dakota, and another blazing blow flies in his direction. Jason leans back from its path as he has before, but Dakota has a plan of his own. Dakota's mouth salivates as he executes his move and takes the moment to step forward as Jason leans back and unleashes an uppercut to Jason's midsection. The powerful fist knocks the wind out of him, sending him tumbling back to the pavement gasping for air.

"Is that all you got?" Dakota boasts. "Surely a man as nimble as you can be more of a challenge."

Jason wants to voice the obscenities that are flowing through his mind, but he is unable to do that and regain his air simultaneously. He instead lies curled in a knot until most of his breath is regained. For the first time in Jason's recollection, a deep fear consumes him. The massive beast he confronts is cunning and above all confident in his abilities. His internal being screams, not only from the pain, but the thought that he's being beaten and outwitted agonizes him more.

He yells loudly, "Aargh!"

He takes a deep breath, thinks *peace*, as in remembering what he should do. His inner self calms; the fear that contaminates him dissipates as if it never existed.

Jason turns over to his knees, rests on all fours and slowly turns his head toward Dakota with a glance that indicates not again.

"What?" Dakota asks. "You're not giving up after one little punch."

"Concede to you," Jason says confidently. "I can't punk-up like that. I underestimated you once; that will not happen again," he announces while springing to his feet.

The area where Dakota's fist connected with his body not only pains him, it feels as though it is on fire under the skin. He unknowingly rubs the spot and his actions produce a comment from Dakota.

"Want more?" he states as he glances at Jason's hand still caressing the area of pain.

"Plan 'C,'" Jason replies.

"You can go through the entire alphabet and you still will not have a plan capable of defeating me," Dakota boasts.

Jason shakes his arms loosely at his side, rolls his neck around in a circle and sighs with frustration. He moves toward Dakota and flinches. Dakota swings and misses as he has three of the four previous times. As if Jason is a one-move boxer, he flinches inside of Dakota's dangerous punch again. This time as Dakota's fist starts toward him, he sidesteps to the left, times a grabbing move and catches Dakota's wrist as it crosses in front of him.

Jason yanks his arm forcefully, combines his effort with the momentum of Dakota's homerun punch causing Dakota to stumble forward. Jason unleashes a left-cross to the unbalanced Dakota that connects solidly on his chin. Dakota awkwardly stumbles forward but miraculously manages to keep from hitting the pavement.

"Not bad for a little man," Dakota confesses. "But, it's not good enough."

"Thanks for the props," Jason boasts with added confidence. "But that's just the beginning."

"Actually, it's the end for you."

For the first time Dakota makes an aggressive move toward Jason. He fronts him and charges like a raging bull.

"Break down," Jason states while bracing himself for Dakota's assault.

Before the words register in Dakota's mind, Jason switches to his side, cross-steps, and lifts his leg as the beginning of a martial arts move. Dakota's defense system raises his arms above his waist to protect his head and chest. His charge is constant, moving forward to inflict his deadly intentions. His protection against Jason's swiftness is perfect except for the fact that the height of Jason's leg is a deception.

Jason's goal is to connect and kick through his intended target. His kick attaches itself onto Dakota's knee, well below Dakota's raised arms. Dakota screams violently as his knee buckles, cracks and shatters into many pieces under the force of Jason's maneuver. As Jason expects, Dakota grabs his knee with both hands and bends over holding it with all his strength as if it will miraculously mend back the pieces. Jason clasps his hands together, connects a double-fisted backhand on the top of his head causing Dakota to crash to the ground.

"Now," Jason states, overflowing with self-pride. "Are you going to cooperate or do I need be more forceful to completely tame you?"

Dakota doesn't reply immediately; he simply gazes at Jason with distress.

"Shoot me," he replies with a look far too serious for Jason's likings.

"I'm sorry, my friend, you're not a maimed animal. Besides, that's not part of the plan. Killing you is giving you the easy way out. Prison, now that's the ticket."

"You don't understand…I can't exist knowing that a little man like you beat me. I may as well be dead."

Jason doesn't show it externally, but he is smiling to himself inside. He has conquered a fear once again and he is feeling damn proud of it.

"As you sit in your prison cell," Jason replies calmly, "this moment will eventually fade away."

Dakota's gaze matches the previous one with the exception of his obvious pain.

"Once I get you and Mrs. Mayor into the vehicle, I'll get you proper medical attention."

Jason manages to get Crystin's body in the front of the vehicle with more than a minimal struggle. Her dead weight tests every ounce of his remaining strength. Jason rolls Dakota onto his stomach and reads him his rights. He grabs and twists both arms behind him, removes his tie and uses it as a makeshift pair of handcuffs. He helps Dakota to his feet and hobbles on one leg to the back of the vehicle. Jason wishes that he had a locking mechanism for the rear door, but ultimately decides that Dakota is in no condition to make an escape attempt. When he enters the driver's cabin, Crystin remains unconscious. Suddenly, he remembers that Sharon was sent to the front and doesn't recall seeing her when Crystin was placed in the front. Oddly, *it is of no consequence*, flashes through his mind.

TWENTY THREE

Jason drives to the morgue, leaves Sly's body in capable hands and calls for a squad car to meet him at the hospital. He gives advance notice that the Mayor's wife is in tow and unconscious. When he arrives at the hospital, Captain North is waiting for him as part of the support team. To the best of his ability, Jason explains to his superior that the situation didn't go exactly as planned. He attempts to put a positive spin on his explanation, but his Captain is fed up. Captain North cuts his words off as if they never filled the air.

"Our plan, the one we discussed," Captain North yells, "was a well-designed one that I'm positive would have prevented anyone harm! Now, you're telling me that you modified the plan which led to the Mayor's wife being fucking unconscious and there is a dead body in the morgue!"

Jason tries to explain Crystin's involvement in the incident, but his Captain's hand raises.

"Talk to the hand, because my ears aren't listening. Is that hip enough for you? You, Mr. Jerrard are on administrative leave until this matter can be resolved."

"What!"

"Surely you can't be surprised. Your leave is effective immediately. Right after a full report of this bizarre incident is on my desk."

Jason wants to challenge his orders, but the part of him that makes him responsible for his own actions controls his words. Therefore, he says that he'll go to the station to start the report. Captain North snaps a glance toward him that reads, "You'd better."

The part that bothers Jason the most is that the glance also contains overtones of disappointment. Jason shrugs his shoulders as if saying, "sorry." Under normal circumstances, he'd have one of the squad cars take him back to his vehicle, but this time, he simply waits for a taxi to arrive. He hopes that the solitude will provide ample time to reflect on the forced absence upon him again.

Jason feels as though he needs to take inventory of himself and examine the things that make him defy his superiors. He runs a multitude of questions through his mind and responds to each with not so much of an answer, but with his feelings of each question. At the end, he feels pretty good about himself to include his most recent actions. Once he realizes that his regrets are minimal, his being calms and returns to the part of him that defines who he is. Somewhere, intertwined in all of his self-justification he makes a decision to protest his superior's punishment by writing a detailed letter stating his objection to it.

The more he thinks about it, the angrier he gets. He isn't denying the fact that he failed to follow orders, but he knows that he can't be responsible for the death that occurred.

Jason thinks, "That's right."

His words do more than just enter his mind; they echo through the air loud enough to employ a response from the driver. Jason exits the taxi, retrieves his car and heads to the precinct. He jogs into the station as if his business is more urgent than it really is.

He sits at his desk and poises his fingers hovering over the computer keyboard while evaluating how to begin his report. His keystrokes begin slowly, easily, with no sense of rhythm. Steadily, he quickens the pace until his delicate touch finds their song. When he maneuvers the mouse to save his document, it is then that he realizes that he lost himself while creating the report and doesn't consciously recall the process. As the sound of the printer spitting out the first page reaches his ears, he hopes that his letter disputing Captain North's suspension will flow equally as well. He closes his eyes and begins to type. Moments later, in similar fashion as the previous reports, he finishes the letter to his superior. He reads it to himself and is pleased that it contains a certain amount of emotion. He believes that his letter has enough sentiment in which to convey to his Captain the seriousness of the matter.

Jason puts the document in a letter-sized envelope, places it and the report in a larger envelope, seals it and slides it under the Captain's door.

The next day, Jason anticipates a call from Captain North to discuss not only the report, but its accompanying letter. He waits at home, expecting the call to come, but, by the evening hours the call isn't received.

Monique enters her new home around dinnertime carrying a few boxes. Jason removes the boxes from her care, places them on the floor and embraces her without uttering a word.

"Hello, dear, I'm pleased to see you, too," she states before kissing him on the neck while in his embrace.

"I see that you've been busy…work and then more work," Jason replies as he tilts his head toward the boxes on the floor.

"I'm trying to move the lighter boxes that we packed, but there are a few heavier boxes that require a man's strength. Also, the furniture that is not coming here needs to be placed in storage. I guess now that you have some time, you can arrange this for me."

"I'll start on it tomorrow."

The telephone rings; Monique instinctively answers it. After a short moment, she passes the telephone to Jason. Jason's conversation is brief. He hangs up with a somber look occupying his face.

"What's wrong?" Monique questions.

"My apologies, it seems that we'll have to postpone our dinner plans. That was Captain North. He needs to see me right away. I told you that my letter would raise some controversy."

"He appeared startled when I answered your phone. There was a brief pause before he asked for you."

"He'll get over it."

"I'm sure, but when you return, talk to me. Please don't be evasive as you were last night. Your troubles are my troubles as mine are to you."

Jason nods in agreement.

After Jason's talk with his superior, he heads to his desk in dismay. He is informed that the matter has been turned over to Internal Investigations, therefore, he'll have to remain on administrative leave until the process is completed. He is also advised that I.I. would be responding officially to his letter.

He struggles with the reasoning behind the Captain's impassive attitude with the situation. Jason tries to recall a time when his superior had been so impersonal to the actions of or actions taken against one of his subordinates.

"The cup runneth over," he announces as he sits down at his desk.

Jason begins digesting his life as a law officer, remembering that he has always wanted to be a policeman. He isn't sure whether or not this moment of recollection is a parade, a pity party or simply well past the time to reflect on his career. But, he positively knows that in cases like this, his only recourse is to submit and let his mind take him where it deems necessary. As in amusing himself with his own private joke, he thinks that the only thing missing is the sound of the waves.

He clasps his hands behind his head, props his feet on the desk and simply thinks. He immerses himself in his thoughts and loses all touch with reality. When his consciousness returns to him, he has no knowledge of how long he was under the self-induced trance. Based on the tingly feeling in his legs, he ascertains that it has been some time. He gingerly stands, fighting off the pincushion feeling as the blood returns to his feet. Jason removes the recyclable paper from a box next to his desk, stacks the papers on the desk neatly and begins placing his personal belongings into the empty box. He pays extra attention to the picture of Monique. He stares at it for a small moment before running his fingers slowly down the glass as if he is tenderly stroking her face. The clock boasting nearly two in the morning is not enough to prevent the smile from illuminating across his face as he reaches for the telephone. After the call, he fires up a web browser, downloads, prints and completes a form before placing it in yet another envelope to take with him.

At home, Jason quickly prepares a cup of jasmine tea for his sleeping Monique. He places the cup and saucer on the night table next to the bed and kisses her on the neck several times before she acknowledges his presence. A smile appears on her face.

"If you keep that up, you'll be in trouble. I'd hate to break your celibate rule," Monique jokingly conveys.

"We couldn't have that." Jason smiles.

"Is that for you or me?" Monique asks after the tea's aroma touches her senses.

"It's your favorite."

"Okay, I'll bite. What's going on?"

"Nothing really."

"Tell me the 'really' part; that should be interesting," Monique states wryly.

She sits up against the headboard, holds the sheet over her breasts with one hand and reaches for the tea with the other.

"Why cover yourself?" Jason teases.

"Less temptation for you this way, don't you think?"

"Nothing can be more tempting than sleeping nude with you every night."

"I stand corrected."

"Actually, you're sitting."

"Jason," Monique replies after a sip of tea, "your corny humor isn't going to help you evade the subject. Tell me, how did things go the other night?"

"I survived."

"Obviously," Monique glares.

"It didn't go exactly as planned."

"Things never do...unless..." She pauses. "...you're the one who changes things."

"Sort of like that."

Monique sees the discomfort Jason is experiencing talking about the incident, but decides not to give him a break.

"Gather your thoughts; I'll wait."

"In short, I'm on administrative leave."

"Not again!"

Monique immediately knows the seriousness of the matter by simply studying Jason's expression. She puts her tea back on the night table, places her arms around him and gives him a firm tender hug. Jason grimaces under her embrace.

"Oh God, you're hurt!"

"My ribs are still sore from the fight last night," Jason confesses.

Monique tears open his shirt to view the injury. Under the dim lighting she can see a bruise in the rib area.

"Why haven't you told me about this before now and why haven't you sought medical attention?"

"Honestly, I'm fine. Bruises heal. I'm more upset that Captain North didn't bother to entertain my explanation."

"Seriously, Jason, can you blame him?"

"Well..."

"Well, you should have known something like this would happen because of your past antics. Do you now regret what you did?"

"You want the truth?"

"No, instead tell me the story about the third moon of Jupiter."

Jason smiles initially with Monique's candor, but her facial expression thrusts him back to the seriousness of her sarcasm. He elects not to include the Mayor's wife in his explanation, however, he continues with the remaining truth.

"I'd be lying if I said that I regretted my actions because they yielded the result that I wanted to achieve."

"Your results were?"

"I was able to confront and arrest Alfredo's attacker. Other than a few minor flaws, things went well."

"These so-called flaws...are they the cause for your suspension? Administrative leave, as you put it."

"That would be a correct assumption."

"So, what are you going to do?"

"I've done all that I can. Now, I have to wait to see the outcome of Internal Investigations."

"The more that I think I know you, the more you surprise me."

"Call it a character flaw."

"Your character, as strong-willed as it may be, will possibly end your police career prematurely. I'm not preaching to the choir but sometimes hearing things from another source helps."

TWENTY FOUR

Monique's eyebrows rise upon hearing the doorbell.

"There is no way," Monique states, "that anyone would disturb us at this hour."

"There is a way," Jason concedes.

"If you're expecting company this late, it must be someone to help you sort out the mess you're in no doubt."

"One of them," Jason implies without providing a meaning. "I'll be right back."

Jason greets Kevin Austin at the door. He carries two large bags containing the items that Jason requested while at the station.

"I don't believe," Kevin states, "that this is so important that you'd wake me in the middle of the night. If I didn't owe you, I would have truly told you where to go. We should be even after this."

"Yes we will be."

Jason peers through the opening of the bags placed at his feet, picks up the one intended for Monique and tells Kevin that he can change in the hall bathroom. When he enters the bedroom, Monique is finishing tying the knot on her robe to meet Jason and the late visitor.

"Good, you're up. Please put this on," he states while passing the bag to her.

"This what?"

"Look and see."

Monique places the bag on the bed. Reaching into it blindly, the first item that her hand catches is a veil, ivory in color. Her head turns to Jason, puzzlement displaying on her face.

Jason tilts his head to the side as in a "continue" gesture. Like pulling a rabbit out of a magician's hat, she produces a dress of matching color. She holds it out in front of her by the shoulders and crosses her hands to view both sides. She is surprised that the dress is actually a reasonable facsimile of a designer wedding dress. Non-traditional in nature, its length is short, a minuscule longer than a mini-skirt, very hip-hugging with a sheer fabric covering the low-cut cleavage area. Her facial expression turns to one of concern. Jason ignores it nonetheless.

"I hope it fits," Jason states.

Monique glances into the bottom of the bag. The completing shoes and hat that the veil attaches to remain alone in the bag.

"Jason, what is this?"

"What does it look like?"

"I know what it is but why it's here, now at this very moment, is what I don't understand."

"Will you marry me?"

"Tonight?" she questions with a racing heart. "Now?"

"Yes and yes. That's the idea. Of course, we'll have an official ceremony for family and friends at a later date."

"You're serious?"

"Let's call it a Las Vegas style wedding without the Vegas frills."

Monique shakes her head from side to side, holds the dress against her being, then sits on the bed with it folded in half on her lap.

"So, will you marry me tonight?"

"Yes, love, I'll marry you anytime, as many times as it takes."

She grabs the veil, the bag, and heads to the bathroom to change. Jason leaves to retrieve and put on his clothes. A short moment later, Jason stands with Kevin at a makeshift altar in the living room waiting for Monique to make her grand entrance.

"Is that anxiety I'm detecting?" Kevin asks.

"You know, I do have a small case of the butterflies."

"Surely, not you."

Jason replies to Kevin's statement with a simple smile.

"So, this may not be the right time to ask but, why all of this now?"

Jason reasons that this is the perfect occasion to mess with Kevin's head, and then an identical smile appears on his face, but more devilish in nature.

"I'm horny," Jason states as if the news would not be shocking to Kevin.

"What? You mean, after all of this time, you two haven't…"

Monique steps around the corner preventing Jason's answer. Both of their heads turn to greet her. Jason's eyes widen with excitement upon seeing her. He glances at Kevin who unknowingly has his mouth open in awe.

"You look lovely," Jason announces. "No, more like angelic."

"I'd have to agree," Kevin concurs.

"Thanks both of you, but isn't this a wee bit short?"

"It's perfect," Jason comments positively.

In actuality, Jason has chosen the perfect size and dress for Monique's physique. The liquid vinyl that she once wore will not fit better. The dress accentuates every curve she possesses, highlights her legs, breasts and butt to the point where Jason is fighting hard to keep from drooling.

"Please don't stare like that; you're making me nervous."

"Sorry," Jason replies while giving Kevin a quick elbow into the side. "Angel, you have nothing to be self-conscious about."

With that comment, Monique feels peace. It is also at that moment she recognizes Kevin dressed as a Baptist minister. Kevin nods when their eyes meet. She mentally notes how handsome her man appears in his black European-styled tuxedo. As she nears them, they separate to reveal a podium with a large wooden cross on it. There are two candleholders approximately six feet in height burning candles that radiate the fragrance of lavender.

"The only things that are missing are flowers and someone playing a harp," Monique states as means to dismiss her nervous energy.

"Are you ready?" questions Jason.

Monique exhales heavily. "We could be getting married in a sewer and I'd still be ready for you."

"Okay then, let's begin, but first, for authenticity, please sign your name to our marriage license."

Monique follows Kevin's hand signal, signs the document located on the podium, and returns to her place next to Jason. Kevin steps behind the podium and places both hands on each side but he is interrupted by Jason's fingers snapping.

"Kevin, allow me a moment, please." Jason moves Monique a few paces away from the podium. "I'd like our vows to be spoken from the heart."

Monique's head is lowered. She speaks softy as to keep her conversation private.

"My dearest Jason, I have nothing prepared, therefore, speaking from my heart is my only recourse."

"I know. I just wanted to capture this small moment one last time before you become a Mrs."

"You silly man."

"Shall we?"

"We shall."

They return to the podium, and face Kevin as he recites his prepared words.

"Tonight, two souls become one, existing from the very substance that defines each. Two hearts beat as one, synchronized to the very depths of their joint rhythm. Two people, one love...destined to be all that time could not deny. Blessed with the sanction of God." Kevin pauses, looks at Monique, then Jason. "Now, it's time for you two to exchange vows."

Monique and Jason face each other. Jason motions for Monique to speak first. He holds his hands out, and Monique's hands automatically fall into his. She gazes into his eyes unsure of her exact words, but then Jason smiles and the simple gesture slowly ignites her words.

"This day I promise, life with me will be a journey toward a common goal of love and happiness. I can't promise you all good times, nor can I promise a bed of roses. What I can promise is that you'll have my lifelong desire to enhance your happiness with my undying love. I will do everything in my power to let it grow and expand one-thousand-fold beyond today. This I know because kissing you is as thrilling as our first kiss at the skating rink. I knew then, I know even more now that we were destined to be..."

"Soulmates," Jason whispers, interrupting her mid-sentence.

"Yes, soulmates. Just as you're able to read my thoughts, I do the same with you. Today and all of my tomorrows belong to you, forever."

Jason smiles, brings her closer to wipe the tear draining from her eye. He places his hand gently on the side of her face and the other hand around her waist.

"Monique, ever since God blessed me with my personal angel, I've felt protected in a strange way. The time, the distance, nor separation, changed the way I feel about you. I've had this moment embedded into my being from the very first time I saw you. Your smile, as it was, and as it remains is still angelic. It has moved me, captured me, and continues to possess me. Months ago when we met at Rosalina's, my love for Sasha was strong. Somehow, I thought seeing you magnified the feelings in me and justified everything I felt for her. I came to learn later that this emotional episode I internally struggled with was truly the beginning of an awakening, my personal giant. Godzilla to the rescue. Meaning, I struggled to stay focused on Sasha, desperately tried not to let the emotions I had in stasis overshadow it. Today, I promise you a love with no boundaries, a love that redefines the definition of the word itself. My heart, my soul, my everlasting life is yours...forever."

Jason removes the hand from her face, turns toward the priest and nods.

"Both of you speak so beautifully," Kevin recites. "Now, by the power invested in me, I now pronounce you husband and wife. You may kiss the bride."

Instead of Jason lifting the veil, he removes and places the hat backwards on her head and then engages in a passionate kiss for a few seconds.

"Congratulations," Kevin states after the kiss ends and walks away.

"So, Mr. Jerrard, when did you decide to do all of this?"

"It's just a small part of my personality. Just think about it; I'm very spontaneous."

"You really want to marry me?"

"Correction, I've already married you. Let's call it our learner's permit. Our driver's license..."

"Legal marriage," Monique interjects.

"Yes, will happen in the near future."

"As I've stated, every time I think I know you, you do something new to surprise me."

"That's me."

"So tell me, Mr. Spontaneity, do you have a honeymoon planned?"

"That will be a joint decision as well as our second wedding. All I ask is that it be real soon."

Monique knows that planning a wedding sometimes takes weeks to get all of the pieces in place. However, she nods knowing that if there is a will, she and Jason will find a way.

"I'm done here," Kevin states, relieved of his costume. "I'll leave you newlyweds alone. Just bag up everything for me and I'll get it from you another day."

"Sounds like a plan…be careful going home, it's late. Or early, depending on which way you'd like to look at it."

"Thanks, you two kids don't do anything I wouldn't do."

As soon as the door closes, isolating Kevin to the outside, an awkward silence comes between them. It is as if they haven't thought of the undertones of Kevin's remark. Surprisingly, they gaze at each other, simultaneously thinking "Oh yeah." Once Monique realizes that Jason knows what she is thinking, she bashfully smiles, bowing her head innocently in shame.

"Don't give me that schoolgirl look. What's next, you rotating your shoulders from side to side?"

"So, do we accept this ceremony as ending our waiting period?"

Jason raises a brow, reaches behind his neck and unfastens his bowtie. He starts releasing the buttons on his shirt from the top.

"I'll take your actions as a positive reply to my question."

Jason remains silent, removes his vest before continuing with the remaining shirt buttons. Monique steps out of her shoes and turns to walk toward the bedroom. Suddenly, Jason seizes one of her arms, twirls her into his embrace and positions her with her back pressed against his chest. Jason kisses her politely on the neck. Her eyes widen, a smile flashes across her face as she feels the zipper of the dress slowly descend.

"This is serious." She sighs. "This time."

"Very much so."

"In that case, let me assist you."

"Silly me, I forgot about your aggressiveness."

"Little ol' me," she implies with a Southern belle accent.

Monique faces Jason, nibbles on his chest while she fondles his hardened member. Her shoulders draw back, allowing the dress to fall to the floor. Jason covers her eyes, assists her in stepping out of the garment while tasting her nipple through the bra. Monique instinctively releases his belt buckle, lowers his zipper and traces the curves of his frame from the waist to the ankles while simultaneously lowering his pants. While in the squatting position, she runs her tongue down the shaft of his penis. Jason clears his throat loudly to draw her attention, steps out of his pants and helps her to a standing position. He holds her tenderly.

"Here we go again," Jason states.

"Yes, this place seems familiar."

"Very."

"No turning back," she states intoxicated by his embrace.

"Not this time."

They separate briefly while they hurriedly remove their remaining clothes. Their next embrace is hard, animal-like, devouring each others bodies as if it's a kill. Neither knows how or when it happened, but amazingly they find themselves humping one another madly on the carpet. Monique cries out in a manner that demands no more waiting. It controls Jason; compliance is his recourse. He enters her with a long, slow penetrating thrust that causes Monique to gasp as he fills her. Monique quickly melts on Jason's frame as if a torch is being applied to plastic. Monique's hot juices break down Jason's steel, almost decomposing it from within.

The words "Oh God" enter his ear translating them into a pep rally for his hips. He begins pounding her body furiously with her bucking wildly against his rapid thrusts. Time seemingly advances to a period of five hours after her womanhood accepted him, but in reality, the forwarded moment translates into only five minutes from the time their hunger takes over, consuming them, helping them explode into and onto each other. They lie panting, sweating, somewhat exhausted with their brief marathon.

"I never thought our first true intimacy," Jason recites after catching his breath, "would be like this."

"What did you expect? You tortured us for weeks. Your initial penetration almost got me off."

"I'll let my performance tell you what you did to me."

"It had to be this way though."

"Maybe you're right, but know this. It ain't over."

TWENTY FIVE

L ate the following morning, the smell of bacon and the aroma of freshly brewed coffee stimulates Jason's senses. The pleasant odor opens his eyes. After a quick trip to the bathroom, Jason joins her in the kitchen.

"So, Mrs. Jerrard, you're an early riser."

"Not really, I couldn't lie there any longer without attacking you."

"Oh really, seems to me, you should have followed your first instinct."

"You were sleeping so peacefully. Last night when you said that it ain't over, I openly welcomed a round two. But, I never imagined that there would be a round three. You outdid yourself."

"I aim to please."

"That you did."

"One day, I'll prepare breakfast for you."

"You, that one who is terrified of the kitchen?"

"I can do breakfast. That's fairly simple but the full-course dinners are more complex and intimidating."

"Well, my husband, I'll teach you. In time you'll be a regular Chef Combo."

"I look forward to it. Wifey, I'm going to see Alfredo and I'd like you to accompany me."

"I'd be glad to. After last night, my mood to clean my apartment is less appealing."

"Honey, after I get the remaining boxes, I'll pay a cleaning service to do the cleanup for you."

"That's sweet but this is another shared expense."

"Agreed."

※※※

Jason and Monique walk into Alfredo's hospital room, wishing that his friend has taken a turn for the better. Based on the lip lock he and Delia are engaged in, something wonderful has happened. He thanks God as they walk to his bedside. Alfredo is embarrassed that Jason has caught him in such an intimate act. The look on Alfredo's face is very similar to the one he displayed when he first tried taking the Viagra.

Jason smiles. "Well, I see that you are feeling better."

"Much better, although my ribs are sore."

Jason didn't disclose that he has first-hand experience with the sore-ribs business.

"The doctor says," Alfredo comments, "that there are no internal injuries."

"That's wonderful news, my friend. Do you remember Monique?"

"Of course, how are you Madam? I apologize for my appearance."

"You have nothing to apologize for. You look well rested."

"Oh, this is Delia," Alfredo expresses excitedly.

"We've already met," Jason states. "Monique, Delia; Delia, Monique."

"You've met...so, what did I miss when I was out?"

Jason and Delia glance at each other. Jason nods, gesturing that all is okay. Obviously, he and she are on the same page because her return nod contains a sign of relief.

"Oh, nothing." Jason smiles.

Monique and Delia step away from the bed and engage in their own private conversation.

"When can you be released?" Jason asks.

"I'm told that I'll have to stay an additional night for observation."

"Great, when you're discharged, the four of us should have a celebration."

"That would be perfect, my good friend."

"Let's celebrate away from Rosalina's. We will find someplace neutral to the four of us."

"I'd," Alfredo glances at the two ladies conversing, "we'd love to."

Alfredo's voice lowers and a troubling expression captures his face. He removes his glance from Jason, gathers his thoughts, takes a deep breath and returns to Jason unsure how to proceed.

"There is something you should know about Delia," Alfredo relays with heartfelt words.

"I already know, my friend." Alfredo's eyes widen with shock. "I'm cool with it. Besides, she seems genuine and she adores the hell out of you."

"As I do her."

Alfredo glares at his friend thinking how wonderful it is to have Jason accept him and Delia as a couple. He smiles with understanding.

"Then we should move beyond this," Jason suggests.

Alfredo nods in concurrence. Somehow, Jason's words justify everything he's ever felt about their friendship, revealing to him that their friendship is strong and lifelong. Jason feels connected with what Alfredo is thinking and pats him on the shoulder with assurance.

"There is," Jason announces in a more excited tone, "something I'd like to ask you."

"Just ask, if it is in my power, consider it done."

"Will you be my best man?"

"You're getting married?" Alfredo announces energized. His words carry the girls, commanding them bedside. "Congratulations, I'd be honored to."

"Then it's settled. I'll let you know the date just as soon as I and the Mrs. decide on one. It will be in the near future though."

"But," Alfredo states confused with Jason's prefix for Monique.

"Let's just say that we had a make-believe ceremony last night. Our official one for family and friends is the one I'd like you to be part of."

Jason's pager sounds. The tone oddly startles the group as all eyes turn to him as he seeks the number.

"Captain North," he states while backing away.

After a short moment, Jason rejoins the group and apologizes for being the party pooper.

✳✳✳

At the station, Jason escorts Monique to his desk, makes sure that she is comfortable and then he ventures to see about the urgent business his Captain spoke of.

"Yes, Sir," Jason states as he knocks on the doorframe.

"Come in, Jason," his Captain replies without lifting his head. "Have a seat. Give me a second to finish my thought."

His Captain finishes writing a couple of sentences on a pad, raises his head and simply gazes at Jason in awe. Jason's shifting in his seat is a trigger for his Captain's words.

"Detective Jerrard, I really don't know where to start. On second thought, I do. I should jump across my desk, grab you from behind and perform the Heimlich maneuver on you."

Jason tilts his head to the side. "What purpose would that serve?"

"Maybe I'll be able to jar loose that horseshoe, rabbit's foot or whatever lucky charm you have stored up your ass."

"Captain, it's not like you to beat around the bush."

"No, it isn't. In short, there will be no investigation, well, not a formal one that is."

"I thought Internal Investigations wanted my ass hung."

"They do, but it's bigger than that. The intricate web you've woven is too complex to unravel without taking down others. The press will have the next O.J. media frenzy if they find out about the Mayor's wife's involvement."

"Politics rule again. But, you must believe my report; I had no prior knowledge of her being connected with the people I was after."

"You slept with her," the Captain states matter-of-factly.

"That's another matter and is not part of my investigation of the murders and beatings."

"You know, it really doesn't fucking matter. This thing is so messy; it's being squashed like a roach running for its life when the lights are turned on. However, as your Captain, I have to warn you that people are watching your every move."

Jason thinks, *that's nothing new*, without expressing it.

"Nevertheless, I'm instructed to reinstate you back to active duty immediately with a commendation for solving another case."

Jason sits unmoved as he watches his superior struggle with determining whether or not his spoken words are correct with his beliefs.

"Again, I seem to have put you in a tough spot."

"True, my emotions are mixed with what has been passed to me, but, it is not me that you've spooked. More like the Mayor and his entourage. You know shit flows downhill. Off the record, what is the true intent of your letter?"

"Honestly, nothing more than my protest to being on another leave of absence."

"News travels fast. Your letter left me to Internal Investigations, from there to the commissioner, from him up the ladder to the Mayor. I don't know this as a fact, but rumor has it that the undertones of your letter are press related."

"What?" Jason blurts in amazement. "You know that is not my style. I'm responsible for my own actions. I didn't like being on leave so I let you know…never did I think of taking it any further than writing you my letter."

"You understand that I had to include it with your report?"

"Yes."

"Well, it turns out that it served you well. Return to work tomorrow. This place can use a Superhero."

Jason smiles with the implication. He gazes at the ceiling for a few seconds, returns his eyes to his Captain, then begins his words.

"You know, all my life, I've never wanted to be anything but an officer of the law. It is this desire that aided me in getting out of the ghetto. This same desire was…is the driving force that drove me to becoming the top of my class at the police academy and becoming the unorthodox officer that you know. In hindsight, this desire, though good for my career, may have been partial blame for the downfall of my marriage with Julie. It definitely was an issue with Sasha." Jason takes a deep breath and continues. "You may be right."

"How so?"

"I may have a horseshoe stuck up my ass or maybe a Guardian Angel because I've been given a third chance to love, to share my life with a wonderful person. This time, I'm going to make her more important than my police work. Will this change keep me from being your top officer? Only time will tell, but, this is my vow to her. My vow to me is to live a little."

"Sounds serious."

"It is. That's why I'd like not to return to work tomorrow. I'm requesting a vacation. I have over sixty days on the books and I'd like to take three weeks of it to put the pieces of my wedding together."

"Wedding, it's very serious. Is she the lovely-sounding person who answered your telephone the other day?"

"Yes, she is sitting at my desk as we speak."

"She's here? Why didn't you tell me, I would not have kept you so long."

"It's fine. She knows what's going on."

"I'll grant your vacation only with two conditions. One, I get to meet this special person and two, I get an invite to your wedding."

Duh? Jason thinks. "Of course."

"In that case, go to your woman and start exercising your vow."

TWENTY SIX

Jason fulfills his promise of taking his soulmate to dinner. They return home for their chosen dessert selection, each other. Afterwards, Monique lies with her head on his chest comforted by the simple but alluring embrace. She holds her hand out in front of her, seemingly admiring a make-believe ring. Jason breaks her comfort, sits up and gazes into her eyes, somewhat caught between a thought and a hard place. Monique glares back, identifying his expression as one of concern.

"What is it, Jason?"

"I want you to have something, but first I need to know if you'd accept it."

"It, as in?"

"It's best if I show you."

Jason excuses himself, travels to the closet and returns with a medium-sized box. He rambles through its contents, finds and hands Monique a diamond solitaire, two-plus carats in size.

"What is this?"

"It's yours if you'd accept it."

"Why wouldn't I?"

"It belonged to Sasha."

Monique looks into his eyes. She sees the emotion they contain and recalls the knowledge of his relationship with Sasha.

"Jason," Monique says carefully, "if my memory serves me correctly, you once stated that it is the memory of Sasha who helped you love me."

"Something like that. As strange as it sounds, Sasha spoke to me some way, somehow. I received whispers from a troubled heart, my troubled heart and her spirit showed me all that I needed. She lifted the pain that I was feeling and released me to love you."

"With this in mind, I'd be honored to wear this symbol of your joint love. I don't want you to ever forget what she meant to you. I'm indebted to her, we both are."

At that moment, Jason realizes that this and more amazing times are in store for him. He takes the ring from her hand, places it on her finger, and politely kisses her on the lips, causing Monique to blush.

"Excuse me," she states in an excited state. "I could definitely get used to this."

For the next few moments, they coexist in silence. Monique lies curled in his embrace. They seemingly have blocked out the television playing in the background until the words "twenty-eight days for twenty-eight million" awaken their consciousness. They leave their solitude and pay attention to what the newscaster is saying. When the segment goes off, they shake their heads in awe.

"I know that the person who bought that ticket is feeling sick," Monique states.

"Probably not, Dear…it seems to me that if someone has twenty-eight days left to claim twenty-eight million dollars, then it stands to reason that this person either lost it or does not realize that he or she has the winning lottery ticket in their possession."

"That makes sense. I can see myself doing that. Sometimes I can't remember my words, much less remember to check a lotto ticket."

"Say that again."

"I'm saying that I often forget to check my ticket after a drawing."

"No, you said, remember my words."

"And?"

Jason doesn't respond. He basically stares through her, attempting to recall why those words are so familiar to him. Out of the blue, his subconscious mind blurts, "Sasha."

"What about her?"

"Who?" Jason states after snapping back to reality.

"You called Sasha's name."

"It is Sasha who said those words to me that night I proposed to you."

"What are you talking about?"

"It's a long story. Remember my words," Jason recites again as he sits on the side of the bed. "Remember my words. She must have been referring to her journals."

It is all clear to him, clearer than the brilliant VS-rated diamond Monique is wearing. His mind bounces to a bookmark located in one of her journals and he recalls himself thinking how strange that a lotto ticket would be used for such a purpose. Jason reaches into the box of Sasha's possessions and blindly begins removing the journals in search of what is calling him. He places each politely on the bed as if they are delicate glass.

On the fourth try, it feels right. It is right; a small block of paper is extending from its pages. Jason holds the journal up to Monique's eyes.

Without even looking, Jason states, "This is it."

"Jason, truly I'm lost," Monique confesses.

"That piece of paper," Jason states as his eyes focus on it, "is worth twenty-eight-million dollars."

"No way, things like that don't happen to ordinary people like us."

"Your statement is flawed. We are extraordinary people. Take it."

Monique finds what Jason is saying well beyond belief, yet somehow his conviction to his statement, the sentiment it carries, makes it all too real. She feels her heart racing as she plucks the paper from the pages.

"The prize amount is?"

Monique flips the ticket over, cuts her eyes from Jason to it, back to Jason. Suddenly her mouth is dry; she swallows before she speaks.

"Twenty-eight million," she states with a crackling voice.

Jason stands, smiles and walks into his home office. In a few seconds he is browsing through Virginia's Lottery page. Monique is too nervous to walk. Even sitting down she feels her knees shaking anticipating the outcome.

"Angel," Jason calls, "Come in here, please."

"Honey, I can't, just tell me."

Jason stands in the doorway. "Well, it appears that we have a new-found fortune."

Monique's mouth opens absent a sound. She gazes at Jason in disbelief, seemingly discarding his words. Jason allows Monique to gather her composure before sitting next to her. Immediately, her arms drape him in a strong, silent embrace.

"This is," Jason speaks calmly, "quite a turn of events considering my poor upbringing."

"Remember, I knew you back then; things weren't that bad for you."

"You're looking at it as an outsider because things weren't good at all. I remember one Christmas my mother wanted to get me something to wear and something to play with but money was tight, so she bought me a pair of pants and cut the pockets out."

Monique's face dives into confusion, followed by a smile and then a burst of laughter.

"That was silly."

"Silly enough to make you laugh."

"Here I thought that we were having a serious conversation, somehow, again you manage to add humor."

"We needed something to break the tension."

"It's strange; seems to me that we would be overjoyed with the money, but we are acting differently."

"Believe me...inside there is a fireworks display grander than the Fourth of July celebration at the Washington Monument. I guess the whole aura of how we became wealthy is mind-boggling."

"So..." She smiles. "What are you going to do with your free time?"

"I've always wanted to learn how to play golf."

AUTHOR BIO

Rique Johnson was born and raised in Portsmouth, Virginia. He joined the U.S. Army six months after high school because he believed that the world had much more to offer than his not-so-fabulous surroundings. After his brief stint as a soldier, he made his home in Northern Virginia where he has resided since 1981. He is married and has three children.

Rique has always had a passion for the arts. From his training as a commercial artist to his modeling days during the first half of the 1980s, he has always penciled something.

His imagination comes across in his novels as creative, bold and sometimes edgy. Rique is often called a storyteller. He writes so that the readers can place themselves into the pages of the story and make the pages play like a movie in their own imagination. He is a passionate writer who is unafraid to reveal the sensitivity of a male or himself, thus, invoking an emotional response from the readers.

Every Woman's Man

BY RIQUE JOHNSON
COMING NOVEMBER 2005

D evin Alexander sat at a table for two in the food court of the Galleria Mall. He waited for his guest to arrive with a strange uncertainty. After all, he'd established himself as a financial analyst, a successful one for that matter, and he wondered...actually, deep down inside he knew, that she had very little to bring to the table if the relationship became serious. Still his desire to see her was as strong as it had ever been when meeting someone new.

Devin was six feet three inches tall, in his mid-forties and blessed by the gene pool. Though his exercise routine was nearly non-existent, his body weight fell well within the ideal range for his combined height and age. He wasn't a materialistic person, nor caught up into what someone else had or how much money a person made, but sometimes the opposite words of his father became prominent in his conscious mind. Yet, he sat waiting for someone many years younger. Strangely, he adored her, even though this was their first date.

She was of Spanish heritage, Puerto Rican to be exact. Youth still afforded her the pleasure of a nice body which, even though he hated to admit it, he received pleasure looking at. Devin had become somewhat fascinated with her streetwise ways. She had rough edges, common characteristics of someone who grew up in the hood.

He remembered that it was her vocabulary that caught his attention. There was something about her commonly used phrase "it's all good" that triggered his unique sense of humor. It prompted the response from him,

"All of it?" Whereas, Gabriella followed with, "All of what?" Devin smiled as he recalled saying, "Whatever is good," but he had to defend himself when Gabriella questioned whether or not he was making fun of the way she spoke.

He replied, "I would not do that. Surely, a person as," Devin remembered why he paused and chose his words carefully, "sassy as you, isn't upset over a little harmless fun?"

From that exchange came a luncheon date, where he oddly anticipated her arrival. A few short moments later, Gabriella Rogue—Gabby as Devin was asked to call her—arrived wearing skintight pants of a flowery fabric. Her top was equally fitting. It matched the color of the petals in the flowers on her pants. He thought that it was odd with the recent fashion changes, she'd be wearing a pair of pumps. However, accompanying that oddness was the thought that her shoes accented her legs nicely.

Devin rose from his seat to catch Gabby's attention. As she was about to sit, Devin commented, "You look nice."

"All of this is much more than nice," Gabby corrected.

"I wasn't..."

"It's all good. I just want you to know what sits before you."

"Are you always like this?"

"What you see is what you get. I'm not going to pretend that I'm anything more than what I am. I'm a vibrant, energetic thirty-year-old female who is not pressed to have a man. I'm not in search of one, but I will not turn away someone who may be worthy of all of this sexiness."

"Did someone put orange juice in your cornflakes this morning?" Devin halfheartedly joked.

"No, and before you ask, I'm not upset. I just want you to know who I am. I won't change and would not expect anyone whom I'm involved with to change either."

"Wow! Let it be noted that I understand."

"So," she said on a lighter note, "how are you today?"

"I'm doing fine...work was a bit hectic. So, this interlude with you is just what the doctor ordered."

"Okay, I have to know," Gabby stated, getting directly to the point. "Why are you here with me? It's obvious that I'm not the kind of person you're accustomed to dating."

"Don't you feel that our meeting held a certain intrigue? Secondly, I don't have a customary type of woman. Besides, I can say the same thing about the type of men you would typically date."

"It's all good because I'm here. So, let's get the one-hundred questions out of the way so that we can capture the groove that we had yesterday, yo."

"Sounds good. Let's make the evening fun."

"That be like what I'm feeling."

Devin paused. It had been a long while since he's heard that expression. It caught him off-guard, and made him smile inside nonetheless.

"We'll get through this awkwardness, I promise. The best way to accomplish this is for the both of us to stay true to who we are."

Gabby thought to herself, *as if you are that fine to make me change who I am.* However, she only smiled and nodded in agreement.

After a quick scan of the menu, Gabby stated, "I'd like sushi." The apparent amazement that displayed on Devin's face was not missed by Gabby. She responded, "What's up with that look?"

"Truly, that is the last thing that I expected to hear."

"Don't be surprised. I'm not all ghetto because I live there. Picture me as a survivor."

"I'd picture you as lovely fabulous. But again, I was not implying anything."

"It's all good. There's more to me than what my exterior suggests. We cool?"

"Cool as the other side of my pillow."

A smile splashed on Gabby's face, followed by a nice chuckle that Devin didn't particularly find amusing.

"Listen, Devin," Gabby stated, "Don't front, trying to be something you ain't." She clears her throat before refreshing her sentence. "I mean, you should stick to the polite, square-like, that is...proper verbiage you're accustomed to. Hearing you annotate your words out of your era is quite amazing."

"We had slang back in my day as well. 'Solid' was one of the words commonly used. 'Right-on,' 'heavy' and a few other words, I can use in a sentence. However, that phrase, 'Cool as the other side of my pillow' comes from a Prince song."

"I'm sure that slang has been around a long time, yo. But I'm merely stating that your trying to talk like me sounds out of place. Just like the word 'annotate' feels strange coming out of my mouth. Ah'ight."

The best thing Devin could do is agree with Gabby. He knew that whoever said, "Be true to yourself," delivered the best advice for both of them.

They both had various forms of sushi for their meals, and each enjoyed the raw delicacies. Gabby, however, let Devin keep the squid and octopus to himself. She placed the napkin on the table in front of her and finished the last couple of swallows of her drink.

"That was tight," Gabby pleasingly stated.

As with several times during their meal, Devin had to decipher the true meaning of Gabby's dialect. He smiled internally with the thought of his brain being a Universal Translator from the *Star Trek* series.

"I take it, you enjoyed your food?" Devin asked.

"I just told you, it's all good. This time I mean, all of the food I ate was good."

"So, what would you like to do now?"

"I was thinking," she started saying, but finished with, "I'm flexible."

"Well, how about bowling? I haven't done that in a while."

"Bowling...a while for me is about five years. It sounds fun though. I'm game."

"Fantastic."

Devin and Gabby bowled three games that Gabby found as amusing. She had fun even though she believed that Devin bowled below his ability to not make her look too bad. She appreciated his gentleman-like way. After the bowling adventure, they stood outside of the bowling alley recapping their day together. Devin felt that there was a good chemistry between them, but he pondered kissing her. He gazed at her with his eyes telling all.

"You don't appear to be a shy person," Gabby stated.

"I'm not. Why would you say that?"

"That kiss you want is written all over your face, yo."

"That can't be, I'm not thinking about..."

Gabby interrupted Devin by pulling him near. She kissed his lips softly and left hers pressed against his. The sudden bold move shocked Devin, but when her lips parted, he participated in the kiss as if he had initiated it. The intimate act lasted for a moment until Devin broke the kiss and gazed at her in amazement.

"That wasn't so bad, was it?" Gabby asked.

"That was aggressive and great. Are you always like this?"

"Like what? Willing to take what I want?"

"I suppose that is what I'm saying."

"It's all good. I was just trying to relieve you of the tension of wondering if I'd let you kiss me. Did it work?"

"You succeeded in shocking me."

"I'm pleased that you are pleased. Well," she stated. "Here is my number. Give me a call if you want to do something again."

"I'd like that. I've truly enjoyed my day with you."

"Today has been pretty tight. You're pretty cool for a guy who wears a tie. I've found that most clean-cut guys like you are rather stuffy and seriously borderline boring."

"They are only clothes. They don't make me. I make them."

"Devin," Gabby stated in a serious tone. "I will look forward to your call."

With that, she thanked Devin for an enchanting day. Well, Devin understood her words, "today has been the bomb" as her way of saying that she had enjoyed herself. They left in separate directions, both believing that their day could be best described as interesting.

Devin thought about calling her the next day, but he decided to allow her to reflect on their first date. He succeeded in fighting the impulse to call her even though a better part of him—more than what he wanted to admit—wanted to hear her voice. He found her accent enticing even though her slang confused him most times.

The next day as if their thoughts were synchronized, Devin and Gabby called each other at the same time. Their respective rings were interrupted by two quick tones. Both moved the receiver from their ears, glanced at the caller-ID on the handset and spoke each other's name in unison. The problem with synchronized thoughts was that they both ended their call and waited for the other to call back. After about three minutes, Devin redialed Gabby.

"Hello, Devin," Gabby spoke.

"Hello to you, Spanish Fly. You've just experienced how great minds think alike."

"Yeah," Gabby agreed. "That was mad-crazy that we both called at the same time."

"It freaked me out."

"Like I said mad-crazy."

"So, does this mean that you like me?"

"That would actually be...what words would you use?" She pondered. "That would be correct."

Their brief conversation ended with an agreement of a luncheon date in two days at Roosevelt Island. Roosevelt Island is an island park located in Northern Virginia on the Potomac River just outside of Washington, D.C. Many couples ventured there for picnics and romantic walks. It had the usual trails, eating and cooking areas, but what made it unique were the exquisite tree formations. A brave few who chose to walk across submerged but visible rocks could climb onto a larger rock suitable for sunbathing or fishing.

As scheduled, Devin picked Gabby up about midday and they rode down the George Washington Parkway to their destination.

"You car is mad-cool," Gabby stated.

"Thank you. I'm pleased that you like it."

"Being a money manager must be rewarding, yo?"

Devin thought that Gabby's analogy of his profession was cute. He smiled and stated, "I do ah'ight."

Gabby giggled at Devin's sentence.

"You know," Devin continued. "I said that for your benefit."

Gabby smiled again as an acknowledgement to his statement. Devin parked his car at an area overlooking the Potomac River near Roosevelt Island. When he turned off the car's ignition the click sound of Gabby's seatbelt being unfastened caught Devin's ears. He gazed at her much the same as he did after bowling. This time though, he felt a need to be the aggressor. He leaned over to kiss her politely on the cheek, but she tilted her head to the side which caused his kiss to land on her neck. Devin held his lips tenderly on her neck for a couple of seconds and removed them with a smack.

"That was pretty cool," Gabby admitted.

"It might have been better if I could have tasted your lips."

"It's all good. It would have been muy nice if you'd tasted my neck."

Devin's eyebrow raised.

"You should nibble on the same spot you just kissed," Gabby suggested.

"I should? Here...now?"

"You college types normally have trouble following instructions?"

Devin became obedient and revisited her neck. He tasted her sweet spot, tasted her perfume and tasted her desire all in one kiss. He closed his teeth around a small portion of her skin.

"Right there," Gabby panted.

Devin tenderly nibbled on her neck and almost immediately, her breathing changed. She moaned as if she were being filled and used one hand to lift herself from the seat.

"I'd better stop before you let one of those 'O' things go," Devin stated.

"Sorry," she spoke after releasing a heavy breath. "That's my spot, yo."

"I see that. I will definitely record that into my memory banks."

Gabby smiled.

"So, what are we going to do here?" Gabby questioned.

"Well, on the back seat in a basket, I have cold-cuts, sodas, cheese and other things. We'll have a light lunch and simply enjoy nature."

"You don't seem like the nature type. Especially, coming here dressed the way you are. What's up with the tie?"

"It's just me. Once I took someone's little girl rowboating like this. I'll just say you know, that's just the way I flow."

Gabby shook her head at his humor.

Devin opened the door for Gabby. She turned slightly and placed one foot on the pavement in preparation of exiting the vehicle. Devin held his breath when he saw her luscious leg. But when the shortness of her dress afforded him a glimpse of her laced panties, he felt flushed. It was definitely a stimulus for him, and he hoped that Gabby hadn't noticed him looking.

Gabby chuckled internally and thought, *You like that, don't you?*

She had flashed him her prize and felt a sense of accomplishment when she noticed his embarrassment.

They walked across a long wooden bridge to Roosevelt Island to what Devin described as the Spider area. It was a huge oval-shaped area with benches and tables around the perimeter. Spanning off of the area were eight different nature walks, four on each side.

"See," Devin explained. "These paths are what make up the crawling creature's legs."

"I can see that," Gabby agreed. "Which one are we going to take?"

"I have to get my bearings, but I believe that the third one on the other side will take us to where I want us to go."

"Where's that, yo?"

"Come on now, that would spoil the surprise."

Gabby sat down at one of the tables and glanced at Devin who had already started unpacking things from the small basket. He prepared their cold-cut sandwiches, and after a short while, they had consumed the meal.

"Thank you, Devin," Gabby stated sincerely. "This has been a wonderful day, and your preparation of our meal was such a pleasant surprise."

"Let's not get it twisted; the surprise is forthcoming."

"It is going to happen soon?"

"Impatient, are we?"

"You're the one who added a certain expectation to our date."

"In a small way I did, but it was you who gave me a greater anticipation earlier."

"I don't remember doing anything to you...yet," she smiled.

"See, there you go again."

"What does that suppose to mean?"

"It means that you're all right by me."

Gabby felt that there was something missing from his explanation, but she didn't question it.

"Well, that nibbling on your neck thing has my imagination flowing vividly."

"I see. So, you want me?"

Devin smiled with her bold question.

"You know," Devin stated. "I somehow feel that being intimate with you would be very interesting."

"Same here, yo."

"What you're telling me is that you're not one of those women who give men an unknown grace period to go through before they feel comfortable making the relationship physical?"

"I don't really believe that I've even hinted toward a grace period."

"Come to think of it, you haven't."

"So, when are you going to make a move toward that?"

Devin's mouth fell open. He had given it some thought. He had already tasted her lips, smelled her perfume and pictured her nakedness before him. But he felt that actually doing these things was somewhere down the road. The reality of it was before him. An offer had been extended to him. This same offer caused him slight anxiety.

"In time," he stated lacking anything better to say. "Nothing would please me more."

Gabby looked at him strangely. She knew by his comment that he was too shocked by her invite or suddenly unsure if he wanted to sex her. Either way, his response didn't sit well with her.

"Oh really?" she stated trying to disguise her mild disappointment.

"Yes. Really." Devin smiled. "Let's take that walk now," Devin suggested.

They walked down a winding path for a few minutes and climbed a steep hill before reaching their destination. Gabby parked herself on an open area of short freshly cut grass to rest her aching legs. She massaged her upper thighs and intentionally gave him another peak of her prize.

"You aren't the least bit bashful, are you?" Devin asked.

"Why should I be...surely, you've seen legs and panties before."

"You have a point. If you're not ashamed to show, I shouldn't be ashamed to look."

"Good point, yo. So, how much further do we have to go?"

"We're here," Devin stated.

Gabby looked around. She saw grass, trees and a few flowers, but in her mind, she could not determine what the surprise might be.

"Give it time," Devin suggested. "Do you like the overlook?"

Gabby shifted her weight to the side, looked across the hill and glanced down at the Potomac River.

"It's all good. Water has a calming effect on you."

"Yes, it does. I see myself sailing the oceans in a large yacht one day."

"That would be tight."

Suddenly, Devin picked up a long stem rose from the ground, followed by another, and then another. Gabby gazed up into the sky and saw that it was raining roses. Devin had picked up a half-dozen or so roses before Gabby found their origin. She saw a tandem pair of skydivers descending on their location. By the time they had landed, Devin had a dozen roses in his possession.

"What's this?" Gabby questioned.

"Roses, delivered in an unorthodox way, nevertheless, roses."

Devin approached the couple that descended from the sky.

"You owe me Devin...big time," the male spoke.

"I know that I do. Name it, you got it."

"All right now," the woman broke in. "Be careful how you state that. This guy might ask for something even more stranger than what we just did."

"You're right, Vi. Mike, don't get too crazy in your payback request."

"Don't worry, I won't. Now, take these and get back to your date."

"Thanks. I'll see you in a couple of days at the club meeting. Later."

Mike gave Devin a thumbs-up, but Devin didn't verbally reply. Devin held behind his back a boxed dozen roses that Mike had given him.

"You know those people?" Gabby questioned.

"Yes. I belong to a skydiving club."

"I see. You planned this ahead of time."

"I do strange stuff like this every now and then."

"I'm speechless."

"Well, maybe these will bring back your words," Devin stated as he gave her the boxed roses.

"More roses," she said with bright eyes.

"They're all for you."

"Well, if you set out to impress me, you've gone way past that."

"I should've asked if you like roses."

"Are you kidding? They are my favorite. I don't know many women that can't appreciate their beauty."

Gabby pulled him near. She kissed him hard and passionate. She ended the kiss and whispered into his ear.

"Thank you so very much."

Devin held her at arm's reach, searched her face and saw the exact emotion he'd hoped for. He was pleased with himself.

"Mr. Alexander," Gabby stated. "I don't know what to say."

"You don't have to say anything. Your eyes have told all."

"Did my eyes tell you that I want you?" Gabby unexpectedly asked.

"They didn't exactly say that."

"I do."

"Then, I think that you should have your way."

Baptiste, Michael
Cracked Dreams (October 2004) 1-59309-035-8

Bernard, DV
The Last Dream Before Dawn 0-9711953-2-3
God in the Image of Woman (August 2004) 1-59309-019-6

Brown, Laurinda D.
Fire & Brimstone 1-59309-015-3
UnderCover (October 2004) 1-59309-030-7

Cheekes, Shonda
Another Man's Wife 1-59309-008-0
Blackgentlemen.com 0-9711953-8-2

Cooper, William Fredrick
Six Days in January 1-59309-017-X
Sistergirls.com 1-59309-004-8

Crockett, Mark
Turkeystuffer 0-9711953-3-1

Daniels, J and Bacon, Shonell
Luvalwayz: The Opposite Sex and Relationships 0-9711953-1-5
Draw Me With Your Love 1-59309-000-5

Darden, J. Marie
Enemy Fields (August 2004) 1-59309-023-4

De Leon, Michelle
Missed Conceptions 1-59309-010-2
Love to the Third 1-59309-016-1
Once Upon a Family Tree (October 2004) 1-59309-028-5

Faye, Cheryl
Be Careful What You Wish For (December 2004) 1-59309-034-X

Halima, Shelley
Azucar Moreno (December 2004) 1-59309-032-3

Handfield, Laurel
My Diet Starts Tomorrow 1-59309-005-6
Mirror Mirror 1-59309-014-5

Hayes, Lee
Passion Marks 1-59309-006-4

Hobbs, Allison
Pandora's Box 1-59309-011-0
Insatiable (November 2004) 1-59309-031-5